The ROCK

Center Point
Large Print

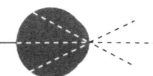

This Large Print Book carries the
Seal of Approval of N.A.V.H.

The ROCK

Sisters of the Porcelain Doll • 1

CARA GRANDLE

CENTER POINT LARGE PRINT
THORNDIKE, MAINE

This Center Point Large Print edition
is published in the year 2024 by arrangement with
WhiteFire Publishing.

Copyright © 2021 by Cara Grandle.

All rights reserved.

This is a work of fiction.
All characters and events portrayed in this novel
are either fictitious or used fictitiously.

The text of this Large Print edition is unabridged.
In other aspects, this book may vary
from the original edition.
Printed in the United States of America
on permanent paper sourced using
environmentally responsible foresting methods.
Set in 16-point Times New Roman type.

ISBN: 979-8-89164-096-2

The Library of Congress has cataloged this record
under Library of Congress Control Number: 2023952052

To my mom.
For encouraging me to not be afraid
to do the hard things.
I wish you were here.

The ROCK

"God sets the lonely in families."
~ Psalm 68:6a

CHAPTER ONE

Meramec, Missouri
March 1846

Rebecca kicked a cold, burnt timber off a tin plate lying in the remnants of their kitchen. She could almost feel the blast that nearly killed Pa and sent her flying out of her boots. "Let's be quick. I can see blood seeping through your pants on your bad leg. We need to get you back to Meramec while you can still walk."

Pa ignored her as always and used the stick he'd picked as a cane to turn the ashes. He uncovered a destroyed piece of copper from his whiskey still.

Always the whiskey. Never her. Never a real home.

All Rebecca wanted to do was guide her limping pa the three miles back to town before he broke open more of his burns. He'd only been healing for two months. What was he thinking? Her foot had healed and her ears stopped ringing weeks ago, but this pile of charcoal they called home only brought back lonely, hollow memories. Even more so, after being around her friends—Heather, Rose, and Cora Mae.

They had real homes, even if things weren't

easy, they were loved and cherished, valued and seen. Rebecca watched her pa search through the soot and wondered what being seen and valued would feel like.

"I'll help with that." She beat Pa to the remnants of an old feather tick mattress, waterlogged after being rained and snowed on—no roof to keep it dry. She crossed in front of him and helped lift or turn whatever she thought he wanted—keeping him from opening any more of his injuries.

"You look like your mother." Pa turned his face away from her.

Rebecca's shoulders sagged. The breath left her chest like he'd punched her in the stomach. *Mother? Now?* Before she straightened, she picked up the coffee pot and tossed it into the dirty snow.

After all the years she'd asked to know more about her mother, he waited until now to bring her up? She stared at him.

One time he told Rebecca that Mother preferred cherry pie. That was it. That was all she knew about her mother, besides the soft, happy feeling she got when she tried to remember. Cherry pie . . . and now this? She let him see her stricken face. What else was she to do? Get back to town, to Mrs. Mabel's cooking, and to her friends—that's what she wanted. This wasn't home. This didn't feel good.

But.

Always the but.

Pa needed her. He always needed her. He stood there and held her stare. "She was some taller than you. Your eyes are the same." Pa turned away and flipped the bulbous copper fixings that were the source of the explosion with his stick and said, "Useless." He tried to pick it up.

Useless is right. Rebecca was forced to join him or have him too sore to walk back on his own. "Let me." She carried the twisted metal and walked beside him, waiting for more—any morsel at all. His scowl told her the memories hurt.

I look like Mother—have her eyes. She tried to absorb it. Tears burned her throat and made her nose runny. All of this was sad. Even she could see what she'd missed out on. She didn't need gumption like Cora Mae's father asked of his daughter. The life she'd shared with Pa out here in the hills was no life. It was hiding. It was living without being alive. It was shattered and twisted like the copper tubing in her hand—beyond useless. They could have died rather than being blown off the porch. Would it have mattered, if they'd burnt along with the rest of their things?

She looked around at the mess, dropped the ruined whiskey still into the frozen mud, and tried to rub the scent of soaked ash from her nose. This place held no tender stories. She'd carried mash and hidden from Pa's customers, and nothing more, for as long as she could remember.

She scrubbed at the dirty sleeve of her calico work dress that Mrs. Mabel and the sewing bee ladies made for her.

She wanted to sit and cry, but what would that change? She needed to get out of here. She needed something different—something more. "I can carry anything you're determined to have."

Back at his side, she shoved her foot into the debris where their beds used to be. She plucked away burned roofing until she found the remnants of her cot. Her hands were black as night.

She dug until she found her tin can full of special rocks. The sight of her beautiful collection made her eyes pool with tears. Maybe she had one sweet memory. She blinked to try to see through the moisture. These treasures had been her only friends during the long months between town visits.

Rebecca fished out the small handful of stones and dropped them into her pocket. She wanted nothing else from the ruins. Desperate to be free of the ashes, she stepped out of the burned shack. "I have all I want, Pa. I'll wait for you."

"Fine. Take this with you." He shoved a dented pot into her arms as she passed him. "Go ahead and start back. I'll catch up."

Rebecca stopped and watched Pa limp-hop away from her over to the large rock next to the well. She didn't start down the trail like he'd asked but followed him. *Is he trying to kneel?* She offered her arm for balance and strength. "Your burns?"

He started talking but not to her. "We got a mess here, Ophelia. Not sure what to do. I kept my promise . . . but not very well." He patted the big stone.

Was he talking to Ma? Was this her grave? What promise . . . and why did it feel like it was about her?

Pa stood, sniffed deep, and spit off to the side. "Let's go back. I need a bed and a hot meal."

Instead of offering her arm for him to lean on, she gripped the back of his elbow. "Pa?" He wasn't going to brush past this again like all the other times she'd asked him questions. *Was this really Ma's grave?* All these years with it only steps from the door and he never said.

He wouldn't look at her. He looked around with Ma's rock right there beside them. Rebecca had assumed Pa came out here to hide from his grief—to drown it in drink. Not to visit a grave. "Pa?"

She kept ahold of his arm as he limped back the way they'd come. He cleared his throat. "Been nearly fourteen years since we lost her."

"Fourteen?" She would have been nearly four. Her eighteenth birthday was only two weeks away.

"Her heart was broken. She never recovered."

Before she could ask or say anything, he added, "April third. I couldn't fix it."

Rebecca swallowed wrong and choked. Her eyes watered.

"Ophelia was all that mattered." Pa tried to escape her grip. He stepped over a charred mash barrel, lost his balance, and tripped over his stick.

"Ahh!" His pain-filled cry was followed by his more familiar string of curses.

She helped him up, dodging his flailing stick, and went around the back of him to check the place where she saw a little blood earlier. Fresh red bloomed bigger and made his pants stick to his wounds. "That's it. We're going back, and you're not going to complain when I get Doc out to the pastor's to check you over."

She drew his arm around her waist, leaving the pot. He didn't need it. There was nothing salvageable here—besides, he would be laid up again for a week or two after this misadventure. Rebecca wasn't sure she was upset by that. She didn't think she was a coldhearted person, but Pa's pain almost seemed fair this time. What would things have been like growing up, if he'd opened up and talked to her earlier? If he'd answered her questions and explained his decisions? Could they have built a true home? He was obviously still grieving. And felt responsible somehow. Was that part of his secret promise?

Rebecca walked with one of Pa's arms pulled over her shoulder for support, keeping a tight grip on his waistband. She looked back for one last view of all that was lost—all that was never found.

Rebecca and Pa came into town when church was dismissing. The noise of the townsfolk pouring out of the building broke the frozen silence between them. Cora Mae, Rose, and Heather spotted her and came running over.

"Rebecca!" Cora Mae waved. "We were looking for you."

Rebecca's mind was so full of the few things Pa revealed—and she was convinced he withheld more things she needed to know. New, unasked questions zipped and buzzed inside her head and nearly made her sick right there in the street in front of her friends.

The trio was around her and out of breath. Heather, the most nurturing person Rebecca had ever met, went to Pa's other side and glanced at his blood-soaked pant leg.

"I'll run for Doc. He's going to need to help you. You might have to return to the Doc's office. Rose, will you watch Mother until I get back?"

Pa seemed to be in too much pain to throw a stink about being moved back to the doctor's office after being settled at the pastor's. While he was tight with pain, Heather was putting

Pa's needs above her own mother's. That's how family was supposed to be. Pa should have done that for her.

Her spinning thoughts changed directions again. If she wanted real family connection with Pa, then she had to do as Heather did. She would put his needs above her own and begin to make a change. She must settle Pa so his leg could heal again, and then she would find a way to wheedle out the things he needed to tell her and hadn't.

Heather ran off to get the doctor before they reached the steps of the church.

"Rebecca! I ain't going in there." Pa's strident voice embarrassed Rebecca in front of her friends. Nurse Roe came out of the building and straight to their side. Pa saw her and made his way in the opposite direction with his stiff-legged gait.

Nurse Roe called after him. "Doc will be none too happy when he sees the mess you made of your leg."

"I ain't going back to that blamed doctor's office."

Pastor Clyde must've heard her father yelling. He came out of the church. "You feeling well enough, Otis?"

Pa made the face. The same one he made after he ruined a batch of prize drink. He was mad and about to let the whole town know. All the lovely ladies from sewing bee would be shocked when they heard Pa's tirade.

Rebecca moved ahead of Pa to the bottom of the stair between them.

"I ain't going back to sleeping at that cursed doctor's office. It smells like death. I want my real bed at the pastor's—at least until I get out of this town for good." The string of curses he let fly burned Rebecca's ears. She watched most of the ladies turn their heads or busy themselves gathering their children to protect them from whatever Pa would do or say next.

Thankfully, he'd had enough and went around the side of the church, heading toward the pastor's home. He made it ten steps when a tall, thin man intercepted him. "Excuse me. Did the pastor call you Otis? By chance, would you be Otis Packwood?"

"I am. What's it to you?" Pa tried to march past, but the man stepped into his path a second time. Pa tipped his head to look him in the face.

Why was Pa so angry? He was the one who kept her life's history hidden. He's the one who waited until she was nearly eighteen to tell her that her mother's grave was right there next to their cabin. How did she die? Why did he feel so guilty? Rebecca was the one who should be railing at the top of her lungs.

"Please, sir. You said you're leaving town. How long until you leave?"

"Not sure." He reached back and almost touched the bloody spot on his leg. Pain evident.

Irritation left Rebecca in a whoosh. Pa was in pain. He'd lost wife, home, livelihood, and his health.

"Not sure why that's any of yer business. Let me pass, you big—" Pa tried using his elbow to shove around the man.

"Sorry, Mr. Packwood. I don't mean to be intrusive."

Rebecca gave a self-conscious look around, relieved the man interrupted Pa's next words.

"I work for the post office. I've had a letter for you on my shelf for a while."

"A letter?"

The postman nodded.

"Who in tarnation would write me?"

Pastor Clyde came around the corner during the exchange and caught up to Pa and the postman. "Why don't you go get it and bring it to the house, John." Clyde took Pa by the arm and led him forward even though Pa was craning his head around to watch the postman leave. "A letter?"

"Looks that way. Come eat. You said you wanted a decent meal. Mabel set a roast on this morning, remember? I can smell it from here."

Pa moved along. His limp even more pronounced. Rebecca followed behind the two men and Mrs. Mabel, the pastor's wife.

Doctor Kane came into view just as they were entering the two-story white house behind the church. He came trotting into the pastor's house right behind Rebecca saying, "Heather said to tell you she'd see you later. She had to tend her mother."

Before Rebecca could respond, Pa turned to him and stood with his fists clenched at his sides, interrupting the doctor. "Don't you go and give me a lecture. These burns are scolding loud enough. But I had to go back. I left things undone." He looked down at the floor and then at Rebecca.

The pain she saw had nothing to do with his burns. She had no right to judge. She could barely even remember Ma. What was she like, that Pa grieved her so? She wished she could know. She wished she could be so loved.

The doctor said nothing more but followed the pastor and his wife as they ushered her pa to the room he'd occupied for the last two months. Most of the winter was spent in this house. Most of the summer and fall he'd spent laid up in the doctor's office.

Mrs. Mabel said, "Let's allow the doctor to use some of his potions and weeds on your wounds before you eat, Otis. We don't want this to set you back. Once you're settled, I'll bring you a bowl full of roast and potatoes and a thick slice of buttered bread." Pa followed Mrs. Mabel's leadings.

"Smells good." Pa gave Rebecca a sheepish look over his shoulder.

Rebecca waited in the hall while the doctor

helped Pa into the night dress he'd lived in for months. She entered his room after he'd flopped onto the bed, stifling a moan of relief and pain. Rebecca watched as the doctor smeared ointment on the red, bunched and puckered, and sometimes cracked and bleeding skin.

Someone knocked on the door.

Pastor Clyde moved to answer it. "That is probably John back with the letter."

"My letter?" Everyone heard Pa ask.

The doctor wiped his hands on a cotton handkerchief.

"That nasty smelling stuff stinks like the dickens."

"I wouldn't have to use it if you listened to me." The doctor met Pa gruff-to-gruff.

"Leave me be. I've had my fill of your doctorin' today." He muttered on. "Enough for my whole life."

"Hold still. And don't give him his letter until he lets me finish." The doctor didn't let Pa get away with it. Rebecca should imitate the doctor's way. Maybe she would learn even more about her past. Did she really want to learn more? She swallowed the lump in her throat.

The doctor didn't let up. "I'd hate to see you deal with a limp forever because you couldn't wait for your skin to heal for a few weeks. Might I suggest you stay here for four to six *more* weeks before you try visiting your home again."

"Ain't nothing left to visit." Pa went silent. His expression was as if he'd swallowed a mouthful of sour whiskey.

Rebecca felt his loss settle like a horse kick to her chest.

The doctor didn't wait for Pa to say anything more. "I'll have Nurse Roe bring more of this to you. Spread it on all your burns, often. You can't afford for infection to set in. I must get back." The doctor pressed past the pastor and didn't even glance at Rebecca as he left.

"Here's the letter." The pastor handed it to Pa and left the room, his wife following.

Pa was lying facedown. He tore the seal open and started to read to himself and then announced. "It's from your uncle Leander."

Uncle Leander? She had an uncle? Rebecca gripped her hands and felt her face match her father's mulish look. What else could she find out in one day? Did she have aunts and cousins, was there grandparents she could meet? Where were these people? And why did Pa keep this all from her?

She knew why. She saw it in the way his shoulders slumped when he talked to the rock that marked Ma's grave. She sagged inside. This was all so much. She craved more. What else was in the letter that Pa was silently reading?

She would read the letter. She would take whatever morsels of information she could glean from it, and she would find a way to discover her past and possibly find a way to a new future.

With their shack burnt and gone, they would have to start over somewhere. Maybe starting over with family made sense. Her stomach tightened. Maybe the letter would tell her if that was even possible.

CHAPTER TWO

Oregon City,
Oregon Country

The wood chair, hard under Clark's backside, wasn't the worst part of the day. His father came out of his office, scanned the bank lobby, and was coming toward him. Clark wanted to stand right up in the middle of the bank and tell his father to go "mother hen" someone else. He gripped the pen so tightly he could feel it bend. Father taught Clark himself, years ago now. Couldn't he simply trust him?

The sound of his father's fine boots clunking on the hardwood floor grated his nerves. Clark was about out of time. *Again.*

He coughed to cover a growl of frustration without stopping his work on the contract his father would put to use in an hour.

Everyone in town knew they could come to his father to lend and borrow as needed. Everyone knew Father would make good on their Abernathy Rocks. Who else would treat marked flint stones as currency? Who else would be as fair and honest as a Sutherland?

A tiny drop of ink splatted on Clark's white page. *Slow down.* He should start fresh after that, but why? There was no doubt Father would take this contract and rewrite it as he did all the others. Did Father think him an imbecile? Clark was so certain of not being allowed to finish that he'd stashed his sanding dish on a high shelf two weeks ago and hadn't had to reclaim it yet. The ink never had time to dry before Father took over.

Irritation churned in his belly. Sometimes, at night, he dreamed of the things he wished to tell his father but couldn't. He loved him, and more, he respected him in all his ways other than this.

Clark could feel the heat of his father's gaze. "Here. Let me take a look at that." Father's voice boomed as if he was the mayor already and the townspeople were listening to his every word.

They probably were. They respected Father. Why wouldn't they? He was helping organize a newspaper, a mail delivery system, and he was a prominent member of the debating society. But until their fledgling town required a *mayor,* Father would hover at Clark's shoulder. His father's manicured hand reached for the sheet of paper on his desk.

"I'm not finished yet." Clark stood so quickly, the chair legs scraped. Teeth clenched against the rest of the things he wished to say.

"I can see that. I wanted to check your progress and lend a hand."

Would Father take the paper from him if he

could see his anger? *Yes, he would.* Clark was convinced. This was madness. Why was he working here at the bank at all? Maybe that was the problem. Maybe he should look into doing something else. Anything else. He forced himself to gentle his tone. "I wrote it exactly as we discussed. I didn't forget anything. I didn't make any mistakes." Clark's shoulders grew tight.

"We shall see."

The growl in his throat became louder, and Clark coughed to disguise it.

His father glanced up from the contract. "Are you ailing? I should cut you off early today. Your mother requested me to send you home in time for luncheon, anyway."

"She did? Why would she do that?"

"Not sure. But you can go. I'll finish this. Take the rest of the afternoon off, and if Red's doesn't have a ready-made shirt, then stop by the tailor and get measured. You ruined that one with ink, and Mother has too much on her plate with Beatrice's coming wedding to fuss with sewing a new one for you."

Again, Clark was being treated like a stripling. He was no child. He was nineteen. He'd stuck out the last couple years of this treatment at the bank because he thought Father was simply being slow to give over freedoms and responsibilities, especially since it seemed like he was being groomed to take over the bank someday. But things were the same now as they were when he started working two years ago.

Clark had a hard time thinking of alternative jobs he could do, but maybe it was time to work harder on that. He needed out. "Do you need anything from Red's, Father?" Clark forced the kindness, while matching his father's professional rigidity. All the while he wanted to shove his shoulder into Father's chest as he passed him on his way to the door. He pulled his coat collar up against the cold March winds and stepped around the worst of the mud.

He had to get out. But what kind of business could Clark start in Oregon City besides banking? What else did he know how to do? Surely, he could find something. He would adapt. He would have to, and soon, or he'd end up giving Father a black eye—and then where would he be? This day couldn't get any worse—or could it?

A picture of his mother crying and carrying on about a breach in his and Father's good relationship would be the outcome of the black eye. And that would be like jumping into hell on purpose. *No thanks.* He needed some time to think. He needed space to breathe. Maybe he would get both after he lunched with Mother.

The house smelled like dessert when Clark entered and hung up his work jacket.

"Clark, you made it," Mother sing-songed from the other room. "I was hoping your father wouldn't forget to send you."

Before he could move to the kitchen, his sister Gwen, with her new short hair styled with combs pulling the sides back, stepped around the corner and found him in the entryway. "Good. I was hoping." She only came up to his shoulder, but she clutched his arm in a bear trap vice grip.

He tried to sidestep her but was careful of her arm. He was the reason her shoulder was broken all those years ago and still giving her trouble. He wouldn't hurt her ever again. "Gwen? What are you up to? I'm not doing anything else like cutting your hair, like I did this morning. So, don't get any ideas. How did Mother react?"

He'd found Gwen out in the woodshed in the chilly air, Mother's good sewing scissors in her one good hand, hacking at her hair. He was shocked at first, until she told him she was making a bolt for her own independence. Short hair and front-buttoning dresses were her first aim to keep Mother from being overbearing. He could relate to feeling smothered, so he succumbed to her requests for help to cut her hair more evenly.

"She reacted as you'd expect. But what can she do? She can't make me sew my hair back on. She was easy to distract, which is why I picked today.

That's where you come in. With a house full of company, she has to back off and give me some space."

"I come in? Company?" *Oh, Lord. What now?* It really was the best prayer for the situation. It wasn't like he could run from the room. Mother knew he was here.

His sister tugged him forward. The table was set with Mother's finest china and surrounded by ladies of all ages dressed in their Sunday best—hats included. The rest of his sisters—Hazel, Matilda, Abigail, and Beatrice—all sat sipping tea, chatting amongst each other and their guests. Once they noticed him, each watched his every move without meeting his eye.

Gwen positioned her fingers to pinch the soft skin on the underside of his arm and muttered under her breath in his direction. "Best behavior. Mother went to a lot of work for all this, and I need her to have a lovely time while all these ladies get used to the shock of my hair."

He backed up a step.

She pinched.

He winced.

"Don't even think about running."

It was inevitable. He'd been caught in his mother's web. The day definitely grew worse. "What is all this?" He shook off his sister's clutches and bent to kiss his mother's cheek, ignoring the sting of Gwen's last pinch.

Mother tipped her head back to keep her hat from banging his face. "A bridal tea for Beatrice. Haven't you heard us planning and talking about it all week?" She rattled on. "But of course, you didn't. You're always running about town with Edward, chasing those beasts of his. Why don't you sit by Viola Evelyn? Doesn't her new lilac dress look lovely on her?"

So, this was his mother's plan. Even here at home he was pressed in a vise between respecting his parents and having his life planned for him. He wasn't even free in his own home. "Looks like a happy gathering for ladies. I should be going." He tried to move toward the door. He patted Gwen on her good shoulder. "I'm sure your friend's dress is just right, if one knows about those sorts of things. Congratulations, Bea."

His mother bounced up and blocked his escape. Then she clutched his arm as Gwen had and used it to bustle him over to the chair of her choice.

And the growl was back. If his mother hadn't kept him in the room, any of his five sisters would have—together they picked out his seat, his food, and his clothes. *Always the hovering.* At least they switched from pinching his cheeks to pinching his arm. *Heaven be praised for that, at least.*

He kept his gaze from landing on any one face, looking at each woman in turn. It was better that way. *I'm trapped.* Before he could loosen his string tie, Clark found himself wedged between two ladies, each with a tiny sandwich in one hand and a flowery teacup in the other.

"Ladies." He greeted them all together, nodding his head, but he couldn't bring himself to smile.

Everyone said there was a shortage of marriageable women around, but apparently, they all came out of the woodwork and sat in his mother's parlor today. "May I?" he asked. He waved at the food.

Mother nodded, and he stacked six of the sandwiches into a pillar on his tiny plate.

He wished he'd looked through the window before he entered the house, but he had been too annoyed with his father to notice. Gwen was onto something with cutting her hair. Mother couldn't make her sew it back, she'd said. He needed to find his own independence. If he did something—anything—other than what they'd planned out for him, what could they do? He needed to come up with a plan and soon. He needed to bring about the changes he craved, but it wouldn't do to be distracted right now, surrounded by unmarried ladies. Who knew what he might accidentally agree to?

He nearly drowned in muslin and lace before he made his excuses and ran to his room. Maybe his best friend Eddie had an idea for a new business. He should meet with him soon.

• • •

Sunday seemed like the hungriest day of the week. Clark didn't know if it was sitting and listening in church that made his stomach seem louder than every other day, or if it was because he saw his mother put in a roast with new potatoes. Either way, he was glad church was over so he could go eat.

Gwen offered, "Do you want to come home with us, Eddie?" as she left the pew. "I'm sure there is enough roast for everyone."

Clark's plan to meet with Eddie might be easier to make happen than he'd thought.

"Roast? I'm coming." Eddie, Clark's best friend since childhood, stood from the pew. "Your mother makes good grub."

Gwen's chin-length hair was a shock, but it looked fetching pinned back from her face, making her blue eyes seem more visible. And if the goggling gaze Eddie was giving her was any indication, he agreed. Clark stepped between Eddie and Gwen. "She does, at that. If we eat fast, we might have time to fish before nightfall. The rains look like they'll hold off."

"Fishing on a full stomach on a Sunday afternoon is perfection. Sounds good to me. Let me tell my folks." Clark watched Eddie track down his parents. Both had the same squat look of solid, hard work as his friend, but only his mother's hair matched Eddie's carrot red.

Clark's stomach rumbled again.

Gwen said, "Mother asked if we would go on ahead to the house and pull the roast off the heat. She needs to talk to the pastor's wife."

Clark knew Mother asked him because Gwen couldn't manage a hot roast with only her one good shoulder. Guilt made his stomach flop. He could never silence the regret. He didn't want to.

"First dibs on her roast? Let's go." Clark moved around his sister and let Eddie catch up.

"Mother also said to keep your digits off the meal until she gets there, or you won't get any apple pie." Gwen's pointed finger wagged under his nose.

Clark was about to push back on her pushiness when Eddie pressed between them. "I'll make sure he minds. No sense jeopardizing apple pie." He reached out and clasped Gwen's wagging finger in his own and gave her a princely bow, before he kissed the back of her hand. "I do beg pardon. We must leave. A perfectly cooked roast's future depends on our prompt departure."

Gwen was smiling at Eddie. "And there's whipped cream for the pie."

"Decadence."

Trying to knock some distance between them and some sense into his blunderheaded friend, Clark let his shoulder bump into them both as he moved down the church aisle and out the door well ahead of them. Eddie caught up before he was down the front steps. "Don't mind me." Eddie shoved him back. "I do beg pardon," he mocked.

"What were you doing back there? That's *my* sister."

"And a fine beauty."

"But it's Gwen." Clark heard how pesky he sounded and turned to make sure that his sister didn't overhear and misunderstand. He didn't want to hurt her feelings, but what man could tolerate his best friend flirting with his sister?

"Look around. We live in man country. Not a lot of ladies dangling about, except in your family's parlor."

"And none interested in waking up to a grizzled-face idiot that resembles the backside of an unshorn sheep. Not even Gwen." Clark winced.

He was teasing Eddie, but his joke could have been very hurtful if taken the wrong way. Gwen would probably be the easiest to be married to out of his sisters—each with their own faults. But with her being crippled . . . it still hurt to think about how one day of his teasing had changed her future forever.

She'd been different since she cut her hair—braver somehow. She made her own jokes now about not being able to pour the water off the boiling corn or having all her dresses be out of style because she had to have the buttons run down the front. But would her limitations keep her from marriage and hearth and home? His heart carried a heavy brick weight of Gwen. And here he was irritated that Eddie was flirting with her. That should be a good thing. Clark aggravated himself.

"What I don't have in looks"—Eddie swiped a hand over his thick red beard—"I make up for in charm and wit."

"You're full of wit, all right."

Eddie laughed and swatted at Clark with his hat, but he dodged out of reach.

"My sisters are off limits to you. If you get snagged by one of them, then your future house will hold one of my sisters. I'd have to endure them to hang out with you."

"But don't you think Gwen and I would make cute babies?" He jogged out ahead.

"Eeeeddieee! You better run." Clark needed to stay close and keep watch over Gwen. There was no way he could bring up his need for a new business venture while Eddie had him so distracted. Maybe after lunch.

They were in the house with the roast settled in the middle of the table, enjoying the smell, when the rest of Clark's family made it home. "Hurry up, everyone. This smells amazing, Mother."

Then it happened again.

A woman, not one of his sisters, came into the room ahead of Mother. *They wouldn't.*

The lady, Widow Jenson, looked right at him with the same eyes he'd seen before. The ones that pleaded "marry me and fix all my problems." They'd done it again—set him up in his own home.

Was there any place safe? He'd seen the widow around town, and he'd seen her at church. She was a fine woman, nearly his age.

Two young kids came around the corner next, talking to Gwen. Gwen's arm anchored to her side with the familiar sling. "You two sit here beside me. Eddie on your other side. He doesn't bite once he's been fed. I can't make that promise for my brother."

The others chuckled at Gwen's joke. Clark didn't laugh. Clark wanted to strangle someone, but he was too busy stuffing down all the cutting things he wanted to say to his mother and sister that he never could. He stuffed them down hard and fast before they flew out of his mouth and hurt the poor woman who looked uncomfortable and terrified in front of him.

She didn't deserve his wrath. He could simmer while eating roast beef and be kind for apple pie. But when the widow left, and he was with family alone, he would let free. He had to. Enough was enough.

Clark's shoulders sagged. Because he knew full well that he couldn't dress his mother down and tell her to back off on the matchmaking. She considered it an act of love and good parenting. Every time he'd tried to make a boundary fence, she jumped right over it.

The things he would have to say to make his point would cost him too much. He loved Gwen, and hadn't he just promised himself that he would make sure he did his part to enhance her future? He loved his mother—even if it felt like she was sitting on his chest, suffocating him with pounds of petticoats.

But Eddie would pay. Clark would make it real clear he wasn't interested in his flirting with Gwen . . . and then he'd ask him for business ideas.

*Eagle Creek,
fifteen miles from Oregon City*

A man stepped out from his hiding place in the trees and watched Leander lead a string of massive horses, stepping with high knees, down the trail. Leander was in the front riding the biggest, blackest draft of them all.

He lifted his gun and aimed. *Ready and steady.* Just skim the animal. Leave no sign. He blew out a tight breath and waited for the barrel of his gun to settle.

Closer and closer the man and the horses came to his chosen spot. Leander would never know what happened. Served him right.

Bang!

The gun bucked against his shoulder.

The bullet burned the beast's rump perfectly. The horse screamed, reared, and sidestepped closer and closer to the edge of the ravine.

Come on. Come on.

Leander dropped the lead ropes, cried a "Whoa!" and tugged his reins, trying to hold his position. "Easy!" Then the horse underneath him stepped off the trail. "Ahhh!"

The crashing whoosh of horse and rider falling down the thirty-foot embankment made the shooter smile. No way Leander could survive that fall, not like last time. The land was nearly his. The waft of gun smoke lingered. The loose horses lunged and scattered, each massive beast finding his own path to safety.

When the crashing came to a stop, the shooter checked a whooping victory cry. He whispered to himself, "Not yet. Not yet, Mama." It comforted him to talk to his mother as if she were really there. What he wouldn't give for her to still be alive and see all his plans go off without a flaw.

When the crashing turned to settled silenced, he crept out from his hiding place, bringing his rifle with him. He tramped randomly through the brush, leaving no discernible path in the wet undergrowth. He wanted to hope. He wanted to dream, but first, he had to know and see with his own eyes that Leander was down for sure—that he'd done what he came to do.

When he got to the spot, he looked over. At the bottom of the ravine lay the sight he'd waited and planned for—Leander, unconscious and on his back with a trickle of blood flowing from his mouth and nose. Completely still.

"Yes. This will work."

He scanned the area, the surrounding hills, at the bare trees that were beginning to push buds, the muddy valley below him, and the horses. When he was sure nothing—and no one—saw him, he scampered back, jumped the dirt trail as he took a slightly different way to the tree he'd shot from. He collected his powder horn and pack and wiped away all signs he'd been there.

No witnesses, no tracks . . . no proof.

Mother would be proud, if she'd lived. "The house and property will be ours. I'll put the oval-framed picture of you on the wall. I'll hang your fringed, Derby curtains, and lay out your fur rug. Reuben and I brought it all, Mother. You would be pleased." He looked around. Expecting to get caught. But no one was there to see. *Perfect.* His secret.

As he ran, his breath came heavy. He quickly untethered his dapple gray, sucked his paunch in, and pulled himself into the saddle—whirling off in the opposite direction of the ravine, rifle slung over his shoulder. The farm would all be his now. *Finally*.

He needed to go home to his brother and behave like normal so Reuben wouldn't suspect anything. His dream was so close to becoming a reality.

CHAPTER THREE

All Rebecca could do was watch as Pa lay there on his stomach, letter in his hand, muttering comments under his breath. She wished and willed him to read it out loud, to include her, but he didn't.

She stayed in her place against the wall and looked around the pastor's cozy home— sermons and hymnals filled a bookcase covered by doilies, no doubt crocheted by Mrs. Mabel, a mantel clock clicked its gentle rhythm, the room was lit by two lamps hung on the wall, and the smell of roast filled the air . . . but nothing gave her comfort.

She was wound tight like a cat watching its prey. She wanted to jump and snatch the letter and take the words that could change her life to her borrowed bedroom until she knew what her next step was.

Pa set the letter on the bedside table. She would stay tucked small and tight where she was until he surrendered to the weariness she saw on him. She wouldn't give him cause to keep her from it. He couldn't keep her from reading the letter if he was asleep.

Mrs. Mabel brought his meal and stayed until she was sure he wouldn't need help to eat it.

Soon all there was to watch was Pa stabbing at his last potato. After many clicks of the mantel clock, he set his empty bowl on the floor, cursed, grunted, and wriggled until he was full on the bed. And then, faster than Rebecca thought possible, he fell asleep, guttural snores coming from his slack lips.

Rebecca listened to her father and studied the angry red wounds on the back of his legs and tried not to think about what it would be like if they had to return to the shack and rebuild to the way things were.

She didn't want to go back. She liked being around Cora Mae, Heather, Rose, and all the townsfolk. She liked Pastor Clyde and Mrs. Mabel. And Ma's grave. That was a new thought. The letter could hold more changes, but would they be good ones? And what would she leave behind to get them?

Now that the letter was free to read, she hesitated. She stared at the back of Pa's snarly hair, running a hand over her own tangled braid. Wherever they started over, she knew Pa would go back to whiskey making. He needed his liquor like people need air. It was the way it always was and always would be. She didn't shy away from that truth.

She swallowed deep and crossed the room, knelt beside her father's bed, reached for the letter, and held it in her hands. The paper trembled.

Rebecca didn't know how long she was kneeling there before she noticed Mrs. Mabel in the doorway. "Pa doesn't care much about what I know, or don't know, or what I do." Those words were as true as his need to go back to his whiskey. But Rebecca also knew she would stay with him, no matter what he chose, like Heather stayed with her mother. She couldn't not. Maybe whatever promise Ma made Pa keep, bound her too.

Rebecca felt frozen—torn between the past and an unknown future. Her moment to push forward and take charge of the room like Doc did was here. Still she didn't move.

Mrs. Mabel came forward and tucked a loose strand of Rebecca's hair behind her ear and took the letter. Before she began to read it, she said, "What is the price of two sparrows—one copper coin? But not a single sparrow can fall to the ground without your Father knowing it. And the very hairs on your head are all numbered. So, don't be afraid; you are more valuable to God than a whole flock of sparrows."

The paper crinkled as Mrs. Mabel moved it. "This I know, Rebecca. If you talk to the Lord and tell Him you want to be His, then no matter where you go or what you do to survive, He'll be there with you. He has a way of making the most dreadful situations bearable. Trust me. I've seen a few moments of despair over the years."

Rebecca believed her. Mrs. Mabel smelled of cinnamon and sugar and had been nothing but warm comfort since she took them in. The woman's words and her peace seemed effortless and unattainable. Rebecca wanted to sit in the quiet one moment and scream for Mrs. Mabel to read the letter in the next. Was her future written on that page? She didn't know, but she didn't say anything. She waited until Mrs. Mabel's eyes came back from their faraway memories. Rebecca held her breath when she started reading.

"'Otis, I'm sure you never expected to hear from me after all that happened.'" Mrs. Mabel flipped the paper over and read the name on the front. "Leander Morton." Then she flipped it back.

"'I'm sure you never expected to hear from me. Especially after you asked to marry Ophelia. And then after you told me my sister died, I didn't think there would be any reason to keep up the connection that would bring us both pain. But, after my own dear Jules passed, I understood a little of your loss. Life has a way of turning things on their head. I have a favor to ask. One I think Ophelia would have been pleased with. It's in keeping with the promise Ophelia made us all make and the inheritance plans.'" Mrs. Mabel looked up with furrowed brows. "Ophelia?"

"That's my mother's name."

"So, this Uncle Leander Morton, have you ever

heard of him? Or this inheritance or promise?"

"Nope. Pa's never told me much about him or my mother. She died. I was too little to remember much. My life has been unknown." Rebecca paused and then added, "I found that out this morning, that Ma's grave was right beside the shanty. I think it hurts Pa to talk about her. *Wait.* He mentioned a promise this morning, when he was talking in grief, but he didn't say what it was."

The soft kindness in Mrs. Mabel's eyes made Rebecca feel like the pressure in her ribs was building like steam in the teapot kept on the back of the stove. "What else did he write?"

Mrs. Mabel read on. " 'I never remarried and I still live on the property Jules and I staked and claimed. I'm sure you remember how beautiful and bountiful the country is out here in Oregon Country.

" 'Here is the favor. I've suffered an accident that prevents me from working the land or the horses. My back won't ever be the same. Hard for me to admit, but if I'm going to keep my claim, then I need help.

" 'There is enough here for both of us. I have little hope of this letter finding you, but if it does and you come, I'll make good on Ophelia's promise and she will have the inheritance that was rightfully hers. I'm sure you remember the way home—head west until you reach The

Dalles, then make your way to Oregon City. Ask around until you find someone who can tell you how to find Eagle Creek. The assayer's office will tell you if you don't find someone else.

" 'Everyone in Eagle Creek knows where the Morton farm is. I will wait a year to hear from you before I make the same request of Jules's kin.

" 'They say "Many hands make the work light." There's plenty to do, that's for sure. If you come, I'm sure we could make a prosperous go of it. Regards, Leander Morton.' "

Rebecca took it all in, but the words that called to her were, "I'm sure you remember the way home." She didn't remember, but the word *home* called to her. She would go. She would help Pa get there once he was well enough to travel.

Mrs. Mabel handed the letter back to Rebecca. "Do you think your father will want to go?"

"I can't say for sure. There's not much left to keep him here with no money and no whiskey still. I don't see how we could afford the trip, but it feels like we should . . . I want to go. But it sounds like he could have gone back any time over the years. Something holds him. Ma's grave? Drink?" She ran her fingers over the edge of the letter. "Home sounds nice."

She said the words to taste their meaning with her ears and heart. They held. Maybe home was with Uncle Leander and Ma's people. Maybe the only way forward with Pa was to take him backward. She would have to leave Cora Mae, Heather, and Rose to reach for it.

Rebecca and Mrs. Mabel sat quietly trying to absorb it, and then Mrs. Mabel, cloaked in her familiar cinnamon peace, said, "Well, worrying about tomorrow—what we can't know—won't help us grow taller or make us live longer. Not that you and I couldn't stand to be a couple inches taller." She laughed a warm chuckle that made Pa stir.

Everyone was taller than Rebecca—even Mrs. Mabel, but not by much.

"Come now. Let's feed you. And while you're eating, we'll figure out how to begin planning for your trip across the Oregon Trail. I'm sure one of the church ladies will know more about the journey, if we ask them at sewing bee."

Making plans sounded good to Rebecca, but seeing her friends at sewing bee sounded better. She had a little time. Pa's legs needed a month or more, if the doctor was right.

A month.

She would leave in a month. She had to talk to Cora Mae, Heather, and Rose.

Though she could still scarcely believe it, Pa had actually agreed. They were going—all the way to Oregon, as soon as his leg was healed enough and the snow had melted. Rebecca lost sleep thinking about how she was going to tell Cora Mae,

Heather, and Rose that she would be leaving. She nearly cried thinking about it. They'd been so welcoming and helpful since the shanty burned. They were the only friends she'd ever had—how could she leave them? What if she never saw them again after she left? She wanted to soak up as much time with them as possible.

Rebecca didn't say much as she walked to the sewing bee with Mrs. Mabel. She watched her feet. Feet covered in shoes Cora Mae gave her after she'd run to town barefoot to get help for Pa after the shanty blew up.

The steps leading up to the sewing bee were freshly cleared of snow—hopefully, the last snow of the year. Mrs. Mabel led the way, holding a conversation with herself about the notions she would need to go with a certain sewing project. When Rebecca opened the door, Mrs. Mabel announced from behind her, "Rebecca leaves for Oregon Territory as soon as her pa heals and the weather breaks."

All chatter stopped, needles froze mid-stitch, and everyone turned toward her. Rebecca's face grew warm. All the ladies came and surrounded her. Rebecca did cry then. Silent tears. Did she really want to leave all this? The women poured kind words over her and offered supplies and necessities for the trip, and they asked questions she didn't have answers to.

Walking off into the unknown wouldn't be

much different than the way she lived. She had to go. She had to see what was on the other side of the letter. There had to be more answers than what she had here. The hope of more was growing in her, but if she couldn't find a real home, then she would walk herself right back here into the hearts of these women.

Someone handed her a hankie. She used it to hide her face. Rebecca was secretly glad Mrs. Mabel broke the news to everyone, especially Cora Mae, Rose, and Heather. The pressure was off now. She wanted to tell them what she'd learned about Ma . . . and Uncle Leander.

Rebecca looked past the women encircling her at each of her friends until they understood what she couldn't say.

Cora Mae was the first to respond. "If we don't have Rebecca for long, then we have to enjoy every second of her until she goes—starting now. Rebecca, Heather, and Rose, I invite you to sup and stay the night with me. Tonight!" Her self-satisfied grin was so infectious that Heather and Rose laughed. The room went back to the normal healthy chatter.

Later that night, after dining on sweet cakes and cream in the fancy parlor with Cora Mae's retired nanny, now housekeeper, waiting on them, the four girls went upstairs and gathered in Cora Mae's room. Before it burned, the shanty could fit in this room four times over.

Rose started out in the only chair, so Rebecca lay across the softest bed she'd ever been on. Cora Mae went to her double-doored closet and insisted Heather put on her fanciest dress and heels. Heather did, and she glowed. Soft tendrils of hair feathered around her face. It was nice to see a smile on Heather's face rather than care and worry. Cora Mae must've thought so too, because she wouldn't let Heather take off the beautiful gown.

Rose gave over the chair to Heather, who sat tall in the straight-back seat with the layers of dark-blue fabric spread all around her dainty feet like a queen on her throne. Long-legged Rose plopped down at Heather's feet so Heather could intricately braid Rose's hair into a crown.

Rebecca tried to memorize the two girls like one of the fancy paintings on the parlor walls downstairs. They would ask questions soon. Maybe they could help her find answers. Cora Mae told them about how irritated she was with her father. "How was I supposed to know he would be irritated I took six dollars off his dresser to spend at the mercantile on a new dress, when I'd done it before without inciting his wrath?"

Rebecca lost track of Cora Mae's voice when she went on and on about her father teaching her how money was really earned and the value of it. It was hard to consider it relative when you had no money. Rebecca couldn't imagine spending six dollars on a dress or on herself. But she might have to find a way to earn more money with things changing so much.

"Father said ideas are worth money after he went on and on about having usable skills. I was so irritated I went on and on about all the things I could do if I had money and how it was his fault I didn't have usable skills, so he might as well give over lecturing me."

"You told him that? Just like that?" Rose burst Cora Mae's tirade.

"Yes. In so many words. And he stopped being angry at me. He said sometimes ideas are worth money *after* I gave a wagon load of ideas. Somewhere in my plans he thought my gumption was worth six dollars. Do you have any new ideas worth six dollars?"

Rose didn't take up Cora Mae's challenge. They all knew Cora Mae was working off steam. She would settle—or more likely move on—in a few more minutes.

Unless Rebecca didn't want her to. Maybe Cora Mae and her friends could help her find skills or gumptions that could possibly provide for her and Pa in Oregon. Maybe she would learn new things at Uncle Leander's place that would lead to income. *Uncle Leander*. Still so foreign to have family she'd never met—to have family at all.

"Did your pa find a buyer for his extra whiskey

jugs?" Rose held her head still lest she interrupt Heather's weaving fingers.

Cora Mae stopped what she was doing and waited for Rebecca to answer.

"When he was laid up, he had the man who supplied the corn sell the jugs and anything else that could be picked up and carried away. Pa grumbled about having to sell everything and having to pay his friend part of the profits to do it, but it had to be done. There's nothing left to salvage. Unless someone is willing to take smoke-damaged wool blankets, burned mattresses, warped pots and pans." Rebecca stifled a giggle. It was a little sad that her life had been reduced to so little.

Rebecca could feel Cora Mae's eyes on her. Since Cora Mae's gumption-dinner talk with her father, she clearly had her nose in the air for even the merest scent of anything that could possibly be turned into a business or a profit. It seemed Cora Mae was as stuck as Rebecca was, if you didn't count the beautiful home, the father who doted on her, and what appeared to be buckets of money at her disposal.

Rebecca wanted to laugh again at the sad truth. As it was, Pa had more gumption than her, selling everything as he'd done. "I'm relieved to not go back to fetching and carrying mash and having all Pa's strange customers lurking around. But I'm afraid we might fall back into selling drink in

Oregon, if I can't figure out another way to make ends meet. Any ideas?"

Cora Mae watched Rebecca in the vanity mirror as she rubbed lotion on her smooth, white cheeks and then brought the squat bottle over to Rebecca. Rebecca held it in her hands and smelled the rose scent.

Cora Mae said, "We should study what you need for your trip to Oregon. I bet Arnie the blacksmith would know what's needed or who to ask. I'll find out tomorrow. Being well prepared could be the same as gumption, and you never know what you'll find at your uncle's farm. You'll have to write and tell me everything—tell us everything."

Rebecca put a dab of lotion on her palm and rubbed it in before she pulled Pa's crumpled letter out of her pocket and smoothed it on the bedcover, wishing it could give her more information on what to expect. "There isn't much here to go on as far as the trip goes."

"Read it to us," Rose said.

Heather didn't look up from braiding. "I'd be afraid to travel that far—not knowing anything about where you're going."

Rebecca kept her eyes on the letter. She wasn't afraid of the unknown. Not knowing was her normal. She was more afraid about what she would find out. What secret was Pa keeping from her? She needed to know if she wanted to build a future, and yet she dreaded what she might find out. She said none of that to her friends. "I'm a little afraid—of leaving you." Rebecca's words were quiet, but at least she got them past the lump in her throat.

Cora Mae wagged an ornate silver brush in Rebecca's direction. "Then don't leave. I'm sure Father would let you live here with me. I'll tell him I need a companion." The smooth dark curls she brushed fell almost to her waist. "You can't go. I like things the way they are."

Rose snorted at Cora Mae. Heather objected to Rose moving her head and the intricate braid she was weaving.

Rebecca wished she could stay, but knew it wasn't an option. "If it were only that simple. Pa doesn't always know what to do with me—he doesn't always know I'm there, but he does need me around so he doesn't feel guilty. He's my only family besides this uncle I've never met. I should stay with him like Heather stays with her ma. Plus, I might learn more about Mother."

"I understand that. But I don't like it." Cora Mae continued brushing her hair. "It does sound like there might be an inheritance. That might be interesting, although it sounds kind of shifty." Cora Mae smiled at Rebecca. "But don't forget, we're family too, sorta like sisters."

Rose rolled her eyes. "Living with any of you would be easier than living with Cecil. My half-brother may be older, but he is as wise as a fence post. Today he said he doesn't want me to work with the ledgers anymore. He thinks adding all those sums will strain my eyesight, and he doesn't think glasses would improve my chances of making a suitable match." She snorted.

Heather pushed her final hairpin into Rose's dark coil of hair.

"Pretty, Heather," Rebecca said.

Heather's eyes twinkled, and her fancy dress crinkled as she moved to sit behind Rebecca on the bed. She'd grabbed the silver hairbrush out of Cora Mae's hand as she came. Once settled, she pulled long, even strokes through Rebecca's hair. Rebecca liked the feel of someone else brushing her hair. She couldn't remember ever having anyone do it for her. Her shoulders relaxed.

Cora Mae tossed her smooth hair over her shoulder. "Cecil doesn't know anything." She stood and started pacing the room. "I'm serious. I don't have sisters . . . or brothers. I need sisters, and I say you three are it—whether you like it or not. Sisters naturally separate when they get married and move away, but they keep in touch. They write letters and keep track of each other." Her hands moved when she talked.

"You wanna help me?" Rose said. "March down to the store and tell Cecil I've been doing the ledgers for three years—no spectacles needed." Rose crossed her eyes at Cora Mae.

Cora Mae spun, her hair flying like a black cape behind her. She scooped up her much-loved porcelain doll, Victoria. A gift from her mother from many years ago, before she left her marriage and ran back to England with another man. The delicate doll looked like a small, blonde version of Cora Mae. She plopped back down into the vanity chair. "I might do that. I don't want things to change."

Rebecca saw sadness cross over Cora Mae's face at the prospect of her leaving. She couldn't help it. It made her sad too. "Sisters it is," Rebecca said.

Cora Mae stood again.

Rose added, "I'm in. What do we do now? Spit in our hands and shake on it or become blood brothers—got a knife?"

Heather laughed. "I would like to have you for sisters . . . but no knives, please." Heather stopped brushing Rebecca's hair and sat back on her heels on the bed. Even Heather's voice sobered. "I'm not sure how much longer Mama will make it. It seems like she grows weaker every day." A large tear splashed on the back of Rebecca's hand.

Rebecca thought about seeing Pa, facedown in the dirt after the explosion, with smoke trailing from his hair, clothes, and skin. He could have died and left her alone in that moment. She thought he had for a few seconds, before he moaned. Heather must feel like that every day, all day. Rebecca turned and hugged her, letting Heather's tears soak into her shoulder. Rebecca hung on for dear life. *Not friend. Sister.* "I need you too. I need you all. I might shrivel up and turn to dust with no one the wiser, if you don't be my sisters. Pa certainly wouldn't notice."

Rose came to the bed and stretched her long arms around both Rebecca and Heather. "If you aren't my sisters, then no one will ever really see me—no one will ever know who I am or what I'm like. Uncle Fitch tries, but he is busy guarding against invisibility himself."

Cora Mae, never one to be left out, joined them on the bed clutching Victoria by one arm. She hugged fierce and tight, then she popped up. "I know. We'll make a pact like you said Rose—like blood brothers do."

Rose snorted. "I said no knives, Crazy Cora." The group broke apart.

Heather said, "I like my blood under my skin just fine—sisters or not."

"Heather!" Cora Mae hugged Victoria to her chest. "Not real blood—a pact. A bond of sisterhood stronger than any of Father's contracts, unbreakable by anything except death. This is better than gumption and worth more."

Rebecca saw the excitement in Heather's and Rose's eyes. She sat up on her knees, listening to what Cora Mae would say next.

"Pacts have a seal. Contracts have a letter

in writing. They are legally binding." She left Victoria on the bed and flounced off the edge, grabbed her stationery and inkwell from her desk, and hopped back onto the bed—almost sloshing the coal-black ink on her quilt. Rose grabbed the pot from Cora Mae before she could spill it.

Rebecca watched her friend's flourishing script scratch across the top of the paper. "I, Cora Mae, hereby declare this day marks the first day of sisterhood between myself, Rebecca, Heather, and Rose. This letter legally binds us to stay in contact, help when needed, and always listen until death do us part." She shoved the pen at Rose. "Now here. You sign."

While Rose scratched her name, Cora Mae flipped Victoria onto her back and lifted her little dress, exposing the fawn colored, leather body beneath. She tugged at the seam of the doll's body and when it wouldn't tear, she retrieved the dainty silver scissors that matched the hairbrush from her vanity. "These will work."

"Wait. Cora Mae, no! What are you doing?" But before Heather could stop her, Cora Mae slit the seam at Victoria's back.

Cora Mae rushed each of them to sign the paper and then rolled it into a slim tube, ready to stuff it into the doll. "Now, before this contract is complete, each of us must place something of value that represents the way we see ourselves inside Victoria. We'll be the sisters of the porcelain doll."

Rebecca liked the idea of being forever tied to each of them. If she kept in contact with them, then she would know if she was welcome to return if things didn't turn out in Oregon.

Cora Mae was so proud of her idea. She flopped off the bed, leaving the torn doll facedown on the quilt. She poked through her jewelry box and found what she was looking for. "Something like this." She held up a tiny ruby ring. "My mother gave this to me when I was a little girl. She said she loved me more than any of her pretty jewelry. I can't wear it because Father gets mad when he sees it. And it's too small—made for a baby."

Rose came close to look. "And it's like you. Beautiful, rare, holding back red-hot fire."

"It's a ruby." Cora Mae scrunched her eyes in confusion.

Rose laughed. "If you're not holding back fire, then you can be found fanning someone else's. It's perfect. It represents you well."

"Good. That's what I want. What are you going to put in?" Cora Mae's questioning eyes probed each one in turn. When they didn't have immediate ideas like she did, she relented. "I'll see if Father will let me have you all over again after church on Sunday. Bring it then."

Rebecca liked the idea. No, she loved it. It made her feel small threads of home tying her to these beloved friends. She couldn't stay, but she could write, and that was more than she had before the explosion. She just wished there was more. It felt like there should be more.

Cora Mae stuffed the rolled note and the ruby ring inside the doll. "Heather, do you think you can make this a button closure instead of a seam?"

Heather put Victoria in her lap. They all were bending close as she fingered the fabric when something clanked on Cora Mae's window glass.

All the girls turned.

The candlelight in the room made it difficult to see out the window into the darkness. As they stared, a tiny glow flickered outside.

Heather sucked in a scared breath and Rose said, "What's that?"

Cora Mae left Victoria on the bed and moved to her window. Rebecca was right behind her, more concerned about her impetuous friend than the strange glow.

Cora Mae opened the upstairs window, letting in a frigid gust that blew the branches of the big oak tree. Before any of the other girls could figure out what it was they were looking at, Cora Mae hollered, "Archie Millikin!" She cocked her hand back and swung her fist before Rebecca could stop her. She heard a grunt as the flickering glow flung away and grew bigger as it fell to the ground. They heard glass break in the darkness and a burst of flames appeared on top of the snow.

"You hit me. Why'd you do that?"

"You're spying on us."

"I wasn't spying. Not on them anyway."

"Why you—" Cora lurched forward.

Rebecca caught her around the waist so she wouldn't fall out the window. Archie jerked away and found the weakest branch to balance on. It snapped. He scrambled and grabbed for a replacement, but not soon enough. He slid down the tree more than fell, twigs and branches snapping with every inch of his descent. He landed with a heavy thud beside kerosene flames burning themselves out.

Cora Mae was out the bedroom door, pelting down the stairs with Rebecca and the other sisters behind her. She raced to the front door to get to Archie before he caught his breath and ran off. Once outside, Heather swept past Rebecca and knelt in the snow, looking like a queen with her braided crown and fancy dress caressed by the flickering flames.

Rose moved to the fire and stomped it out while Cora Mae bent over Archie. "You idiot. Don't you think it's high time you gave up climbing tre—"

Archie came up from the ground faster than any of the girls expected and wrapped one arm around the back of Cora Mae's head and kissed her soundly.

Heather squeaked a protest.

Rebecca could only stare. She'd never seen people kissing. She stood shocked and fascinated until Archie released Cora Mae and cried, "Cora Mae!" at the same time Cora Mae gave him a two-handed shove back into the snow.

Before she could even finish saying, "How dare you?" he was up from the ground and scrambling away into the darkness.

All the girls were speechless until Rose said, "I think he likes her."

Cora Mae growled.

Rebecca wasn't sure if the redness in Cora Mae's face was from anger, embarrassment, or from the last vestiges of flames Rose was still stomping. Before she could decide, Mr. Reynolds came out the front door.

He went to his daughter and stood there in his shirtsleeves holding a short glass with amber liquid in it.

Cora Mae didn't wait for her father to ask. "It was Archie Millikin. He was up there." She jabbed her finger in the tree's direction. "He knocked on my window and then fell. And then he *kissed* me."

Reynolds didn't soothe Cora Mae's indignation. He chuckled.

"It's not funny. How dare he?"

Mr. Reynolds bent and caught his daughter's upper arm in a firm hand and led her out of the snow toward the house. "Let's get you inside. It's freezing out here—and go easy on him. He's jumping the gun a little, but he'll mellow."

"Are *you* saying it doesn't bother you he kissed me? Without asking? I most assuredly would've said no."

Her father still held on to her, but Rebecca could see Cora Mae's taut arms and clenched fists.

"I didn't say that. I'll talk to him. He should wait a few more years and be less mulish."

"Now or later, Father, it won't matter. I'm nearly seventeen. I know my mind. He's an unfeeling, selfish beast."

"Most men are, most men are, darling. That's why I said, 'Go easy on him.'" He pulled up at the foot of the stairs, let go of her, and took a drink. "Time will reap a great harvest from that young man. Trust me and be patient with him."

Cora Mae flipped her hair out of her way. "You sound like he is one of your investment schemes."

"Maybe he is." Her father raised an eyebrow.

Cora Mae growled again. "Is this to be the way it is? Any business partner of yours who happens to have a teenage son is allowed to accost me anytime he likes?"

"Not any business partner of mine—just this one." He turned and walked down the hall and ducked into his den.

Rebecca expected Cora Mae to growl again and flounce up the stairs. It concerned her when her friend blanched as pale as the white lace around her collar.

Cora Mae dropped her head, turned, led them back to her room in silence, and then stood in the middle of her room.

Rebecca poured Cora Mae a glass of water and brought it to her. The others crowded close and squeezed her shoulders. "Archie's gone. You'll be fine now," Rebecca said.

Cora Mae took the glass and gulped the water. "Archie will never be gone. And I will never be fine." She chucked the glass against the far wall. It burst into tiny pieces.

Heather squeaked. Rebecca ducked.

"Knock it off, Cora Mae," Rose said. "Now we have to watch for glass. You're just fine, you goose."

Cora Mae turned on Rose. "You think it's fine Father already picked a husband for me? You think it's fine I'm just another pawn in his investment games—that I'm to be used to profit and pad his already stuffed bank accounts?"

Rose held up her hands. "Whoa, whoa. How did you come up with all that out of what happened?"

"Because I know Abe Reynolds. Oh, he loves me just fine, but not enough to put me and my desires above his precious money. I won't do it. I won't stand idle and watch as my father plans my future for his benefit." She paced back and forth. Bits of glass crunched under her slippers.

Rebecca didn't enjoy seeing Cora Mae so upset. Maybe having a disinterested father wasn't the worst thing in the world.

Cora Mae continued to pace. "He can coax and cajole all he wants, but I'll best him. I will not be baited into marrying Archie Millikin. I have to figure out what I'm going to do."

"You can come with me." Rebecca looked to the window. If only that could really happen. The vat of loneliness was already sucking her in. She'd lived around Pa in soul-silence for years, but after being around friends, how could she go back? She knew Cora Mae would have to say no, just like she had to turn down Cora Mae's offer to stay with her and her father. She offered anyway. "As soon as his burns heal, that's when Pa said we leave. The snow will melt off by then."

Cora Mae stopped pacing and seemed to soften. She climbed onto her bed, kicking her slippers off as she went, and sat cross-legged—very unladylike—next to Heather perched on the edge of the bed. Cora Mae picked up the porcelain doll, finished tucking their signed sisterhood pact into the body, and hugged it tight. "I might do that, Rebecca, I might do that."

Heather and Rose collected as much of the broken glass as they could easily pick up and placed it into the bowl of her wash pitcher. Rose added, "Well, if you go with her, Heather and I might have to go too. We'll march across the prairies and deserts with our arms linked, defying any man who comes close. We'll make Rebecca's pa pull our stuff in his little cart."

Rebecca grinned when Cora Mae quirked a dark eyebrow. Rose was trying to tease them all out of the doldrums.

"Was the kiss any good?"

All of them gasped at Rose's audacity.

"What? If we march off defying any man who comes along, then that"—she pointed out the window—"might be the closest thing any of us get to a kiss. Since I will be denying my lips all their future pecks and smooches, in the name of sisterhood, I think I should know what it was like. Tell us, Cora Mae—did you like it even a little? The way he grabbed—"

Cora Mae pulled the pillow from behind her and swung it toward Rose. Rose caught it and armed herself against all the other pillows that came after. The four girls deflected their concerns for the future with bops and pops of the pillows.

Rebecca let herself play. Soaking up the sound of fun and laughter, at the same time tucking away the desire to cry for her loss of these three.

Mostly Rebecca avoided the fear of what was to come that hovered right outside the window. How were she and Pa going to provide for themselves? What would they find if they made it across the Oregon Trail?

CHAPTER FOUR

Three weeks later

"We leave tomorrow," Pa said. He ate his egg breakfast standing up with his backside away from the warm kitchen stove. He was healing nicely, but his new pink skin wouldn't tolerate the heat of the oven.

Rebecca froze. All she could think about was having one last chance to see Heather, Rose, and Cora Mae together. Her throat tightened. She couldn't eat another bite.

She needed to see them. She wanted to finish their pact. She'd found the right thing to put in the back of the doll. More than that, she needed to claim Heather, Rose, and Cora Mae as sisters—like clutching a log when she swam Beaver Lake, they would keep her afloat. They were all that tied her to anyone who cared.

"Let's get an early start. I need to gather a few more things for the cart. Be ready early."

Rebecca didn't even try to hide a shudder.

He scraped his tin into the pig bucket on the kitchen counter and put the plate in the soaking tub.

"So soon?" Mrs. Mabel placed her drying towel

over her shoulder and turned toward Pa, folding her arms to listen.

Pa didn't say anything to her. He limped out of the kitchen. Both women heard the front door close behind him.

Rebecca said, "There won't be anyone but me and Pa. I don't know if I can face the silence and the unknown." She shrugged, unsure if Mrs. Mabel could understand.

"Oh, pretty Rebecca, there will be other folks—other friends. Dr. Elijah White took a hundred wagons over the Trail last year. You never know who you'll meet. But you will meet someone. And when you get there, you'll have an uncle—who I'm sure will be ready to love you after all these long years."

"Will he? Or will he be like Pa—happy to live alone in the wilds of Oregon Territory instead of the Missouri mountains—jug and drink his only love?" Frustration and tears clogged Rebecca's throat. Somehow the coming silence felt like it was sucking her down, despite the initial excitement and conviction she'd had that this was the right choice. She knew what she was leaving behind. She'd changed so much over the past few months. To go back would be . . .

Mrs. Mabel came to her and pulled her to her feet and smothered her in a cinnamon-scented hug, rocking Rebecca right there where they stood.

"Shh, child. He knows . . . He knows. He collects your tears in a bottle—never be afraid to cry out to Him—He'll listen. He hears. If you don't know what tomorrow holds and your going is blind, He'll lead you down the paths you don't know yet. He'll guide you. He makes ways where there's no way—won't ever forsake you. He wrote it in His book for you and me to hear." Mrs. Mabel's words cut through her fears.

"Courage, Rebecca, courage. You can't go anywhere the Lord can't find you. You will never be alone. Don't you worry about all the tomorrows that are sure to come. Live today. It's what's important." Mrs. Mabel's hug settled into her bones.

"You ready to sew? One last sewing circle?" Mrs. Mabel winked. Both of them knew Rebecca had yet to sew anything at the sewing bee. It had become her routine to be with Heather, Rose, and Cora Mae the whole time the older women worked on their projects.

"Yes."

A blast of wood heat met them at the door when they slipped in. Rebecca took off her coat and hung it on the peg, wondering how long after tomorrow it would be before she had wood heat and a wood floor under her feet. She prayed as Mrs. Mabel did—simply. *Do I really have to give it all up? All I want is a warm home and a family that lasts.* Rebecca felt a warmth that was more than the heat and then a whisper spoke inside her.

I'm not trying to take something from you. I'm trying to give something to you.

She looked around the small entry room, unsure whether she thought it up herself or if someone had said it in the other room and she'd overheard. She didn't decide before her sister-friends poured into the tiny space, grabbed her by the wrist, and tugged her upstairs to the guest room that they had claimed as theirs.

Once the bedroom door closed, Cora Mae asked them all, "Did you bring it? Did you figure out what to put in Victoria for our pact?"

Rebecca was self-conscious of her choice, so she'd held hers back until last.

Cora Mae held Victoria facedown on her lap with her little doll dress flipped to expose three neat white buttons holding the middle seam together. "This is what I imagined, Heather. You're so clever. You always make things nicer."

"She does. And she makes the best doughnuts around."

"We aren't here to discuss food. You would waste all day if that's what we were doing," Cora Mae complained.

Rose gave Heather a goofy grin and waggled her eyebrows.

"I thought of a few things." Heather fingered a sleek ribbon. "But they have to be tiny to fit in there. This is my choice. Mama gave it to me when I was little. She said she had the pair of ribbons woven into her hair when Daddy met her. Her folks weren't thrilled she moved away from them, but I can see in her eyes, she would do it again if she had the choice." Heather held out the thin ribbon with tiny roses printed on blue satin.

Cora Mae took it. "It's perfect—like you—simple, beautiful, and full of beauty and love." Cora Mae curled the ribbon around her finger until it was in a tight roll, and then she tucked it inside the porcelain doll.

When she finished, Rose said, "I have nothing that's truly mine. Cecil didn't let me bring anything from home when our folks died. He said he had his own household things. I thought about tearing a page from one of my favorite books, but they're Cecil's too. I couldn't bear to have anything of his seal our pact. So, this is what I chose." She held out a dried, wild pink rose blossom. "An old lady patron gave me a handful of blooms a few springs ago. They were so pretty I put them in a vase by the cash register."

Rebecca watched Rose's brown eyes sparkle.

"Cecil bumped it and knocked a few petals onto the counter when he was ringing up a customer. When they left, he shoved the vase into my chest and said they were creating a mess and needed to be thrown out."

Each of the girls reached out and touched

Rose. "I had to do what he said . . . . I always have to do what he says. But I couldn't bear to see them go, so outside the back door of the store, I placed the bouquet in the ground like the dirt was their vase. I wanted to look at them for a little while longer. It worked. I enjoyed them until the blooms faded and the petals all fell. And then I forgot about them. Until the next spring. I couldn't believe it when there was a bud of green leaves on the stem. It took root. And now there's a rosebush hedge by the back door. This year I cut a piece off and planted it to make more. Cecil never noticed." She grinned.

"Nice—a wild rose to match our Rose—sassy, strong, and a little stubborn," Cora Mae said.

"And beautiful to look at." Heather elbowed Rose in the ribs. The two girls contrasted in looks. Heather petite with feathery curls. Rose tall with long, black hair.

"That, too. How about you, Rebecca?"

Rebecca could see all their faces saying, *I can't believe you leave tomorrow*. But none of them spoke the words out loud. She would. "When I was alone on the hill with Pa, I didn't realize how lonely I was. With Pa, things are quiet for days. I don't mean he didn't talk. He did—but it was always to tell me to fetch or carry something. It was a different quiet. It would press in, I could feel it. The silence would squeeze me until I had no breath. On those days, I would wander down to the creek and look for beautiful rocks and agates."

She held out her palm, the first rock she'd added to her collection in the middle of it. Light from the window shined off the small stone. They could see its many colors—blues and silver and white. "This rock was buried in the muddy bank. It was the first one I collected." She moved her fingers. The rock rolled over. "I am nothing, like this rock. I have nothing. When I found this, somehow, I found a way to press back the quiet. The rocks helped me. Sometimes I talk to them." Rebecca felt uncomfortable saying so much. She groaned inside to think of what she sounded like to them.

Cora Mae must've been able to tell. "But like your rock—you were destined to be found and treasured. We treasure you."

Rose and Heather agreed. Rose said, "And you will never face the quiet alone again. Even if you move a long way away, we will be your rocks." Heather hugged her.

Cora Mae nearly bounced in place. "We did it. We sealed our pact. This binds us like a contract. No matter what, we are sisters. Victoria, our porcelain doll, will keep watch over our things and we'll work hard to stay in contact. Rebecca, you are the first to leave us. When you get where you're going you *must* mail us a letter immediately—here to my house and we'll read it together. Whenever you need to talk, just write. We'll listen. Same goes for us."

Cora Mae pulled forward a small box that held paper and pencils and gave it to Rebecca. "I didn't think sending ink with you on the Trail would be a good idea. I put my address on a couple, so you would know where to send it. Don't lose it. We *have* to stay connected." Cora Mae took hold of the hand of each girl beside her.

Rebecca did the same, completing the circle. She squeezed the hands she held almost to the point of pain. "Thank you," Rebecca said.

"I know you're leaving tomorrow, early. I'm not sure Cecil will let me get away to see you off. I brought you this." Rose handed her a small leafy plant. She turned to Heather and Cora Mae. "I have one for both of you as well." Then she went back to talking to Rebecca. "If you keep the dirt moist until you get to Oregon, you can plant it there. Then you can talk to plants and rocks. People will think you're less crazy that way . . . or maybe crazier?"

Rebecca laughed with her but couldn't stop the tears from falling. *This is it.* All was set. The cart Pa found, the kind that required no cattle, was pitched and sealed for river crossings, and it seemed every member of the town had given them something to tuck around Pa's whiskey jugs to better prepare them for the arduous trek. Mrs.

Mabel sewed a canvas to keep their things dry in the rain.

By this time the next day, she would be miles away from these women, her sisters. She smiled through tears and studied each of their faces to remember forever. She determined to write along the whole trail and immediately, once she was in Eagle Creek.

Eagle Creek

He watched from hiding. *Naantam, that blasted Indian, is making my job harder.* Why would he go to all the effort? He saved Leander. Again.

Why would Naantam care for Leander? This should have been over weeks ago. With Leander out of the picture, there was no one in place to take over the farm. It would be his.

If Naantam had just minded his own business, he could celebrate and move into the farmhouse. *But no.*

What did the Indian owe Leander that made him so attentive to all of Leander's moves, and to pack firewood, cook his meals, and plant his garden? He had to get something out of it.

The fool Indian played hero. It galled him that Naantam was hunting in the area when the horse fell. At least he was too stupid to notice the mishap wasn't an accident. Naantam got in his way, again.

Leander should be dead twice over. The first

time, it was crazy to watch the pock-faced idiot grab Leander and jump off a cliff down into the frigid river to miss the avalanche he'd started. And now this? Maybe he should come up with a plan to take them both out. It might be harder to pull off as an accident, but it could be done.

Leaning his shoulder on the side of the barn, watching the Indian work, he spat. *I can't rush this.* Something would come to him. Reuben wouldn't be any help. His brother was too busy playing house on the rotten plot Leander shafted them with. The place they lived wasn't worth a crate of canned peaches compared to Leander's place, and Leander knew it.

"I won't be swindled," he whispered to himself. "I won't let him take what's ours. I still got time to fix this."

He wished Mother were here with him to come up with a new plan together. She was good at that. But if she were here, he would see disappointment in her eyes. Knowing that kept him from a good night's sleep. He spat again, wishing he had a smoke instead of a plug. But the Indian would scent him if he did.

He left the barn and walked back toward his brother and his house. He would find a place he could sit and blow a cloud while he imagined another way he could take out Naantam and get his hands on the property that should rightfully be his.

CHAPTER FIVE

Oregon City

The creak of the stairs woke Clark. He opened his eyes to predawn darkness. Who was coming up to his attic? Being the only boy that lived in the house meant the third-story attic was his sanctuary.

Knock. Knock.

"It's me, Gwen. I'm coming in." Gwen came in and sat on the side of the bed. "You awake?"

"I am now." Clark pulled his blanket over his bare chest, torn between waking enough to know why she was up here in his room and going back to sleep.

"Awake enough to listen?"

She patted his shoulder—normal for her, a little strange for him. She was his sister, and she could cherish him all she wanted, as long as he was standing on his feet. He couldn't remember the last time one of his sisters came into his room.

"Mother sent me with news."

He opened his eyes enough for her to know she could say her piece. "What is it?"

"Mother is fixing to set you up."

He sighed. "Again? I can't get away from it—not here or at the bank."

"At least you can do something about it. I told her I'd tell you, but mostly I figured I owed you a favor after you helped me with my hair. So, here's the news—you remember Widow Jenson?" Gwen played with the fabric of the crazy quilt Mother made for his bed years ago. Sewing was one of the things Gwen could still do—if she kept the work low in her lap to protect her shoulder.

"Yes." A simple answer to a silly question. How could he not remember the woman they'd ambushed him with? The woman who still looked at him from across the church as if she was praying for him to be her next answer to prayer. He turned in the bed instead of groaning.

"What you may not know is she is being forced to give up her homestead. Mother told her you'd be available to help her move off the farm and into the boardinghouse. She's already sold off the animals and farm equipment. It's so sad for her."

"And you agreed to tell me this, why?"

"Because I thought you might consider this one. Think of it. A homestead. You could have all the freedom you want. I'd take her up on it, if I was a man." Gwen's sigh held the weight of all of Widow Jenson's sorrows plus her own. "If she only had a husband."

Clark came fully awake and sat up. "You want to live on a farm? That would be your dream?"

"I want any opportunity to live on my own and make my own way. If I can't find that through love and marriage—I'll find it as a crazy, old spinster. You avoid Mother and Father's schemes, trying to buy time to create your own, because you *can* create your own. I'm stuck unless something unusual happens or I make myself unusual." She reached up and tugged one of the springy curls that haloed her head in a very fetching manner.

It was shockingly short. Clark fully understood her motives, but folks still stared when she came into the bank or church. He watched her press her lips together, stand, and cross to look out the window, her back rigid.

"What? I didn't even say anything yet."

"No. That's just it. You didn't say anything. But worse. You haven't done anything."

"You came up here at the crack of dawn, what are you expecting me to have done?" Clark knew she meant more than today. She was going after something that he felt in his own bones every day. He wanted to face his future with confident knowledge. He wanted to have a plan that was as easy to do as following orders at the bank.

But the next step was his alone to make, and he had no ideas. It felt like he was trying to shake the trunk of an apple tree to make apples fall, but it was spring and the apples were too green to fall. He was too green. He put both palms to his face and rubbed the weary sleep from his eyes.

"If you don't marry the widow, fine. But then

stop stomping about this place like Father and Mother are forcing a martyr's life on you. I've learned the hard way." She fingered the stitching on the tether that held her sling tight to her waist. "Feeling sorry for yourself doesn't make or create anything. It leaves you cold and empty and crying alone. I have an excuse. You don't. You are not a coward, Clark." She looked down at her hands folded at her waist and whispered. "Stop acting like one."

Her words knocked the wind out of his chest. Clark could feel the intensity from his sister. Gwen was wrestling with her own loss and heartache and was winning, and she was going to drag him along to freedom with her. She was the bravest person he knew.

He witnessed her struggle first with pain, then with the loss of mobility, and then with loss of identity. Peter, the boy who was courting her before the accident, came around for the first few months, and then when she was in the kitchen with Mother, he stole back his mother's cameo brooch that he'd given her and left a note saying he didn't want to marry a cripple.

Clark had mourned with her. He hedged her in and protected her where he could—stopping her from dreaming and wishing—just like Mother and Father. He hated swallowing that truth.

He was trying to keep her from getting hurt again. That seemed like the right choice, but wasn't that protection the smothering bondage she was trying to break free of now? Wasn't that well-meaning protection what he was trying to break free of?

"You, of all people, aren't allowed to give me that look. If I could have a penny for every time someone pitied me, then I'd at least have a steady income." She gave a light chuckle at her own sally. "Unless the pity I see in your eyes is really fear?" She paused and let that sink in. Then she grinned. "Fear that I will find you and live in your root cellar, if you're lucky enough to end up living on a farm?"

"I don't feel sorry for you." He felt guilt and responsibility, but not pity. Her injury was his fault, after all. Gwen was stronger than him. She was making a move toward her future. "You can live with me wherever I end up—I'll give you heck, but I won't hover like Mother and Father."

"That's a mercy. One I may take you up on someday." She stood from the end of the bed. "But seriously. If the widow isn't the future you want, and being here working for Father isn't what you want, the least you can do is what I *can't* do." She lifted her sling an inch. "Figure out what you do want and seize it . . . for both of us. What's stopping you?"

She went to the door and before she went quietly out, she added, "Do it for me. That would be more valuable than watching you beat yourself up for what happened to me when I jumped off the manure walk. I jumped, Clark. Me. I chased after you, tried to snatch the letter back. I fell wrong and busted my shoulder. I'm done crying over spilt milk—you should be too."

Gwen was right. He didn't want to think about her accident right now, but as far as his future, he had a choice where she didn't.

After she left, Clark lay awake in the dark. He couldn't entertain marrying the widow for even a second. But if that wasn't an option he was willing to take—then what was? He'd planned to talk to Eddie twice and hadn't done it yet. He pulled back the quilt. It fell to the floor in a heap when he got up. It was early enough he could catch Eddie before his shift at the bank started. He needed something new to think on. He needed a plan.

He made swift work of his morning ablutions, dressed in his old clothes, and was out the door with a cold biscuit and bacon while it was still dark outside.

Clark jogged down the walk in the darkness and took the shortcut path that led to the back of Eddie's parents' house. He turned up his collar and pulled his coat tight. Spring was here. Daffodils poked their yellow heads from several nooks and crannies, but the morning air was still cold. He hadn't spent much time there since

Gwen's accident. Not because the old farmhouse haunted him, but because life seemed more about growing up than playing after her accident, and Father brought him on to train at the bank.

Eddie came out the back door at the same time he did every day carrying a small pail. Crossing the porch, he headed to the barn for morning chores as predictable as the sunrise.

"Eddie!" Clark blurted.

Eddie did a little hop step before he turned to him. "What are you doing here? No paper cuts today?"

"Soon enough. I have a few ideas . . . maybe you can help me with?"

A cow bellowed in the background. "That's my call. I can talk and milk, come on."

Clark stayed with Eddie as he entered the barn.

"I can help too, while I'm here."

"Sure. Let's get the ladies. There're two milk cows now. We're taking in Widow Jenson's animals. She couldn't care for them all anymore. You really want to help, grab a stool and milk with me."

"It's been a long time, but I can try."

Eddie gathered milk buckets, stools, and the cloth to clean the cow's udder before they began. He set Clark up on one cow and he sat down to the second. Eddie was experience-fast. He had half-a-bucket before Clark could get a good position and get a thought out. "I don't need to go into my situation at the bank or with Mother. You know all that."

"Right. Heard it all a dozen times over. What's changed?"

Clark pressed his forehead into the cow's side and focused on the milking as he talked. "Nothing's changed. Not yet. That's the problem. I want to change, but I always get stuck at this point. Should I try and find a new business? Do I go work for someone else?"

"What is it that you want to do? You have the luxury to ask that question." Eddie finished filling his first bucket and traded it out for the second.

Clark wrinkled his forehead as he concentrated on aiming the teat and getting the milk into the bucket. Two barn cats rubbed his ankles, anticipating a good meal from all the missing he was doing. The sound of Eddie's repeated, fast-draw sprays tinging the bucket mocked him. "Luxury? What do you mean?"

"Work is work. That's why it's called work. I do things I don't want to do or don't like to do all the time. You have a good job at the bank. A job that you don't have to leave unless you find something better—meaning something you like doing. You have a job and a choice."

"You make it sound like I'm spoiled." The bucket was nearly full. Clark wanted to smile and show off, but the cow needed to be milked until stripped empty, and there were two more buckets' worth to draw from this one milking.

Eddie was already finished with his cow. His friend moved around the barn and collected chicken eggs from a few stashes hidden in hay piles while he watched the cow he just milked finish her grain. "Not spoiled, but having a choice to do something you enjoy isn't a question that everyone gets to think about when they must find work."

Clark knew Eddie was right. Most put their hand to the plow—wherever the plow presented itself. *Plowing?* Did he want to farm? Did he want to work with his hands? Did he want the life Eddie had?

Just then, the cow stepped and put her foot right into his bucket of milk, splashing his pants. "Oh no." Clark caught the bucket before it spilled, but bits of mud floated in the milk after the cow stepped back out. *One simple task and I failed.* His shoulders sagged.

Eddie laughed. "Happens. Let me take that. I'll save it for Widow Jenson's pigs I'm picking up in a few hours. You want to start a pig farm? She has two fine breed sows already ripe with piglets." Eddie put the ruined milk up out of the way of the cows and cats and brought a fresh bucket over along with his wooden stool. He sat on the other side of the cow and finished milking her.

Clark said, "That's a lot of milk."

"Six gallons each milking, when you put the two together. We'll get this much again tonight. And they nurse the baby between them. Want to start a cheese and butter business? There's always room for more of that. Especially with all the new folks crossing the Trail, floating the Columbia, and stopping at our doorstep."

"I'm still not sure. But now that's three ideas more than I had before I came. How did you end up with Widow Jenson's animals?"

"At your house, when you were avoiding looking at anyone in the room, I asked her how the farm was faring without her husband and she told me."

"Mother was trying to set me up."

"Obviously. I knew she and her husband had a large farm and the work was probably stacking up, so I asked if she needed help. You could save up and buy a farm. Not hers, the property already sold. The new owner is a wheelwright. He's bringing in his own animals."

"I'm surprised you're not halfway down the altar with all the help you're giving her."

"She wasn't looking at *me* with her heart in her eyes. If she had been, I might be halfway down the altar. There are worse things in life than a situation like that."

"But what about Gwen?" Clark felt sheepish. Eddie wanted to be married, and here he was keeping him at arm's length around Gwen. He was also in the way of the widow. Silence hung heavy. Clark didn't know how to fix what felt like a blunder.

Eddie skipped over it. "There's lots of job choices for you. You could do almost anything. You could take up at the paper or the post office and learn that trade, or learn to be an assayer. You could put the math to good use with that job. Or you could work in the woolen mill. Don't try the forge. You're too soft-handed for the forge."

"I could learn to forge."

"But would you want to? Blistering, back-breaking work with nary a break. The bank would be better. Besides passing something up, like being a blacksmith, is one step closer to a solution. Do you want to stay in town?"

"Again, my only answer is I don't know. It feels good to think about something different than working under Father, but every other job feels like playing house—like pretending. I wish I could try a job for a few weeks to see if I can do it. See if I'd want to do it for the long haul."

"Whatever you do, you'll be at the beginning," Eddie said. "Lots more spilled milk before you get on your feet. You need something that has grace for learning."

They put the milk supplies back to rights, put the cows out to pasture, fed the rest of the barn animals, and gave Eddie's ma the milk. Clark liked the work. He liked being outside, he liked the variety of it.

Standing together on the back porch, Clark asked, "You need help around here? Maybe I should start working after the bank or come again early, like this."

Eddie rubbed a hand over his fiery red hair and itched his chin. "I can't pay you except in eggs, milk, and garden goods, but sure. You can learn, get a little dirty, get some calluses on those lily-white hands of yours. Start today. I still have to move Widow Jenson's pigs this afternoon. Pigs are the easiest of *all* the animals to lead." Sarcasm dripped off Eddie's last words.

"Sounds like a picnic."

Eddie collected a shovel and a hoe from their place leaning on the porch. "Yes, a real walk in the park. I told her I'd come after her children are done with school. Her oldest will be home, and he's more help than you will be, for sure. Join me or don't. It's up to you."

"I might. I'll see if I can take the afternoon off. Father won't like it, if he knows what I'm thinking."

"Just tell him I need the help. He likes me."

"That might work." If Clark didn't use that reason, Father would find a way to keep him at the bank all afternoon. "I should probably get back to the house and clean up before I go to work." He looked down at his dirty hands. "This was helpful."

"It was? You didn't decide anything."

"No. Not yet. But I milked a cow and I decided not to be a blacksmith."

Eddie grunted, and the men went their own way.

On the way home to change, Clark met his father on the boardwalk. Father carried a roll of papers and his customary newsprint.

People in town knew Father liked to read about anything happening in *any* town. The lady who ran the hotel, several restaurants, and the tavern gave papers left behind by clients to Clark's father. "You're out early. You eager to get to your desk this morning? Did your sisters tell you last night?"

"Tell me what?"

"They didn't tell you?"

"I'm not sure. What are you talking about?" Clark watched the dirt street for coming wagons waiting for Father to speak.

"Bea's fiancé asked to join the bank. If Max can prove he has a head for figures, then Sutherland & Son might change to Sutherland & Sons. After Bea marries him, of course." His father stepped closer to Clark and lowered his voice. "I think Max will be a good fit."

Up until now Clark had thought Father's primary goal was to train him to take over the business. He'd acted like Clark was the future—his legacy. He'd said it so many times. But was it true? How could it be true, if he was willing to bring on his son-in-law?

Maybe this was a good thing. Clark felt a pressure all along, but this opened his options and made the possibility of leaving the bank more manageable.

What should he say to Father's announcement? All he wanted to say was "Good Luck. You'll need it." To Max. *Poor sap.*

Before he could form adequate words, his father shoved a stack of accounts and contracts into Clark's chest. On a quick glance, Clark noticed none of the names and numbers matched any of the folks in town. "What are these?"

"Practice. Look them over and see if you can find any errors. There is at least one—I'll be surprised if you can find it."

Why would Father want him to check them over, if he already had? Wasn't that what he did everyday with real accounts? Here it was again. The reason he wanted to leave—he needed distance or he was destined to run in his father's wagon ruts—never allowed to blaze his own trail.

Clark would rather help with the needy widow's animals than try to figure out what his father was doing pitting him against Max. If Clark wasn't careful then they would both end up living in the Sutherland shadow.

"I didn't get a chance to say—Eddie asked if I would help herd Widow Jenson's pigs to his place. I was over there this morning, helping with the milking." Clark felt a twinge at making it sound like Eddie needed the assistance rather than admitting he was tagging along for his own benefit.

He didn't wait for Father to object. "Here." He shoved the stack of test papers back into his father's arms. "You might need these for Max. I'll be in like regular tomorrow." Clark left Father standing on the boardwalk, and instead of going home to change his clothes and go to the bank, he turned around and jogged back to Eddie's. His friend would have plenty for him to do before they left to get the pigs, and Clark could use the time to think about his options.

He almost felt free.

Almost.

CHAPTER SIX

Rebecca's heart broke. She cried for days when they first walked out of town, but then her tears dried up and the weeks turned to months as they clumped over the South Pass and farther until they found Snake River and eventually said good-bye to it at Farewell Bend. They stayed after it and made good time crossing. She thought they would walk the bottoms off their shoes in the desert sage, but eventually trees—trees so tall she craned her neck to see the tops—appeared around them.

The trees introduced them to the great Columbia River. They walked parallel to the mighty water for days until they reached The Dalles. After months of walking with the cart bumping along behind the wood, wheels, and canvas had become a part of her. Handles molded to her palms and her stride adjusted to the confined space between push rail and wheel. But they were nearly finished with it.

It was June seventeenth when they walked down the last hill, stepping over rock and sage with a view of the mighty Columbia River stretching wide to the right and left before them. In a couple hours, they would leave behind the cart. Rebecca and her father would carry everything they owned onto a raft and float the Columbia until it met the Willamette River. Then, they would step off the raft in the great Willamette Valley. Along the Trail, Rebecca listened to all the pioneer talk of the valley's bounty. If even a thimble full of their words was true then farming would be made easy.

Rebecca tucked a loose strand of hair behind her ear and kept ahold of the cart handle so it wouldn't barrel over the top of her and Pa on their way down the last hill. When they came to a stop, she stepped out from the traces and went back to the bed of the cart to check on her rose. She fingered the leaves. She'd cared for it like a newborn the whole way through dry and rocky terrain. She wrote about her plant when they rested at the forts along the way. Its care was her priority until it was safe at her new home.

Close to the end—only a raft ride away from Oregon City—and still, Rebecca thought if each one of Pa's words was the size of a pebble, she wouldn't have enough to fill a coffee tin.

She wasn't sad about it anymore, or even angry. She was resigned—too grateful he never stopped helping her pull the cart.

An old-timer tried to talk them into walking Lolo Pass up and around Mount Hood. But Rebecca knew all Pa could see was a peaceful float down the Columbia, then a quick trip on the Willamette River to Oregon City—with no walking for days.

Pa sat on the ground, pulled off one of his boots, and unrolled the ankle of his sock. He uncovered a dirty, ratty handkerchief with coins enough to pay the high price of the float. All his wheeling, dealing, and selling whiskey jugs along the way was for this moment.

A friendly Indian was to be their guide. They emptied the cart and hefted only the little gear that would make the final float of their journey. Rebecca latched onto her ceramic pot with her writing tools and her rosebush. She climbed onto the raft and tucked herself as much out of the way as possible as another family joined their raft. When they shoved off, she watched the steep mountains on both sides of the river glide past, including Mount Hood's massive white brilliance.

They floated all night and into the dawn of the next day. Rebecca hoped and prayed they stayed afloat through the rough waters. She pulled one sheet of paper from her crock and a pencil. She used the rough-hewn logs that made up their lifeboat as a desk. While listening to Pa explain to the Indian how to make firewater, she wrote her letters small and tight so she could fit as much as possible onto the one sheet. Her dry soul took a drink. When she was finished, she tucked the letter back into her crock. She would send it tomorrow when they reached Oregon City. It might take a long time to get back to her friends, but it would get back. And if this one didn't, then another would. Maybe in the next letter she would be done walking and her rose would be planted.

White kid gloves adjusted Clark's collar. "Hold still. We don't have the time for you to go rogue. The wedding starts in a few minutes."

Clark batted his sister's hands away from his hair and shirt. "I can do it. Don't touch me, Hazel." He swiped at his own locks. Gwen fussed over him as much as Hazel did. "Traitor," he whispered to her. She ignored him.

"Matilda left it to us to make you presentable. She is in charge of the details for Bea's wedding day. You may be used to being in trouble, but we aren't. Hold still. Your shirt needs proper tucking."

"I said I'd be ready, and I aim to be." Clark shook free long enough to tuck his own shirt in and straighten his string tie. He stood tall, so he towered over his sisters.

Gwen stepped to him, lifting her hand to fuss with his hair. If he had been outside rather than on the wood-floored church, he would have spit and narrowly missed the hem of her Sunday best dress. He learned long ago that spitting kept all his sisters one step back where he was comfortable having them.

Gwen licked the thumb on her good hand and

used it to scrub a spot on his cheek and chin. "Ew." He tried to step away, but Hazel stood behind him. He scrubbed his sleeve across the wet. He could escape, but he'd have to bowl one of them over. Father would be livid if he tussled one of his princesses—especially on Bea's wedding day. But how old did they think he was? He wasn't a child. He was a grown man.

"I think he passes inspection. What do you say, Hazel?"

Hazel stepped around to look up at his face. "We did the best we could. At least he's cleanly shaven."

Clark glared at them both. This was a day to survive. He tried to think of a few of the things he'd learned or done going to Eddie's before and after work—how to check and clean horse hooves, how to render lard, and his arms were still sore from splitting a cord of firewood.

Both girls grabbed his shoulders and dragged him out of the back room and through the sanctuary.

Clark let them. "If you don't leave me be, I'll come up with something special for your wedding, Hazel, if that day ever comes. Speaking of which, have you posted an advertisement on the store board yet? 'Bossy spinster, ready for marriage, can clean, can't cook.' "

Hazel growled at Clark and released his arm. He chuckled when her face flushed. Gwen intervened.

She reached up and pinched his ear, dragging him down another hallway. "Hey. Ouch."

Gwen let go when they gained the room at the back of the church where they would wait until the wedding started. She pretended to brush imaginary dirt off his sleeve, and Clark darted away, weaving in and out of his other sisters, friends, and family to get across the room from the fussing and nearly collided with his oldest, very pregnant, sister Abigail.

"There you are. Did Hazel hog-tie you?" Abigail took her turn smoothing his shirt collar and fussed with his string tie.

He pulled it out of her hand. "Not you too. Where's Jesse?" Abigail turned to look for her son. When she spied him pulling a petal off a flower decoration, she went to his side, belly leading the way. Clark grinned, pleased he'd fobbed her off.

"She might fall for that, but I won't." Calm, sensible Beatrice handed him a comb and a cup of water. "Here. There's a mirror on the wall over there. It starts in five minutes. Don't leave." She looked so calm on her wedding day.

He didn't think he could handle any more female attention. Why would he ever want to get married? Why would he ever need to with this flock of chickens clucking over his every move? He jammed his hands through his hair, messing it up worse. Beatrice's look warned him of her seriousness, even though she tempered it with a smile.

Clark took the comb from her. "Thanks. I'm here now, and all of you have pawed over me. I feel sorry for your new husband."

Both turned when someone came up behind them. "You shouldn't. He's been . . . how'd you say it . . . 'plucked and stuffed for the last hour.'" Matilda came into the room and straight over to Clark. She pulled off a delicate white glove and picked an imaginary fluff off his shoulder. "Let me see you. Did they get it done? The candles are set. And the pastor is waiting down front. It's almost time, Bea."

"I stand corrected. *Now* I've been fluffed by all five of you." Clark used the comb and gave the mirror a darting glance.

"Thank you," Beatrice answered. "Clark's as clean and orderly as can be expected. The wedding can go on."

Clark's sisters formed a line. Abigail strolled over to them with eighteen-month-old Jesse on her hip, his chubby little legs accommodating her expansive middle. Beatrice dipped her fingers in a cup of water and smudged at Jesse's face. Jesse whimpered.

"Trust me, Jesse. I know how you feel." Clark scooped the heavy boy from his sister. "But, unless you move to the North Pole, you better get used to it."

"Who is moving to the North Pole?"

"Me, if you don't make them stop, Father."

"You can handle it. You've done this before and you'll do it again. It's time." On those magic words, the five sisters pushed away from him, each with a hand to their own clothing and a word of approval for each other.

Clark's mother gracefully crossed the oversized room. "You first, Abigail. In order now."

All cinched and bustled, ready to walk down the aisle in front of Beatrice, Matilda followed Mother and Hazel. Gwen converged on them. She was already using her white hankie to dab a tear from the corner of her eye.

Clark kept Jesse on his hip until it was his turn to enter the sanctuary behind Gwen. He then set Jesse down and held his hand. Jesse didn't take a step forward with him. Clark bent down and said, "Our turn. You ready to walk with me? It will make Aunt Bea happy."

Jesse put his thumb in his mouth and looked at Clark with sleepy brown eyes.

"They wore me out before the real show too. You want a ride?"

Jesse bobbed his head and lifted his free arm up. "Here we go, big guy. Let's get this over with so we can get out of here and be comfortable again."

Gwen turned from in front of him and said, "At least until next time." She wasn't wearing the ever-present sling, but anyone who knew what to look for could tell things with her arm weren't right.

Clark was about to say, "If there *is* a next time," but his mother—who'd been able to read his mind since he could talk—said, "Save it, Clark," before he could even get the words out.

Instead, Clark did the right thing. He turned around to Beatrice and gave her a kiss on the cheek. "Happy for you, Bea. Max is a good one. He'll do right by you."

Her eyes filled, and she dabbed at them. His father grunted his approval. "Yes. He's a *sensible* man."

Clark couldn't look at his father. The word sensible was regarding his soon-to-be brother-in-law's willingness to go into the banking business with him. He shouted inside his head. *I'm nineteen years old and well able to choose my own way. I don't know what way it is yet, but I am sure-in-tarnation certain that it isn't banking.* If he said any of it out loud, it would do more than ruin Beatrice's special day. He looked at Jesse, who was still working his thumb. "Let's get this over with."

CHAPTER SEVEN

They finally floated to a stop, and Rebecca climbed off the raft and stood with wobbly legs on the banks of the Willamette River in the middle of the bustling town of Oregon City. People came and went. The banging of several hammers rang out, and the scent of fresh cut lumber hung in the air.

The happy sounds of a piano came from the whitewashed building. As she was looking, people poured out the front. Little children and pretty women dressed in their Sunday best came down the steps toward her.

Pa moved up the bank ahead of her with his hitched step. Rebecca kept pace with him. She was lost in thought and trying to take it all in when the echo of thudding footsteps coming fast behind her made her turn. A man with stocky shoulders and tousled blond hair was barreling down on her, closer than she realized. She clutched her crock securely, bracing for him to knock into her.

"Clark!" An anxious female voice reprimanded him from the church doors at the same time he narrowly avoided a full collision and was spinning to catch her, keeping her from falling, as he rolled past.

"So sorry, miss. I'm trying to make good my escape before my sisters catch me." His blue eyes danced as he put Rebecca to rights and smiled at her. Then he was checking behind him for the ladies standing on the top step. One pointed to Clark and shouted his name again.

Rebecca watched him shrug and heard him mutter under his breath, "I'd rather be tarred and feathered. Try as you might, sisters, I will pick my future—both bride and career, and sooner than you think."

Clark released her shoulders and then finally really looked at Rebecca. He gave her a sheepish look and quirked an eyebrow. "I really set them straight, didn't I?" His look softened, like he saw into her somehow.

She didn't know what he would say next and needed to deflect the sense of being too close to a campfire. She looked over his shoulder. "They're coming."

Clark jerked to see if his sisters were close. They were still on the church porch steps. He laughed and turned back to Rebecca. "Pure evil."

Rebecca smiled. "You could say all that, again, loud enough for them to hear?" And why did she feel the need to tell this stranger to stand up for himself when she was barely managing her own independence?

"Someday." He winked at her and moved down the packed dirt street.

Pa, well ahead of her, called back, "Rebecca?"

Rebecca watched Clark skip into a jog that turned to a run.

She was still smiling when she entered the assayer's office behind Pa. She set her crock on the counter and pulled out the letter Leander sent her father and the letter she wrote to her sister-friends. She opened the first. She wanted to make sure they had the right directions.

The older man with snow-white hair running the counter grunted.

Pa asked, "Can you tell us the way to Eagle Creek? Have family there—Leander Morton."

The other man grunted again. Then he drew out a sheet of paper and dipped his pen in an inkpot that seemed to have more ink on the outside than the inside. Several drops fell from the pen before he drew a rough sketch of where they had to go. A road with a few barns drawn marked the paper. "Here you are."

Rebecca watched another ink drop sprinkle onto the man's desk before he had the pen secured. "How far, sir?"

"Fifteen miles or so."

She looked to Pa to see if he was up to it and added, "I can walk. Let's walk, make camp near the place, and greet Leander first thing in the morning."

Pa shook his head. "I'm powerful thirsty. Let's

stay a night here and see what this town has. Then we can walk the rest. Stay tomorrow night on the trail."

She nodded, but didn't say anything to her pa. She would have finished as soon as possible. One more day walking wouldn't hurt. She handed the other letter to the man. "Can this be sent back along the Trail?"

He grunted and pointed to a mail sack that sat half full at the opposite end of the counter. She slid it into the sack. *This is it, Rose, Cora Mae, and Heather. Rest tonight. Walk tomorrow and then we are there. I'll set my stuff down, plant my rose, sit, and never walk that far again.*

Her heart wanted to add, *I'll be home.* But she was fighting the idea that she needed to add, *unless this is a complete failure and I must walk back to you all.* She squelched the possible disappointment. She hadn't even met Uncle Leander yet. Those thoughts were for another day.

The day after the wedding, Clark was back at work at the bank. He stood and came around his desk to stand behind the oak pillar blocking him from Father's view. He pretended to read the account papers in his hand, so no one else would wonder why he was standing there, growing angry and hiding. *Like a fool.* Guilt swam through his middle. He looked out the window and saw people coming and going down the street. He needed air—not bank air, not his father's used air.

Father meant well. He stood tall and proud at the front of the bank greeting Mr. Fritz with his customary, firm handshake. The grip, Father said, imparted trust and went a long way toward making loyal customers, especially when paired with his barrel chest and booming voice. People trusted his father. There was no room for Clark to thrive here, Father took all the room. In a few moments, Father would bring Mr. Fritz over to his desk and both men would critique his work.

The string tie at Clark's neck, mandatory to his father's code of dress, felt like a noose. Nothing would change. Father wasn't retiring anytime soon. If Clark didn't make a move, if he let things continue, he would still be hiding behind this pillar next year.

Every day at the bank screamed for him to grab Gwen's advice and run.

Echoes of companionable male laughter retreated to the big office. Clark darted to his desk, ducked his head, and put pen to paper.

He sped through the numbers before him with all the ease of experience, working the numbers until they fit the family's story neat and tight, happy or sad. He enjoyed the work. Numbers showed no bias, no favorites. They were constant and steady, but the numbers couldn't change themselves to make the client's life easier. The numbers never found new innovative ways to solve cash flow problems. No. The farmer, or the restaurant owner, or the businessman did that.

He wanted to do something—to see the change too. He wanted to know he'd done the work to bring increase or failure one day to the next, one year to the next. How would that happen if he stayed in his father's shadow? How could he make that happen? He could learn to do something, surely. It was the when to learn and where to learn of it that were the challenge. And the what to learn. And he wasn't going to find the answers to those questions hiding here at the bank, spending all his time growing more frustrated.

He raced through the notations. His hand nearly cramped. Father and Mr. Fritz would be out soon. He shook it and went back to it. If he could finish one project without his father's interference today, he would walk home head tall.

Father laughed at something Mr. Fritz said. The sound closed in. In a few short steps they would be out of the office and Father's warm hand would press on his shoulder—a moment of warm affection and pride would lead to the papers being slipped off Clark's desk, out of his fingers, and out of his control. *Just once. Lord?*

The two men talked as Clark wrote. Father's footsteps came closer, as he knew they would, and finally, the hand of warmth rested on his shoulder. It might as well've rested across his mouth and nose.

"Your boy here is making you proud." Mr. Fritz's gravelly voice didn't make Clark look up.

Clark checked the frustrated words that chased in circles through his mind and leaned forward to block their view of the numbers. The last three columns slanted and wobbled with his haste. He figured the math like a madman, ignoring everything and everyone around him just to finish. *I'm so close.*

"He works faster than any of my clerks. Has a real knack for numbers."

Clark knew Father wanted to add, "Wish I could get him to commit to the business with that much enthusiasm. Wish he would do what's best for this family." Or something similar. But how could Clark think of it when each day stripped him of a little more of his freedom and pride? He continued to tally numbers, even when the bell on the door announced new patrons.

"Gwen, my dear, how good to see you. And who is your lovely companion?" Father greeted Gwen from across the lobby. His hand lifted from Clark's shoulder. He would be back.

Clark glanced at Gwen to see who his sister brought. Heat fired his neck.

Gwen met his gaze and raised an eyebrow. Then she put her hand on her hip in a way he recognized as a challenge. *Matchmaking again.* Even after the last fiasco with the widow. Gwen was daring him to do something about his own situation.

He had to change the course of this day or he would choke on it. He looked down at the columns of numbers, refusing his sister any more eye contact. He swiped his pen in the ink and wrote three more columns of numbers and finished.

I finished. I'm finished. He was done. Even if he didn't know what was next. The completed papers made it possible for him to smile. He could see his way forward. He batted his irritations away, lest he hurt those he loved most, and reached for the only escape he could think of.

"Here, Father, I finished." He walked across the wood-paneled lobby and handed the papers to his father as he slipped into his jacket. "I have lunch plans with Eddie. We're talking about a new business venture."

Mr. Fritz spoke to Father as if Father didn't know Eddie. "Eddie is a good fellow, good family. His father helped build my house when we first came to town." But Father knew about everything and everyone in Oregon City. He was probably there when Mr. Fritz's house was built.

"Yes. The best of fellows. Do what you can for him, Clark."

Clark maneuvered around his father and Mr. Fritz. "And Father . . ." He waited until Father looked at him before he said what he'd wanted the courage to say for weeks and months. "I quit." He would face an endless scold when Mother found out. He would deal with that when it came.

Father's mouth dropped open. He stuttered a few times and then Mr. Fritz caught his attention. Clark turned to go. Gwen's skirts stirred and settled to a stop when he brushed by her. He squeezed her good shoulder but never slowed. As he passed Gwen's guest, he made his eyes nothing more than bland, warm, and friendly. He knew better than to even glance at Gwen's companion.

He was out the door in the fresh air before Father said more. Clark would've wondered if Father heard him at all, if he didn't have that stunned look on his face. Clark took a deep breath. "Freedom." Weight lifted from his shoulders.

"That place making you talk to yourself?"

Clark turned to see Eddie beside him and grinned.

"Work there much longer and you'll be one of those people touched in their upper story." Eddie tapped his temple with a thick finger and joined Clark stride-for-stride.

"That's the beauty of it. I don't work there

anymore. I just quit. Besides, lots of people talk to themselves."

"Not when they're as young as you. Either they're turning you into an old man or you already are touched in the—wait. What? You quit? Well, I'll be." Eddie sounded impressed.

"I may be a little touched in the head. I quit without a clue what I'm going to do next. I told Father I was heading to consult with you on a new business venture. They assumed it was you getting advice from me. So maybe it's you who's the crazy one taking business advice from a lunatic?"

Eddie snorted. "Huh."

His friend was average height, shorter than Clark, and squat like an ox with flaming red hair. Both men knew Eddie had a business mind to rival Father's—only he wasn't afraid of risks or hard physical work. The idea that he needed advice really was laughable.

"Huh, is right. But I didn't lie. I am coming to you for advice on a new business." Clark grunted when his belly clenched. He wasn't afraid, was he? The jittery jumps in his gut said he was plenty afraid, but he still wasn't going back to the bank.

Eddie said, "Suppose I better make an honest man of you then. My first question is where do you want to eat?"

"Anywhere but Betty's Bakery. It's Gwen's

favorite and sure to be her next stop. She wasn't alone . . . *again*."

"The Chuck Wagon is open behind the blacksmith. I've smelled his barbecue all morning." They crossed the dirt street. "Why do you always act like the hammers are working on scaffolding for your hangman's noose when your sisters play matchmaker for you? Others, myself included, would consider themselves lucky if the ladies were introduced to them instead of the other way around."

They walked down the narrow alley between two tall buildings, following the sound of clanking iron and the smell of the livery mixed with cooking meat. They nodded at the brawny man wielding the glowing spike and moved behind the building to the food wagon.

Several men lined up, receiving heaps of shredded beef on steaming sourdough biscuits. Turned over crates made seating for any who wanted to sit. Both men were silent as they worked through half their plates.

Clark didn't answer Eddie's question about being set up. He had other questions on his mind. Tomorrow morning, he would wake up and do what? He had to go home tonight, how would that go? What would Mother say? Should he, would he be able to, sleep in his own bed after sitting across from his mother's disappointment at supper? What was he going to do?

Eddie used his handkerchief to wipe his titian beard clean, muffling his mellow laugh. "I haven't seen you this twitchy since we set traps."

"Traps that caught skunks. Who wouldn't be twitchy after that? I've never stunk so bad. Just the thought of it still burns my nose."

"We got paid, didn't we? Paid enough for me to buy my first worn-out oxen pair." Resting up oxen that had trekked across the Oregon Trail and reselling them was Eddie's primary income.

"I spent mine on a new jacket. I couldn't get the reek out of mine."

"No return on your investment." He shoved another bite of food into his mouth. "And you're the banker?"

"Not by choice, Eddie, and not anymore."

"So that's what has you grumping. If you work cattle or the land, you might realize you don't enjoy getting your fancy pants dirty. Be careful how you play this. You might want to go back to banking."

Clark looked at his pants and compared them to Eddie's heavy, worn denims. "I'm not afraid of hard work. I've just never had to do any, except when I visited Leander with you when we were young. He showed me enough not to be a total dandy. I don't know if farming is for me, but I won't be going back to the bank." It felt good to say it out loud.

"I could use the extra hands, tomorrow. Come

work for me for a few days, while you're trying to decide. I just got a slew of rundown oxen. I'm headed out to check on Leander. They need to rest in Leander's wide open pastures for a while. If you want to go with me."

Clark thought about it, scraped the last of the meat from his plate, and set the tin in the water barrel that held the other dirty tins. Here was his chance. He could take up Gwen's challenge and break away and choose his own future. There wasn't much to think about. Today was a day of action.

"I'll come. Tonight, if possible. I'm sure Gwen will invite her friend to dinner, and I'm sure Mother will have a thing or two to say about me quitting. None that I want to listen to."

Eddie's tin plunked into the barrel. "Yellow belly."

"You want to come to dinner? Mother will have a full spread, and I'm sure Gwen could convince the latest pretty miss to change her affections to a certain redhead."

Eddie's eyes bulged.

Clark laughed. "See? I'm coming back over tonight. I'll sleep in the barn, if I have to. What will I need?"

Clark worked the farm until late afternoon and then he rushed home to get what he needed to stay at Eddie's before it grew dark and, if he was honest with himself, to get in and out of the house before Father was home from the bank.

He came in the back door, the same one he used when he came across Gwen with her new short hair. He avoided the kitchen and headed for the stairs. Before he got there, the sound of his mother's tears told him he wouldn't have the clean escape he was hoping for.

Father's voice called him from the parlor. "Clark? Is that you? Will you come in here, please?"

Clark's stomach sank.

His mother's whispered words were not for his ears, "Please don't. He may not come back."

Clark took a deep settling breath and faced his future straight on. He'd quit the bank. What could they do about it now? Like Gwen's hair, they couldn't sew the job back on . . . or could they? "Yes, Father?"

"I see you didn't tell your mother of your decision today? You waited for me to spring it on her when I came home."

None of Father's words were worth responding to. He had done that. By not coming home right away, he had left it to his father. And he probably wouldn't have said anything now, when he came home to pack for the night, if he'd had the chance. He waited. Father turned to look out the window instead of at Clark.

Clark reminded himself that he spoke of his

desires today, but he'd made his decision over weeks. The least he could do was be gracious as his parents caught up to the changes.

"Not only have you left us in a lurch with the contracts and clients, but you embarrassed me in front of Mr. Fritz."

Mother spoke up. "I'm sure all of that can be remedied, Clark, if you come back. Your father has planned for you to be a partner alongside him for years. I'm sure you can appreciate all he's trying to give you." Her eyes added how much she felt he was disappointing Father and letting them all down.

Clark wanted to dart up the stairs, pack up a change of clothes for overnight, and run back to Eddie's, but he waited in silence. He couldn't say what his mother wanted to hear, and he knew more was coming from Father.

Father turned from the window and sized him up like he did the time he'd accidentally thrown a rock and broken the upstairs window. "So you are quitting?"

"Yes, sir."

"Have you thought this through? Do you have another job lined up?"

"Nothing for sure. I'm working on it."

His parents exchanged a look, and his mother put a hankie to her face to stifle a cry. She wasn't normally so dramatic or emotional.

Clark began to feel an unease that didn't fit

with how he thought things would unfold. "I'm exploring job possibilities with Eddie. We've—"

"Possibilities? You quit without something lined up? You're trading a career and an inheritance for a possibility? Clark, you're good with numbers. I can see you enjoy the work, and I know you've studied enough contracts to fully understand the risks others take when it comes to starting a business from the beginning. It's unlike you to take such a foolish risk."

Foolish risk. Clark knew that's what his father would think his decision was, but Father's words still stung. Clark could feel his father's anger coming up beneath his lack of understanding, but what could Clark say? *You are impossible to work with. You're overbearing. I can't breathe with your hovering. It wouldn't be living at all, if I had to do that forever.*

He couldn't say any of that, but he had to say something to help them understand. "I appreciate the opportunity you created for me to work at the bank and follow in your footsteps, but I need to try something of my own. You went all the way around Cape Hope to chase your dream of starting a bank. You understand?" He reached his hand out to appeal.

"I did that to make the way easier for you. My father never handed me anything but the back of his hand across the face." Father paused to suck in a breath, and Mother reached out and touched his hand. "You can thank me for putting this much distance between him and us another time."

"I can appreciate that. I'm sure that took courage to change your world that much. I haven't had to prove my independence in any way, because you . . . and Mother . . . have provided so well for me and given me so many blessings. But I still need to try my hand at forging a future of my own making."

"You can say that, but the only future you can forge, while living here, is by standing on the back of the privilege and opportunity *I've* given you." Father cleared his throat. He flexed his fists a couple times then cut a glance at Mother.

Clark didn't know what he was supposed to say or do. He wasn't about to go back to the bank. It would be worse if he did that. But he couldn't exactly leave for Eddie's with this much tension between them. He waited, hoping Father would get enough out on the table to vent his irritation and start getting used to the idea.

After the silence grew long and uncomfortable, Clark said, "Maybe Max can be trained to take my place. He seems eager to learn."

"He is, and at least he is grateful for the golden future the bank will lay before him. I'm not sure you understand what you're throwing away. If you quit, don't expect to come back anytime soon."

"Yes, sir." Clark's fast agreement didn't soothe.

His father's face flushed red, and he went back to the window. Mother didn't make eye contact with either of them.

"Maybe we made things too easy for you. That can be changed."

Clark didn't know what Father was alluding to, so he stayed silent and held his head tall. He'd desired change for a long time. His father's pain from a lost dream wasn't his responsibility. He was feeling more relief with each word Father spoke. Once this was clear between them, he could dig into his next choice with all his focus and attention.

"We have made it too easy on you. I can change that. You really want to start from scratch and *forge* your own independence?" The way he asked the question gave away the depth of his offense.

Clark didn't want to hurt him. He waited for Father to look at him instead of out the window, and he nodded.

"Then I can help you gain the full experience. You are done with school already, and since you are not planning on learning any more of the banking business, then I'm asking you to find a place of your own. You are nineteen. Of an age to cover your own expenses and find a place to live."

Mother gasped.

Father quickly added, "We aren't expecting you to stay away—come for Sunday supper each week and come by when Mother asks or whenever you'd like. But to be clear, you're to provide your own way. Your own income, place to live, and provisions." He turned to Mother. "You can bless him from time-to-time, but if he's going to appreciate the bank job, he needs to see how good he has it."

Mother nodded her agreement and then stood to leave the room. Her emotions were high on her face, she was running from them so she could cry. "Supper will be ready in an hour."

"Thank you for the offer Mother, but I have a lot to do to help Eddie take a load of oxen up to Leander's in the morning." He crossed and gave her a kiss on the cheek before she darted out the doorway.

"Ungrateful pup—"

"And Father," Clark interrupted Father's muttering. "Thank you for the opportunity to train at the bank. I have a real understanding about the value of money and the risk involved with borrowing. I have a lot to think about going forward, and I know what you taught me will come to good use." Clark extended his hand, unsure if Father would be able to shake it.

He did and squeezed more firmly than usual. So much was said in the pressure of it. They held eye contact. "I'll stay in touch," Clark said.

Father looked away at the door Mother left through.

Clark added quiet words his mother wouldn't

overhear. "I'll be careful with Mother. I'm leaving the bank . . . and moving out, but not leaving the family." He hoped Father understood.

Father left the room without saying anything else.

Clark stood there for a long minute, his day coming full to his stomach. He no longer had a job or a place to stay. A jolt of real fear squeezed his belly. The pressure to find a new way to make a living doubled. And where was he going to stay while he figured it out?

Father was right about one thing—this was a different experience than he had when he was talking it out with Eddie less than an hour ago.

He went up to his room and began to pack his things in the trunk that had sat at the end of the bed with a quilt over it for years. He left more than he took, and he figured out how long the money he had saved would last him. He had enough for a few months of room and board, but that security drastically dropped if he had to invest into a new business.

The room around him was cool, but sweat beaded on his forehead despite it. True to his word, he left the house before the hour was up, with a tender good-bye to his mother and his trunk hefted onto his shoulder.

What came next was up to him. Whether or not he had to come crawling back to his bank job was also up to him.

CHAPTER EIGHT

Rebecca wanted nothing more than to be done walking. Pa was finally shaking the leftovers of a night of heavy drinking. They picked up their pace, like horses heading back to the barn, hopefully making up for the late start.

Pa shuffle-stepped beside her. "It's been less than a year? He said a year, right?"

Rebecca heard Pa's insecurity. "Yes. Less than a year. He should expect us still."

Nervous pain pinched Pa's face. She wished he'd soften and let her into his thoughts. If he could open up to her, then she wouldn't feel such great solitude. He didn't say anything. She didn't ask. They continued in familiar silence.

"We must be close. Look." She pointed to a soaring white-headed bird. "Eagle Creek's way of saying hello."

Her father grunted. After several hours of walking, they made camp for the night with a simple supper, each one silent with all the thoughts of the changes ahead. The trail behind them, the unknown tomorrow.

The next morning, they were up before first light with only a few hours of walking left, Rebecca was anxious to get done. The trail went up a hillside with craggy boulders on either side.

The incline was steep. Thick green foliage made a canopy overhead. Then finally, they huffed the hill and went up and around the bend and found a cabin and barn tucked neatly across from them.

The closer they walked to it, the tighter Rebecca's stomach clenched. On closer inspection, it wasn't a cabin but a log home with a barn bigger than she first thought—oxen and draft horse cropping in the afternoon sun.

Rebecca and Pa were fifty yards away from the front step of the cabin when the door opened and a tall Indian with deep, craggy pockmarks came out. His crow-black hair streamed in the breeze. He stood with his arms folded in front of his chest.

"Pa?" she rasped.

Pa cleared his throat. "We're here for Leander Morton, the Morton place? This it?"

She tucked herself behind Pa even though his short, lean frame didn't do much to conceal her. The man on the porch took his time taking their measure. He turned and went inside, leaving the door opened.

Pa looked at her as if she knew more than he did. Then he walked the final steps toward the cabin. She never let him be more than one step ahead as he slipped in the door in front of her. "Morton?"

"Back here! You'll have to come to me."

As they crossed through the house, Rebecca

looked around for the Indian and saw no trace. They passed a family-sized, wood table and a rock fireplace sitting fat in the middle of the wall to their left.

At the door to Leander's room, Pa spoke, "It's me, Otis."

"I know it's you. Naantam told me the ugliest man he'd ever seen showed up at my door with a pretty little brunette. I knew it had to be you. Does she look anything like Ophelia, now that she's grown? Come on in. Come back here and let me see."

Rebecca moved into the room and stood at the foot of the bed behind Pa.

"Why, don't that beat all. It's like seeing her from beyond the grave." After looking at her for several long seconds, he passed a hand over his eyes. "Don't mind your old uncle. I grow more sentimental with each gray hair."

She straightened her lips into a half-smile since the man's head was covered with coarse salt and pepper strands. "How do you do, Uncle Leander?" She bobbed her head.

"Your pretty, brown eyes are the image of her. Come in. Sit. Sit."

All the references to her looks and her mother swelled inside Rebecca. This was the beginning of what she was hoping for. To know about her mother, to have family, and to have them share with her some of her unknown history.

Satisfaction almost erased her weariness. Overwhelmed, she watched Pa look around.

"You won't find him. Naantam isn't here. Disappears and reappears like a breeze. He helps me. I owe him my life. I suspect we won't see him again for a few days."

"He's your friend?" Rebecca's question surprised even her.

"Sure. We have an understanding. We keep taking turns saving each other. I nursed him through smallpox, that's why his face is marked. And ever since then, we decided it's good to keep close. Well, he decided—and I'm grateful. I downsized things around here after my fall, but he's been holding down what's left of the farm chores since I was injured. I'm hoping now that you're here, he might have a choice about things again."

Leander looked out the window that gave a perfect view of the barn. "It won't be me getting better that will give him that choice. My back is shot. Now that you're here to help, I'll send a letter to my nephew to send the animals back. We might just save this place."

Leander listed to the left in the middle of a large, log bed propped against a headboard. "I imagine you two would like to sit down a spell after all that walking, before we get into all that."

Pa sat on the only chair nearby.

Rebecca looked around for another. A cherry

wood dresser with an attached mirror held a prominent place along one wall. A lace collar hung from one of the ornate knobs that framed the mirror. A heavy chest was positioned at the end of the bed, with folded quilts stacked on top, and another sat under the window. A rocking chair with long runners rested dusty in the corner. Books were stacked on the small vine table beside it.

Leander smiled at Rebecca. "I can't imagine walking as far as you have. The load of us—Ophelia and Albert, you Otis, and my Jules and her brother—we took the easy way, when we came all those years ago." He laughed. "If you could call it that. We floated around Cape Hope, crossing land and sea until we landed on the California coast." He paused. "Such a long time ago, ah, Otis? We're getting old and crusty."

"Speak for yerself," Pa grumped.

Rebecca looked at Pa. Cape Hope? He and Ma had traveled around Cape Hope, with her grandparents, to come here, and Pa still needed to separate from family and cross to Missouri? She pushed down irritation. Uncle Leander told her more in five minutes than Pa ever had. If this was what she found out in the first conversation, what else would she learn? She wanted to yell and scold Pa, but there was no point to that. Pa lived in his own mind, and in a bottle of his brew.

As fast as she was angry, she withered. She

leaned against the end of the bed instead of sitting.

Leander must've been watching her. "You look travel worn. There's smoked ham and coffee in the kitchen and maybe leftover corn cakes," he offered. "If Naantam didn't eat them all. Why don't you refresh yourselves while I muster these old bones out of bed? Having you stand over me feels a little too grim."

Rebecca led the way out of the bedroom, trying to curb the final traces of her irritation with Pa. Pa bent to place her crock with her rose and papers in the corner. She stretched her back and walked around the large table, enjoying the feel of the log timbers beneath her feet. *No more trail dust.* She was here.

Rebecca pulled a skillet down off a nail in the wall. With Leander's encouragement, she wasn't shy about making herself at home to the food. Pa either. He sliced thick sections of ham as she chopped up new potatoes to be fried alongside. The kitchen seemed to be built different than the rest of the house. It had no windows. The living area, which held the table and the fireplace, had windows flanking both sides of the long room.

The only thing impressive about the kitchen was the walk-in larder, which spanned the entire width of the kitchen, to the left of where she was cooking. The solid cookstove sat squat next to the door.

All the cooking utensils and pots and pans were

stacked and scattered in odd places. Rebecca thought it was the surest sign of all that there was no longer a lady in the house.

The scent from her cooking hung in the air and made Rebecca think of Mrs. Mabel. She denied the warm rush of tears with a swallow and kept her fingers busy making the best meal they'd had in four months. The first meal without the smell of smoke or ashes. She made fresh coffee without stooping over a fire. Her body felt like it was still walking.

Just as she and Pa sat at the table and started eating in the sheltered silence, Leander's door creaked. She came to attention. Without waiting to see him come into the room, she dished a hot plate of food for him and set it at the head of the table and prepared to pour his coffee.

"Here please, Rebecca. If you don't mind." Leander pointed to the place on the table closest to him. He was dressed in what looked like his Sunday best. He stood tall with his shoulders back, steps short and measured, but strong.

Rebecca moved the food and ignored the creaking sound that came from the distinct lumps under his shirt. He must be wearing stays of some sort to support his back, and it seemed impolite to notice.

A pinch of pain crossed his face as beads of sweat formed on his lip. He sat on a log-round cut to look like a chair, creating a relentlessly straight-backed seat. She brought everything to within his reach. "Thank you, my dear girl. Take a seat. We have much to discuss. However, before I fill you in on the details of our place here, I should thank you both for coming and say welcome home. We'll have to set up a cot and a bed pallet for you two."

Rebecca sat back in her chair and held her warm cup. Did he say welcome home? Or had her tired mind made it up.

Pa talked with his mouth full. "Our cabin burnt. I was burnt before your letter came. We would be startin' over, there or here." Pa shoveled a too big piece of ham into his mouth.

Leander watched him chew. "I hear ya. Still glad for the help. I made a decent income purchasing oxen used hard on the Trail—draft horses too—before I got hurt. My nephew gathers them from Oregon City, when folks are fresh out of money, then he brings them here to fatten them up, and then we sell them back to the new folks in town for a profit after they've had a chance to settle into their homesteads."

He ate a bite of his food. After he swallowed, he said, "I used to have more than I do now. More of everything—cattle, pigs, chickens, goats, sheep, and my favorite draft horses. My plans ground to a halt because of my injuries. This past year I sold everything off. Now that you're here to help, though . . ." Leander continued to talk about the land, the trees, the barn, and the letter he was going to send.

Rebecca's heart was too full. He'd said, "Welcome home." *Home?* She looked around this main room. A hand-stitched scripture hung in a wood frame beside the mantel of the fireplace. AS FOR ME AND MY HOUSE, WE WILL SERVE THE LORD read back to her from its nest of hand-stitched flowers. The room showed wilting signs of a woman's touch. Some of them fading away into dust and cobwebs, horse tack, and boots.

". . . Sheba's my only draft left, and she's due to foal anytime."

"Sheba?"

Leander smiled at Rebecca. "She's the prettiest draft you ever saw—as black as night. She lives up to her name."

"Can I grow corn?" Pa interrupted.

"Yes. That's what I said. It's a bit late in the year. But if the frost holds off this fall, you'll be all right. You'll have a hard time getting copper for your still out here, though. Not much of it around. I can't say I'm excited about the idea, but this place is as much yours to work as mine. If I'm to keep it, and if we're to put enough by to make it through the winter, we need all of us. We can't wait a day more getting things back up and running. I don't want to move to town. This is my home—my memories of Jules and Ophelia are here."

Leander pushed his plate aside and looked at Rebecca. "Your mother was strong and capable. She was a good friend to my wife over the years. If she hadn't lost Isaac, she might still be here."

"I didn't make her leave," Pa blurted. "She's the one who drug me to Meramec. I never wanted to live in Missouri. I just wanted her happy. That's all I ever tried to give her. She was always so sad."

Rebecca looked at her pa. Who was this man who shared so much? It even sounded like he cared for Mother—loved her, even. "Isaac?" she asked.

"I kept her secret. I didn't break her promise." Pa was twitchy-irritated.

Rebecca hadn't seen him like that since he was forced to stay in bed for his burns past the point he thought he was well enough to get up.

"She didn't expect you to keep that from Rebecca. You know what was at the heart of what she wanted."

Kept from her? Secret? Rebecca needed to know what they were talking about. Her past was the only way the roots of this new future would really take hold and grow. Knowing where she came from was the only way she could really set down roots and find a home. "Isaac?"

"Your brother. We lost him just days after he was born too early. We almost lost your mother too. It broke her heart." Leander was candid but sad.

A brother. She would have had a brother. It felt

good to know about Isaac, even though it was sad. Would she feel the same about the secret promise? Would she learn enough to feel whole?

Leander added, "We all grieved when we lost your brother. Your mother most." The room got quiet and still. The moment lingered, and then Leander switched topics. "Yes, to growing corn. What I meant to say is that the work of getting us all through the winter will need to come first, but I don't see why you can't grow a crop."

Rebecca watched Pa listen to the things his brother-in-law told him as if the words were dropping on his ears straight from heaven. It wouldn't be long before he was back to making his brew. She was fine with it. There was room for them both out here in this beautiful country. As long as she didn't have to go back to that nothing-life she had before her sister-pact, before the shanty burnt.

The coffee churned in her belly. She could almost smell the sour mash and Pa's burnt hair and flesh from that day. She couldn't look away from the burns on Pa's forehead and ear. A shiver shook her—like when a rat jumped from the shelf in the mash shed and ran down her leg—at the thought of going back to drink-making.

She knew better than a hundred-year-old saint that Pa would never change, never be different, but she couldn't stay there in mind or body. She needed roots. "Can I plant my rose?" she blurted.

She longed for this to really be home—to have something to write to her sisters about.

"Certainly, you may. And anything else you might take a fancy to. Jules was notorious for digging up mere weeds she deemed pretty and planting them close to the house where she could see them. She tried to bring a climbing rose from California with us. We built the cabin with a place in mind for it. Sadly, it never thrived. Yours could take its place with my blessing."

When Rebecca stood right then, her chair scraped on the floor.

Leander's mouth gaped. "Now?"

As silent as Pa, she claimed her flower and moved to the door.

He stood, winced, and said, "Her spot was to the right of the steps on your way out. If you want a shovel or a spade, they're in the front bay of the big barn." His stays creaked.

Rebecca was out the door and down the steps before he finished. She set the rose on the steps and jogged to the barn for the shovel.

I can't live like Pa. I have to put down roots. I have to tell Cora Mae, Heather, and Rose about Eagle Creek. I need them to know I'm here—that I'm home—that my rose is planted. That I have more of a future than packing mash for Pa's whiskey. She was halfway back to the porch steps with the shovel in her hand when her own thoughts settled her.

A pair of goldfinches flirted and danced past her. The confident yellow birds knew what they wanted. Rebecca knew the same. She wanted a home—a home that wouldn't shift and move like the sandy shores of the many rivers they crossed to get to this green place. One home that wasn't reliant on Pa's odd whims and withheld secrets. *I had a brother.* There was more to that part of her history. She would stay until she found out all there was to know—and more.

She would stay, learn how to help Leander with his farm, and put down roots to grow as large as the oak, and maple, and fir trees that stood around this farm as thick as her father's cornstalks would stand around her. She clutched her rose to her chest and looked to see where she would plant it—where home would begin.

CHAPTER NINE

Rebecca knelt next to the stairs where Leander had directed her to plant her rose. "Home." She said the word slowly and on purpose. It tasted as sweet as clover nectar on her tongue. "Home." She whispered it again and again as she cleared a spot and dug a hole for her sister rose.

"Thought I saw someone come past the place." A man spoke close to Rebecca.

She squeaked and tipped from her knees to her backside, using the shovel as a shield.

A large stranger stepped back. "Sorry. I didn't mean to scare ya. Thought you heard me coming. Folks tell me I make the noise of ten oxen."

Rebecca scrabbled to her feet. "Can I help you?" Her voice sounded rude to her own ears. "I'm Rebecca Packwood," she said to soften the greeting and offered her hand covered in brown dirt. He shook her hand.

"Not sure if I heard of no Packwoods." He scratched his unwashed scalp. "I thought I'd check on Leander, feed the stock, and get on home before dark. It's what I always do, when our cows is eatin' Leander's grass—though there aren't as many animals this year."

Leander must've heard the commotion on the

steps. He yelled, "Afternoon, Reuben. Reuben, meet my niece Rebecca. Will you take her and my brother-in-law, Otis, with you as you feed? Answer any questions they have. They're family, and they'll be living here and helping me get the farm up and running again. And don't leave without collecting a letter. I'm writing one to Eddie right now."

"Will do." Reuben crooked one eyebrow at her.

Rebecca turned away from him and finished pushing her rose into the dirt and tucking the loose soil around its roots. Planting it must come first. While she worked she said, "I can help with the animals, if you show me." She left the shovel leaning against the house. Before he answered, she asked, "Can you show me where to get a bucket of water?"

"Pump's over there. Bucket's by it." He pointed to a well that was nearly grown over with bushes.

After she watered her rose, she led the way to the barn. Pa didn't help feed, but he followed. Reuben stopped and leaned on the split-rail fence, looking at the solid black bull standing with his head bent and cropping the grass that came up to their shoulders. Rebecca joined him, admiring the sea of green grass shaded by a grove of massive oak trees.

"That's Baron the Bull. He's not friendly. Stay clear of his pen." Reuben pointed back behind the house. "The pond is over there." There was a line of tall trees on the far side of a large pasture. "I can show you after we feed."

They moved into the barn. Pa asked questions about the tools and supplies he would need to break ground on his corn crop. She ignored the conversation and tried to watch everything Reuben did to take care of the animals.

"Your uncle has been sharing his spring grass as a trade for feeding his stock. We—my older brother Joe and I—live down the steep hill you came up on. Our place is tucked back in the trees, by the creek. Under the trees, in the shade, our grass is a month or more behind Leander's up here on the hill in the sun."

Rebecca thought the farm was the most beautiful she'd ever seen. The evening sun shined warm on their backs as they looked over the field that, at the same time, somehow was covered in gray clouds. The combination cast an eerie gloom around them accented by the vibrant sun. It was as uncertain as she was about whatever she would find out about her mother's promise or secret.

"Let's feed before the rain starts." Reuben led the way down the well-trodden path to the second smaller barn.

Pa followed behind them. "Where's the garden? Leander said the field for my corn is behind the gardens."

"Yes, over there." Reuben pointed the direction

and traipsed past her and filled grain buckets. "I'll get this done as fast as I can so I can show you both the garden and the pond before the rain gets serious. When it gets warm enough, we all swim in the pond. I want to help Leander down there for a soak, when it warms enough. He'll love it."

"How long ago did he get hurt?"

"He took a spill last year, then another in March. He led a string of drafts into town to sell. Something spooked his horse. The horse reared and stepped off the trail, and they both tumbled to the bottom of a small ravine. His horse came down on him and messed him up. Naantam, the Indian, found him and carried him home. I think how he is now is as good as it's going to get."

"We met Naantam."

The few cows complained their hunger as they came from the far field. Each stopped, one-by-one, as they fed.

"If you want to see the pond, we should go now. Let's grab the shotgun."

While Reuben collected the gun from somewhere in the barn, Rebecca looked around to see if Pa was coming to join them. He seemed happy to break ground on his corn plot. Reuben handed her the shotgun. "You never need a gun until you don't have it on ya."

She took it, tucked the butt of the gun under her arm, and pointed the barrel to the dirt as she followed Reuben down the path.

As they came up to the water's edge, two bullfrogs squawked and jumped into the safety of the water. A wave of peace settled around her. "This place is something beautiful."

"Ain't it? Prettier than some of those Frenchie art paintings I saw when I was a kid. The stream runs off this pond and goes underground over there." Reuben pointed. "It must join up with the creek somewhere along the way." He shifted his weight to rest on one heel, pulled a blade of grass out of the ground, and squatted down to poke it into the wet dirt.

Rebecca couldn't picture Reuben as a kid or around French paintings, heavy whiskers and unwashed black hair poking out in all directions preventing it.

He took a deep sniff of the sodden air, said, "I like it here," and picked up a rock. He skipped the rock toward the middle of the pond and startled a pair of wood ducks into flight—one dull, one covered in vibrant blue and green. "We met Jules and Leander in California a long time ago. I think Leander felt sorry for us and had us packed up and following him up here. It was just Joe and me."

"How long ago was that? How long ago did Jules—?" Rebecca didn't want to talk about Jules's death. She looked back at the water and could see a salamander beneath the surface.

"Nigh on thirteen years. I was seventeen and

Joe twenty. We lost Jules, ah . . ." He scratched his shoulder. "She got the side sickness. Sad. She was in pain and gone within a week."

Reuben's shoulders drooped. After a long minute, he stood and looked at the sky again. "I best be going. I left my nag standing at the rail." He lifted his hat in her direction. "Can you find your way back?"

"Yes. I'll be fine. I'd like to sit here and take it all in. Nice to meet you and thanks for showing me the chores. I want to be as much help to Uncle Leander, to this farm, as I possibly can."

"Naantam will be back. He has been helping with the feeding. If he doesn't show in the morning, I'll feed them double when I come tomorrow evening."

Rebecca resettled the heavy gun. "Or I can copy what I saw you do just now?"

Reuben gave her a toothy smile. "Sounds good. I won't turn down help."

He made his way back up the trail as she moved over to the large rocks and stood on the muddy bank where he'd stood. She looked at the pond and all the green growth surrounding it. When she knew he was out of earshot, she whispered it again. "Home."

She tried to settle into the place, letting the surroundings pour through her. Then she studied the ground at her feet, picked up a small, blue-black rock, rinsed the mud from it in the pond, and sat on the nearest boulder and was still, enjoying the novelty of not walking all day.

What did she need to do to help Leander's farm provide enough for her and Pa to stay here? What was the secret promise Mother made both men agree too? What was the inheritance the letter talked about? Could the inheritance be this farm? An injured man might be thinking of his heirs when he was writing a letter in which he admitted he couldn't keep the property going. Maybe Leander would tell her soon. *A girl could hope.*

"Home." Listening to the chatting birds, she looked around her again, memorizing the details she would write to Cora Mae, Heather, and Rose about. Staying here didn't feel real yet. They'd stopped and stayed at a couple forts along the Trail, and this had that passing-through feeling. She stayed at the ponds edge. No need to be in a hurry. Her feet didn't believe they wouldn't walk miles tomorrow.

She fingered the new rock. She needed to talk about Reuben, Leander, and Naantam. And a letter to her sisters was what was needed. She wasn't alone. If she sat here in this peaceful beauty a little longer, then maybe her heart would believe it.

Sweat droplets clustered on Clark's forehead while others dripped down his back. The oxen lowed as they trudged up the last hill.

Leander must've heard or smelled them coming. He was out on the front porch, leaning heavily on the railing.

"We're here, Leander," Eddie called out. "I know you're not up to caring for these brutes, but I needed a place to put them. My barns are full."

One hand rose to block the bright sun from his face. He waved with the other. "Hello, Eddie. And Clark, it's been a few years since I've seen you. You've gotta be taller than your pa, and he's no small feller."

Clark came forward and shook Leander's hand. "He's still got me by a few inches. I'm sure I look different than when I was here last."

"Got your mama's coloring. She has the prettiest yeller hair a man ever did see. I told her so once. Your pa almost blackened my eye."

"That must've been before the Cape Hope trip?"

"It was. Feels like a different life to think about it."

Eddie patted the side of a tired ox.

"It's providential you came. I had a pen and paper out just now to send for you and these animals. I can take them and care for them."

"You feeling better?" Eddie asked as he reached to shake Leander's hand.

Leander said, "No. I'm not better, but I have help. Looks like a fine mess you brought me. Go ahead and put them out to pasture. We'll let them have the afternoon to nap and feed. Then we can sort them. Or I should say, you fellows can sort them. After that, I have a plan you'll need to hear. It involves you, Eddie. I'll fill you in over vittles, after these beasts are settled."

Clark asked, "Pond still where it was?"

"I didn't move it." He laughed. "Go cool off. It's shaping up to be almost warm today. The water will be cold. June sky doesn't know if it should be sunny or stormy. It will be nice when spring finally gives way to summer."

"Cold, yes. But at least it will wash the stink from him." Eddie punched Clark's shoulder as they moved the oxen to the gated pasture.

Eddie and Clark left Leander and made swift work of the animals. They were on the trail to the pond in a dozen minutes. Clark's long strides set the pace to the water. "One point in favor of banking—a bath every day of the week. You smell like a hog."

"I smell?" Eddie ran a hand over his red hair.

"Yes. When I try to get a fresh breath of air, beyond my own stench, it smells like a hog—that's you." Clark stopped and tugged one boot off and then another, tossed them aside, grabbed the collar of his shirt at the back of his neck, and pulled it off, still moving along the trail. Bare-chested, he trotted, working his leather belt and the top button on his grimy new jeans. "It's been six long years since you and I were here together. If I remember right, I owe you something."

Eddie shed his clothes as well.

Both men were down to their drawers. Clark stopped and glared at Eddie, making him stop in the trail too.

Eddie flung his shirt over a bush. "What?" He hesitated.

"Cow pie? Ring any bells?"

Eddie laughed. "I was just remembering that myself."

"Yes." This place held many fun memories. Even the air smelled free compared to office work. But there was no way he would ruin the perfect moment by thinking of banking, or not having a place to live, or not having enough money to pay for a place to live. He slugged his friend hard on the shoulder and took off at a dead run toward the pond.

"Hey!" Eddie chased. "At least it was a dry patty."

Clark weaved and bobbed through the trees, bare feet tender on the path. He would never forget this trail. Every turn, every bend, every boulder was stained on his childhood brain. He had only been here a few times for short stays, but he loved this place. He sped up at the sight of the mound of boulders that trapped the water into the deep end of the pond. He balanced on one rock after the next without slowing.

He could hear Eddie trying to catch him. He shouted, "It was a cow pie. They could never be dry enough!" He leaped off the last rock and tucked his knees to his chest, scoping out his watery landing.

Before gravity did her work, he made eye contact with an alert, doe-eyed woman pointing the business end of a shotgun square at him. He disappeared beneath the surface of cold water. Eddie plunged in on him before he broke the surface—sucking him down a second time.

A branch snapped. A shiver of terror came over her when heavy thuds came her way. Was the bull out?

A bird flew.

Then all the birds went silent.

The clomps came faster. She stood and lifted the gun, eyes wide, breath still. What could it be? She hadn't been around these parts long enough to know what she should be afraid of. Her head shouted for her to run, but her knees locked. Then she heard yelling.

She pulled the rifle tight into her shoulder. This could be her last moment. She thought of what Rose, Heather, and Cora Mae would do if something happened to her. They wouldn't even find out for a long time. She lined her finger alongside the trigger, waiting to see the danger.

A bare-chested man came running toward her in nothing but his britches. Never slowing, bellowing as loud as a donkey, he jumped off the highest rock. Wavy blond hair hung loose about his head. He saw her and the gun she pointed at his naked chest before he splashed into the pond.

Another uncouth cry followed. A second shirtless man leaped off the high rock right behind him. His hair was almost as blazing red as his scarlet drawers. The second splash sent a cascade of drops sprinkling around her.

By the time their heads surfaced side-by-side, she bent the muzzle to the ground. "Thank you, Lord." She could've pulled the trigger easy as not—she could have pulled it by accident with the waves of nerves crashing over her.

The redhead hadn't seen her yet. He lurched up and broke the surface, a crown of water following behind him as he tackled the first jumper. He smothered him back under the water, crowing like a rooster until his feet were pulled from under him. The pond water muffled his squawk.

The fellow that saw her struck out a few swim strokes away from the redhead. When both were standing in water only covering half their chests, he said, "Stop, Eddie. We have a guest."

Eddie changed directions mid-lunge, turned toward her, and froze.

Rebecca studied the blond man. She spent no time with men her age. Archie didn't count. Reuben was at least ten years older than her, and his hair wasn't the color of dried wheat, and his chest looked nothing like—

She stopped her thought, gulped and swallowed, but her mouth felt like she'd eaten a dandelion puff.

He passed his hand across his chest. "Sorry to barge in on you like that. We didn't know anyone was about."

The redhead, Eddie, lowered himself in the water so only his head stuck out. "I'm Eddie, Leander's nephew, and this buffoon is Clark. We brought weary oxen to pasture in Leander's fields. Hot work." He looked at the blond.

"Clark?" Was this the same man who swept past her in the street?

"My name is Clark. I'm helping Eddie even though he smells just like oxen. We decided to clean-up." He patted the water's surface. "You live around here? You know Leander? Have I met you before?"

Rebecca wondered if her heart would ever return to its regular, controlled rhythm. It was dancing around in her chest like it was lost. She loosened her grip on the gun and relaxed her stance, shifting her weight, buying her voice a few more precious seconds before she had to speak to this friendly boy. *Not boy. Man.* Her heart fluttered.

She looked at the muscle lines on his chest again. He must've noticed because he flexed. She cleared her throat. "Oxen? Already? That didn't take long. I thought Leander was going to send you a letter today. I'm Rebecca, Leander's niece. I came through town."

The redhead said, "He didn't send it. I ended up with more than my pasture and barn could handle when a large group of pioneers came to town after walking around Lolo Pass. They were a really good deal. I rounded up what I could manage and brought them here. Looks like we need to work on the fencing back there?"

"Yes." Her voice trailed off. She shrugged and the gun at her hip raised and lowered. She didn't know a thing about what the farm needed.

"Good thing you didn't get a shot off. Would've surprised me for sure. Big gun for a little thing like you."

Eddie kicked out under the water.

Waves rippled, and Clark scowled at his friend. "What?"

"Never mock someone that's armed." He slapped the water, and a handful sprayed over Clark.

Rebecca slung the shotgun over one shoulder and put her hand in her pocket, rolling her new-found rock around. The movement was awkward, inexperienced, and she knew it showed.

"I think we met, outside the church?"

Clark shifted his weight from one foot to the other. The water swished around him. "Yes. We did. Fancy that. Here. Let me help you." Clark walked toward her and the edge of the pond. The water lowered as he came, revealing more of his bare chest and eventually the top ring of his drawers.

Rebecca couldn't turn away. Her face warmed. She was sure it matched Eddie's hair, but Clark kept coming. He never noticed.

"Wait. Clark!" Eddie's booming voice shook her.

Clark obeyed. "What?"

"No pants, you idiot."

"She needs help."

"Sorry, ma'am." He grabbed Clark's wrist as he spoke to his friend. "She got out here fine without your help, now leave her be. Stay in the water." Eddie grinned at her. "You can go ahead and shoot him. He's dumb as a rock today."

Rebecca maneuvered her way around the end of the pond and across the large boulders, trying not to think about how much she liked rocks—even dumb rocks.

Her steps were quick, light and agile. She felt both of their eyes following her, but she didn't have the nerve to turn and face them. Clark wasn't the only one being dumb. "See you back at the cabin!"

She thought Clark was the one who yelled a response. She was off the rocks and out of sight when she heard Eddie mock and rebuke Clark. The sound of splashing drowned out Clark's response.

She was nearly back to the cabin before her

heart settled into its normal rhythm. What was she going to do now? She couldn't ask about the promise or the letter with two new strangers listening. But she could learn about the farm and what was needed before winter and for it to thrive enough to hold them all.

Going back to the cabin felt more like retreating and running away than making determined plans for her future. Pa did that. He avoided the hard. She went up the steps calling for Leander with thoughts as murky as pond water. The only thing that was clear was that she refused to run. She wanted to be different than Pa.

CHAPTER TEN

Clark shook the water out of his hair and watched her go.

Once she was out of sight, Eddie lit into him. "You sounded as daft as a hillbilly."

"I wasn't that bad. She startled me, that's all. She had a gun. My sisters would faint. Father made 'em scared to death of guns. She could probably outshoot me." He hadn't had much need to practice in town. He looked down the path she'd just taken. He smiled when he remembered nearly knocking her down in the street the first time he met her. There was no way he would tell Eddie about that.

"I've never seen you like that. You almost walked out of the water in wet skivvies. Usually, you have a poet's charm with the ladies, or at least a dancer's light foot as you strategically bolt." Eddie laughed. "Your mother would've shot you herself, if she was here. Either that or, knowing her, she would've used the business end of Rebecca's gun to point you two to the preacher."

Clark stared after where the lady had gone. "That wouldn't be so bad. I can see myself married to her."

"What? Did you hit your head on a rock when

151

we jumped in?" Eddie stood up in the water and tipped his head to the side, trying to drain his ear. "You all but swore off women for life. You just ran away from town—from the fairer sex—like they had leprosy. And now you tell me you could see yourself marrying a girl who almost shot you—that you just met?"

"Yup." Why was his friend looking so thunderstruck? Hadn't he seen her big, brown eyes and thick hair the color of morning cocoa? "You'll see. Everyone in Oregon City knows a Sutherland man can talk anyone into what's best for them. It's the family way."

Eddie started toward him, splashing. "Ah. I see."

Clark said, "I'm going to marry her. I'm pretty sure I'm the best thing that's ever happened to her." Clark stood tall on the outside, but inside he was quaking. *What if she doesn't like me? What if she can see "marry me" in my eyes and runs?* "At least I hope so."

"Sutherland charm, eh?"

Both men splashed and scrubbed until their skin was pink. Eddie washed his armpits and mimicked, " 'My, your gun is big. I see you are a *tiny* woman, and even though you stood ready, locked, and loaded like you thought I was an intruder, you look poised and confident, but you must be fragile and weak and in need of *my* big strong muscles.' Yah—Sutherland charm. What a bunch of hooey."

He was right. Clark treated her like she was fragile. Did she think he was a simpleton? *Hope not.* Her brown eyes stained his memory. There was no trust in them—they seemed skittish. How was he supposed to gain her trust? He never tried to do such a thing before.

Before he could figure out his next step, Eddie's full weight collided with his and submerged him. Water flooded his nose. They wrestled until both were water-logged.

Out of breath, Eddie huffed, "Are you serious? About her? We barely got her name."

Clark climbed from the water and stood behind a thick tree, checking for Rebecca. When he was certain she was long gone, he shook the water out of his hair, stripped, and wrung water from his under shorts.

He thought about what Eddie said and considered the little he knew about the petite brunette. He couldn't form any answer other than yes. He was serious. It was like he could see her old, with gray hair streaking her temples as it flowed back into her braid, her tiny curves tucked perfectly under his arm after years of care.

A stick poked him in the neck.

He jerked and swiped, thinking it was a bee.

Eddie laughed and then pretended to lash him with the branch. "You really are gone for her. You've been gazing at those rocks where she was standing like you're expecting a visiting angel."

Clark did not understand how he knew. But he did. "I will marry her, Eddie."

His reverent whisper checked his friend. "I can tell you're serious, but how can you know that? How can you be sure?"

Clark shrugged. "I guess we'll find out soon enough." He couldn't hold back his wonder. "She never scolded or fussed." He stopped and looked across the pond at the rock. "And her eyes weren't desperate and begging. In fact, I think she could have used that gun."

"You are in for it. I predict you will be covered in more manure than just cow pies by the end of this trip. I can hardly wait to see it." He climbed out of the water and began to dry as well. "If Leander is really ready to bring this farm alive, you could ask him if you could work on his projects in exchange for room and board for the widow's pigs. There is plenty of time to drive them up here before they whelp. You could be Clark the pig farmer."

Clark knew exactly how much money he had and exactly how little he knew about any other career path other than banking. There wasn't much to think about. The timing of the pig idea was a gift. They were a beginning, and if he could get permission to raise the pigs on Leander's place, he would truly have an opportunity to begin a real business of his own. And he would be close to Rebecca.

"Yes. That's a good idea. I'll talk with Leander when we get back to the cabin, and I'll buy the pigs when we go back to town."

His stomach grumbled, reminding them both of the primary reason they were down here—to get clean so they could enter the house to eat without stinking it up. They finished dressing with Eddie telling Clark all he knew about pig farming.

Then they made their way back to the cabin, one talking about the heavenly smell of meat frying, the other thinking about the person cooking the meat.

Rebecca went into the cabin talking, "Did you know that Clark and Eddie are here and they brought us oxen?" She crossed the room and hung the shotgun back in its place on the wall. Did she just announce that like this was her home? Was this her new life? She and Pa arrived only this morning and already they were building toward a new future. At least she was. Pa was stuck. He was still out turning the soil for his future corn crop. Repeating history.

Leander called from his bedroom. "Yes. I saw them and the animals. I'm glad you met them. They'll be hungry when they come in. Would you mind putting more food on? What we had this morning was wonderful."

Rebecca found a place inside the food larder, brushed and rebraided her hair, not thinking about her motives for cleaning up at all before she put her hands to work making a second meal. Meeting Leander's needs was the perfect way to put her thoughts in order.

Potatoes were sizzling and the ham smelled good when Leander came to the table, slowly, sat in his special chair, and said, "How is that for timing? The Lord's goodness for sure. The same day I was going to send a letter into town for more livestock, they arrive. It will give us a head start on getting things rolling again." Leander reached for his knife and fork. "Rebecca, you'll have to learn about the oxen's care. Eddie has his own animals back at his farm. I'm sure he won't be able to stay for very long. I don't know about Clark."

She left Leander to his own thoughts so she could focus on hers. She wasn't any more settled when she heard the men coming up the steps.

"Go ahead and come on in, boys."

They came into the cabin—Eddie ahead of Clark.

"Take a seat. Rebecca's fixing us a solid feast." He pushed a full coffee cup in Eddie's direction. "Eddie, do you have access to any draft horses? That's where the real money is, or at least that's where it was. I'm ready to bring this place back to life."

Rebecca didn't know Leander enough to understand the depth of his feelings, but anyone could have heard the emotion in his voice and seen the excitement in his eyes.

"I only have a few cows and enough chickens to keep me in eggs, which won't be enough, now that you're all here. We need to bring the garden back. End of June is awful late, but we'll need more than what Naantam has put in to sustain us." Leander nodded to Rebecca. "Maybe even bring back all the livestock. You do realize, I'm making all these plans and I won't be able to do more than put up a little capital to get the animals here, right? I'll need all of you, for the long haul, if this is to work, and whatever help Otis gives."

Rebecca would have reassured him. His plans were fast becoming her plans. If his plans didn't work, then she would be out of a home too.

Leander didn't slow. He kept talking, "I kept Baron because he is irreplaceable. Well, mostly I was too sad to see him go. But if we can bring in some cows and a handful of older heifers then we could begin to turn a profit next spring. I think there's enough growing season yet to get a second cropping out of the garden."

"I'll do that." It was a relief for Rebecca to hear about a part of bringing the farm back that she could handle. She didn't know how to store food, sell food, or butcher or smoke meat, but if she could get the garden going, then she could learn about each thing as it came up. She would put down her own roots at the same time as the garden.

Eddie was nodding along. "We'll help get the soil turned. Here's an idea—if I go back into town and bring out a pair of drafts, like you want, if they have already been trained, then even if they are worn out and trail tired, they could make the heavy lifting of garden prep easier. We'd have to go slow. I have a dozen or so pullets that will start laying eggs in a month or so. I hatched them out under a broody hen back in February. But there are too many chickens at my folks' place."

Rebecca watched Clark out of the corner of her eye. She noticed when he sat forward and put his elbows on the table, following the whole conversation. He said, "I didn't have time to tell you before, Leander, but I recently quit my job at the bank to be a pig farmer. I'm pretty new at it, but excited to find my way. I don't have my own land yet. Could I possibly bring my first pair of breed sows to your barns? I'll trade chores for their room and board."

Eddie laughed and smiled after Clark asked.

Clark joined him. "Room and board for me too. I don't know what I'm doing, yet. But I'm willing to work hard and learn."

Rebecca didn't know what they found so entertaining about the request. She could feel Leander agreeing before he answered.

"A hearty yes from me. I'll take all the help I can get. And put me down for two piglets. The two that are out there are nearly ready to butcher.

I'll raise them out for the smokehouse. The larder has shrunk quite a bit with just me running things, without my Jules, and to an almost dangerous level of low since I got injured."

Rebecca looked around at all the men at the table. "You'll have to tell me what it is you think needs doing. I am planning to be worth my keep too." Heat bloomed Rebecca's face. She said the words out loud that she meant to keep to herself. She didn't want Leander to regret his request for them to come join the farm. She wanted him to relax enough around her to tell her more about Mother and all the other hidden things.

She was embarrassed by her words, but also determined to do everything Leander talked about. He was talking about feed crops, bees for honey, and putting up hay for the barn. There was enough work for a lifetime. Rebecca wanted to be around to see it all.

Leander rattled on, but all Clark could do was try not to stare. Rebecca looked tame and quaint beside the cookstove, turning the ham steaks. She looked neat and pressed after the pond. Her dress squeezed her petite curves, her white neck exposed. So delicate and fragile with her braid tucked and pinned tight at the base of her skull. He caught himself staring. He would do well to remember Eddie's teasing.

Leander must've picked up on his gawking.

He moved between them—like he was guarding her. "Uh, sorry. I've been a little remiss in my excitement. Boys, I'd like you to meet my niece, Rebecca. Rebecca, Clark's been a friend of the family for years. His pa came around Cape Hope with Jules and me. Good man. I owe him much."

"He'd say the same about you, sir. Even gives you credit for saving his life. I'd love to hear the reason, one of these days. I can tell he's keeping something to himself on that score."

Leander chuckled but gave no explanation. He continued his introductions. "And Eddie, he's my nephew—my Jules's brother's boy. These two have been as tight as two sides of a coin for as long as I can remember. And it sounds like that will continue, if you're going to be a pig farmer and not a banker, Clark? How are your folks doing, Eddie?"

Leander turned his attention to Eddie as he answered the question, freeing Clark to steal glances at Rebecca. She moved about the kitchen quietly, loading the fried potatoes onto a serving plate. Nothing about what she was doing was fancy or attention seeking, but he couldn't look away.

She scooped a handful of her skirt and used it as a hot-pad as she carried the vittles to the table. "Ham steaks are done."

"Thank you, dear." Leander moved to his specially built chair.

"You boys will have to make yourself a bed in the hayloft. You've done that before. If you search around, those plank beds are still under the hay. Better the planks than the straw blades poking you in the back all night."

"That won't be a problem, he still sleeps like a fallen log. A fallen log that snores like a bear," Clark said.

They all heard a heavy thud on the front porch.

Clark watched the color drain from Rebecca's warm cheeks. He stepped between her and the door. His turn to guard her.

The door opened and a man carrying three jugs came in. "Don't just stand there, give me a hand, girl. I don't want to drop 'em."

Rebecca moved from behind Clark, back straight and tall, an irritated glance scolding Clark as she passed to grab a jug. Why would she be mad? He stepped forward to take the heavy jar she'd just claimed. His fingers brushed hers and felt like a match touched to dry tinder. His whole body felt like it was on fire. He checked her eyes to see if she felt the same.

Her eyes flamed, but not like his. More like a riled yellow jacket. He let go of the jug and stepped back. Was she annoyed with him or her pa?

"Have you decided if you're going to stay here on the farm for good or make your own way, Otis? You came a long way. You're not obligated.

We're making plans for the farm and we're willing to include your corn field." Leander asked the questions as if he expected a yes.

Clark watched Rebecca's stiff response. She tucked the jug away in the larder, but she still looked annoyed when she came back out. If her pa didn't stay, would she go too? He didn't like that question. He would have no way or reason to get to know her or follow her. Whatever this captivation was would be over before it got started.

"Yeah, for a while anyway. Need to make more of these." He gave the room a toothy grin. And limped to a chair.

Leander made introductions, again. "We're a fine pair. Otis got burned when his shanty exploded, and a horse rolled over me. You fellas should be a sight more careful. You only get one body."

While Leander went on, Clark fixed it so he sat at Rebecca's elbow. Eddie sat in the chair opposite—one eyebrow raised—smug and daring, and still mocking.

Otis talked to the room without looking to see if anyone was listening. "I bought these off the neighbors in the two-story white house. They had a few chickens stolen and few other things go missing."

Leander grunted. "That doesn't sound good. We've never had trouble of the seedy sort before.

All kinds of people are coming across the Trail. You know how to shoot, Rebecca?"

Rebecca looked right at Clark. They were both thinking about the pond, no doubt. "I've shot a gun enough times to know I need a refresher."

Leander smoothed a hand over his shirt front. "I can walk you through that. And I'm sure Naantam will want to teach you to hunt. He's a fantastic archer. He's always bringing me something he shot or trapped. It will be good to add those skills, and it will add more variety to the larder."

Clark perked up. "I'm game to learn too. I may have lots of questions on a lot of these things, but I'm not afraid of working hard or learning."

Leander folded his arms over his chest, looking at them both. "Good. We'll start with a shooting lesson. Keeping you safe is foremost. I don't like that a thief is about. We'll do that after we eat and I get a chance to look over the oxen more closely. And I want to introduce you to Sheba. She's about to have her baby. She's my pride and joy. I'd appreciate you all keeping your eyes on her."

Clark agreed like everyone around them. He would make himself available to the shooting lesson too. The farm was the best open door he could have found for his new business venture. He had a lot to learn and Leander needed the help, so he was willing to teach. Clark planned to be the best student around.

"It'll take a couple days for these oxen to settle. Once they do, and once the stalls are ready, I think I'll get back to town, collect a couple drafts, crate the chickens, and bring your sows back," Eddie said. "I know the structures are here, but we should probably check fences and gather feed."

"I can do that." Clark was glad to have the duties laid out for him. And he could ask more questions about the pigs when they were here. He was a farmer. He would check fences, tend a barnyard, and learn to shoot. He wasn't sorry at all that his life had changed so much. He needed to work hard enough to earn his keep and have a more permanent plan in place by the time winter came. He wouldn't be able to sleep in the hayloft when the weather turned.

CHAPTER ELEVEN

Joe came riding up the hill toward home, tired and dirty after being gone a week. He reined his horse behind thick trees and watched his brother Reuben go about his evening chores. He climbed out of the saddle and sat leaning his back against a log. He fell asleep thinking through his new plans to take out Leander and Naantam at the same time without any suspicion falling on him.

He thought of poison and all that could go wrong, then he thought about a fire, but that would take out the cabin or the barn, which defeated the purpose. No, he needed an accident that involved both men. The timing was tricky, and he needed to be one step ahead of Naantam.

The smell of meat cooking awakened him. "And that's my call." His horse nickered. The plan would come to him. He would be patient until it did.

Joe left for a week every couple of months to get away from the monotony of the farm and Reuben, and to think. He would go to town and keep his eyes open for information and opportunities. He managed to keep money in his pocket that was a lot less backbreaking to acquire than farming provided. He went the rest of the way home and was sitting at the table by the time Reuben was dishing steaks. "Smells good."

"You always get home in time to eat." A fat, furry dog lay on the floor watching Reuben's every move. "Find what you want this time?"

"Not particularly. The good properties are taken. We should've looked around more when we first came." Joe did manage to come home when the chores were done and the meals were hot. He prided himself on using his mind more than his muscles, and he intended to keep doing that until something, mainly Leander's farm, fell in their favor. Then he would spend the rest of his days reminding Reuben how much he owed his good fortune to Joe's cunning.

Reuben put two more steaks on to fry. When the raw meat was sizzling, he sat back down at the square table across from Joe. "What is it 'zactly you want that we don't have? If it's pastureland, we have that taken care of with Leander."

"We shouldn't depend on anyone else. We should be self-sufficient. Trusting Leander was our first mistake."

Reuben checked a predictable huff.

He and Joe had argued the same point on the regular for years. Neither saw the situation the same as the other.

Reuben, ever the peacemaker, without an ambitious bone in his body, never stopped trying to get them to agree. "I thought you might say that. I've figured a plan of my own. But I'm not moving, even if you find a place."

"If I find the right one, you will." Joe would find a way to make Reuben move, even if that wasn't his brother's preference. *I can do that.* Leverage was easier to come by than people thought, and Reuben wouldn't even notice if it was Joe creating the leverage . . . he hadn't so far. Joe took a bite of the hot meat and smiled to think of how well he played his brother.

"All I want is here." Reuben flipped a piece of gristle to the dog. The dog caught and swallowed the morsel without getting to his feet and never blinked his piercing blue eyes. The dog also watched Joe.

Reuben didn't notice that either.

Reuben was full of his new idea. "We've had this conversation enough times to know what the other is gonna say. I've decided on something new. You might be right about not expecting the deal with Leander's pasture to last. I plan to make money to pay for feed and grass by making shakes and shingles. Every home needs 'em, and not everyone wants to make 'em.

"Next time I go to the city, I'll take a load and see how it pays. I won't be able to do it forever, the trees will run thin, but we need a plan for if Leander doesn't want to share pasture. That might even happen, now that his brother-in-law and niece are here. Suppose they'll get more stock, eventually." Reuben flipped another gristle strip to the dog. The dog's teeth clicked when it caught it.

They both licked their lips and thankfully missed the way Joe stiffened. "New neighbors?"

"Yep. Nice folks. Otis, Leander's brother-in-law, is a belly burner without his copper fixings. He's pretty bent on getting his still set up and put back together. His daughter, Rebecca, is pretty—a tiny little thing. She seems eager to learn all she can about farming. She's saved me a weeks chores already. Kinda nice having help. There's a couple other fellas up there too."

Joe flipped his own meat scrap to the dog and thought about what his brother's new information really meant. Reuben's jab about help was ignored. Joe'd been using his excuse about looking for new land to get away from the farm and its daily grind for months, but the truth was, he had no intention of moving anywhere except up the hill.

Leander led them amiss all those years ago. He'd taken advantage of two kids back then, and he lied too. Leander said he didn't have any family to speak of. He'd said it more than once. He talked about a nephew but the nephew showed no interest. He seemed to have his own prospects in town, that Joe could tell, and he was paying attention. Besides, if Joe was on the land and living there, let the nephew try and run him off.

Joe rubbed his hip where his revolver was still

slung. *I want Leander incapacitated. I want him so far behind on the farm he had to ask for help—to depend on us.* That was his plan.

He took another bite and chewed his frustrations out. A brother and a niece? *I must see how bad things are.* A drunk and a girl? *I wonder what she looks like.* If Reuben was the observant sort, he might have noticed the irritation turn to a gleam in Joe's eyes that matched the expectant dog's look. "In the morning, I think I might walk up the hill and introduce myself. It will be good to stay friendly with Leander without depending on him. Good luck on the shingles, even though I can already tell you it won't be enough."

This time his brother ignored Joe. Instead he said, "Otis, the brother, spent his day digging in the cornfield, but she plans on working the farm. It will be good for Leander. You want some blueberries?"

Reuben turned to a crock on the counter and dumped a couple fists full of berries onto each of their plates. He also forked the finished second steak for each of them.

Joe grabbed a handful of fruit and stood. "You can have my steak; I'm going to water Jep." The dog went to the door with him. Joe could feel the animal watching his back with a leery eye. He closed the door behind him before the dog could follow him out. The mutt made it harder to stay hidden.

Joe ate his berries as he walked his horse to the small stream that ran behind the barn and the cabin. Then he put Jep away, slipped out the back of the barn, and walked the trail to Leander's.

When Leander's cabin was in sight, he could see a few changes already. Mainly more animals in the pasture. *This doesn't look good.* Leander wouldn't need him, if these newcomers took care of him. Joe climbed over the split-rail fence and found his way closer by staying behind the thick oak tree trunks. There was someone outside working the garden. Even without seeing the long braid running down her back, he knew it must be Leander's niece. "What did Reuben say your name was?" His words were so quiet they were barely louder than the wind in the tall grass.

Joe pulled his mother's favorite opera glasses out of his pocket and watched her alternate between digging, watering, and weeding. "You're a per-tty little thing. Maybe there's an even better way to go about claiming this farm." Joe imagined he had all the time in the world to make his mark on this family—on her.

He looked at the solid log cabin—three or four times the size of his and Reuben's. He studied the mature fruit trees that needed pruned. They hadn't been tended since before Leander's accident. But they were evenly clipped underneath—a sure sign of healthy deer in the area. The grass, the barn, the pond, the sunlight, this was it. This was the place that should be his.

A hot poker twisted in his gut when he remembered traveling with Leander all those years ago. Leander may have said he was looking out for him and Reuben, but it was a lie. *First choice. First choice, my eye.* He only offered them first choice because he felt sorry for two young orphans on their own. If he was truly looking out for them, he'd have traded them places that first week when he saw how much better situated this place was.

The girl was spilling water a little at a time at the base of each plant. He daydreamed of living in the house, eating fresh fish from the pond, having his horse tucked away in the barn. A familiar daydream, only this time a delicate brunette with a sun-kissed nose served him the fish.

Joe sucked the air between his teeth and made himself calm down. If he was going to meet her, he needed to make a good impression. Even he knew he didn't make a good impression when his face was intense or puckered with irritation. Mama told him that often enough when she was alive.

Now watching her, dreaming, his face grew warm with the very opposite of irritation. He tossed the blade of grass aside, spat, and moved out from behind the tree. It was as good a time as any to lay on the family charm and stake a claim on his farm.

Maybe it was good Leander hadn't been killed in the accidents. Her back was to him as she crouched and dug in the dirt. At the same time he moved in, a more familiar form, clad in buckskins, stepped into view in the tree line beyond her.

Naantam looked him straight in the eye from across the yard. Joe hated it when he did that. His black eyes cut right through him. The hair stood on end and made his scalp itch.

Joe watched the Indian do many freakish things over the years, but jumping off that fifty-foot ledge into icy river waters fully clothed to save Leander always set the standard. The crazy pock-scarred, wild man messed up his well-laid plans before, and he was sure the Indian would do it again, if he could. He knew better than to meet his new neighbor with Naantam watching on.

Leander's niece didn't notice either of them.

Just then another person came out of the barn and moved to the pig pen with a bucket full of tools. That must be the nephew. Joe flexed his fist. He could take out the nephew if he tried to play the hero. Joe scanned the yard for anyone else before returning his focus to Naantam. Naantam never blinked or turned his gaze away. Joe would have to come back later to figure out who the other fella was. He turned to leave, retracing his steps.

CHAPTER TWELVE

Rebecca squeaked, sat with a thump, and spilled the tin of water down the front of her dress. Naantam stood towering over her, sunset reds and oranges silhouetting his fierce face. She wondered if he delighted in scaring her—second time in two visits. She stood and faced him, suppressing her instinct to look for a path of escape.

Naantam pulled his ears, pointed at his eyes and looked across the yard to the tree line, and then tapped his nose.

"Always listen. Always see. Always smell."

He seemed intent on training her to watch her surroundings.

How was she going to explain him to Cora Mae, Heather, and Rose?

She almost swallowed her tongue when he went back behind one tree and hefted the body of a deer forward. He dragged it to her feet. She had to make herself not look around for Clark to come to her rescue. *He saved Leander. He saved Leander*, she repeated to herself to keep her rooted to the spot. Curiosity was the only thing that kept her from running to the cabin as fast as she could.

She tried not to stare at the pockmarks that made his face rough as gravel as he reached down and continued to drag the deer. Was he angry with her when he first came out of the trees? Was that why he said to see, smell, and listen? She waited for him to be focused on moving the deer before she looked around, wondering why he was telling her to pay attention.

Clark was working in the fenced paddock that was probably going to hold either pigs or chickens. She'd explored the buildings and fenced yards before she found a row of raspberries in desperate need of weeding. Naantam didn't stop pulling the deer forward by the forked antlers until he'd cleared the garden and was stopped at the entrance to a wooden outbuilding.

She left her weeding and joined him, watching him for what he wanted next.

Naantam pulled the larger of the two doors open before her and pulled the heavy animal inside. An old smokehouse scent still lingered in the wood, declaring its purpose. The door banged closed behind him, leaving Rebecca with the choice of following him or retreating unseen back to the cabin. She looked back at the cabin, ready to leave, but the memory of Leander's low gruff voice telling Pa how the Indian saved his life gave her the courage to pull the squeaky door open and step into the darkness. The room was still stocked with the equipment and tools needed to process any kind of meat. Steel blades hung from their hooks.

Naantam had the deer up on a large table and was working his knife—tracing the edge between the hide and food. Rebecca watched him swiftly unwrap the animal, exposing red meat that would be their future meals. Naantam separated a leg from the rest and deposited it in front of her and pointed to the white canister at the end of the table. "Sal." And then he pointed at the wall that held cleavers and knives of all sizes. "Cut." He mimed the chopping motion.

Rebecca looked into the container. It was full of salt, and there was a ladle hooked on the rim. She scooped it full and brought it to the hunk of meat and sprinkled salt on the exposed flesh. Naantam reached over and made her sprinkles thicker and heavier, and rubbed and patted the salt into the meat.

Rebecca imitated his movements. He seemed satisfied. They worked side-by-side until the animal was separated, salted, and hanging from ropes and hooks. She would have a story to tell Clark. Her hand stilled. Did she really just think of Clark without thinking of Pa or Leander? She didn't dwell on it; she cut a few sections of meat she could cook up for their supper—for all their supper, including Eddie if he managed to make it back.

Then Naantam pulled something out of his pocket and worked with it until he had a small fire growing in the large, rusting cast-iron pot that sat on a flat rock in the corner. Black marks on the stone walled area said many fires had sat there. Smoke filled the small space and chased her out. Naantam stuck with it until he was happy with the amount of heat and smoke coming out.

When he came outside, he grabbed her arm and pulled her awkwardly around the side of the barn until they were at the pen that held the few cows and oxen. She bobbed her head when Naantam pointed to two of them and then back to the smokehouse that now lived up to its name as white puffs escaped the cracks around the edges of both doors. "Snow. Eat."

"Yes. I understand. Winter is coming. You want me to smoke beef." She could tell by the shift in Naantam's eyes, he understood her words even though he didn't speak much.

He turned and walked past the garden and into the brush beyond without looking back or saying another word.

A cow meandered over to her looking for a handful of grass. "How am I to get you from here to there? You can't go in there alive?" Back at the shanty, smoked ham and jerky showed up ready to eat in trade. "For the first time, I kinda wish Pa had his whiskey still up and running." She spoke to the cow and then quit talking when she heard Clark coming her way.

"Eddie gives me a hard time when I talk to myself. Should I be worried for you?"

She blushed. "Depends. Are you willing to help a girl butcher two of those cows? Naantam just left. He gave me an assignment. And he gave us a deer. Which is now in there smoking, and he said we needed to do two cows."

Rebecca pointed to the smokehouse and then began walking to the barn to feed the animals early, glad she'd found a way to act normal around Clark. She couldn't seem to shake the need to always know what he was doing or where he was. Maybe it was because he was so different than Pa. Pa was all she really knew. And she didn't really know him at all.

She had a lot of questions about more than the secret promise and the inheritance in the letter sent, and she wanted to leave time to write to the girls. Everything that had happened in just one week on the farm was definitely enough to write the girls about it. She looked at the cows chewing their cud. "That oughta count as a gumption for sure."

"What's that? Gumption? I can help with the cows, but I don't really know what I'm doing either. My banking job ended just before we came out here. I can hardly believe I'm out here working a farm at all."

"I had no idea. You seem as comfortable out here as a duck on the pond. I wouldn't have guessed it. Do you know how to butcher the cows?"

He shook his head. "Let's go check on Sheba and then ask Leander to work with us."

"I'm sure he can help, if we haven't tired him out too much for one day." Rebecca led the way. She tried not to think about what Clark thought of her or what she thought of him. She didn't even make it to the grain bins when she heard Sheba scratching at the hay and restlessly pacing her pen. "Hey there, Sheba." The horse dipped her head down, and her tail arched up and to the side. She grunted and pawed at the straw again.

"That look normal to you?" Clark was watching the horse as closely as she was.

"I think she's in labor. Shooting lessons might have to wait." After a few more minutes of watching in silence, Rebecca was sure the mare was in labor. She looked behind the animal's full belly at her udder. White waxy-drops were plain to see. "Time to get someone who knows what they're doing."

"I second that. Eddie is going to wish he'd stayed."

"Yes, but we needed the drafts to work the garden—and your pigs."

"You're right. But still."

"You stay here while I go get Leander." Rebecca sprinted across the yard and banged into the cabin. "It's time. Sheba is ready."

She didn't wait for an answer. She went back to Leander's bedroom door and found him dressed and sitting in his other straight-backed chair working at his table. Two books lay open in front of him.

He was writing lists and numbers beside them. "She's ready? You're sure?" He quirked a salt and pepper eyebrow at her.

"Sure enough you need to come check even if I'm wrong. Clark thought so too."

"I'll meet you down there."

"I'll bring your chair." Rebecca couldn't bear watching pain streak his face and jaw when he stood too long. She left him to make his slow but steady way to the barn. She hefted the log chair—grateful it was dry seasoned wood and more cumbersome than heavy.

When she came into view of the barn door, Clark came out and took it from her. She was glad for the help. She smiled back when he smiled at her. Clark put the chair in place and dropped several forkfuls of straw into the pen by the time Leander got there.

"Should I run for Reuben?" Rebecca offered. "He'll be able to help better than us."

"No. She doesn't look like she's in trouble. We'll have time. I'll send you if we need him. Hopefully, we won't have—"

Sheba's water broke and spilled onto the floor. The horse worked the hay and eventually lay down and half-rolled up on her side.

"She's making good progress. Your pigs will

be a lot like this, except multiple times in one birthing."

Rebecca saw Sheba's belly tighten in a contraction. More water expelled, and then a hoof appeared wrapped in its protective covering.

"You okay?" Leander asked Clark.

Clark's face was contorted in pain as if he was the one with a hoof protruding.

Rebecca laughed.

He turned to her. "I wouldn't laugh too hard. I may go through this with Sheba and my pigs, but there is no chance it can happen to me."

Rebecca blushed and looked away. She was suddenly very serious inside.

"Sorry." Clark had come close to her side and whispered it. His breath blew the tendrils of her hair. She nodded, and they both watched Sheba.

It was such a forward comment, but understandable with what they were facing, and it proved he really was as green as her. It made her think of Ma. From the little Rebecca had gathered, her baby brother Isaac hadn't died in childbirth, but the sorrow that followed the birth was still felt many years later.

"The other hoof will follow soon. See how the hoof is angled? That's important. Needs to be that way for things to be easy." Leander was invested only in Sheba.

The mare grunted and moaned. Her legs extended straight out at her effort. The second hoof pressed out to meet the first. Rebecca could hardly believe what she was watching.

They all three watched together as Sheba labored through several more contractions. Leander must have seen how tense Rebecca was. He reached from his straight-back chair and clasped her hand. "She's doing fine. Look at that, here comes the head. Here is where you can help. We don't want to interfere too much. Pull back the white film that's covering the nose. Make it easier for the little one to breathe. Same with pigs, Clark."

"Like this?" Rebecca slipped into the stall and behind Sheba. She knelt by the coming foal and used both hands to tear a hole to expose the baby's nose. Sheba pushed again, and the full head and neck came out.

"If she can't finish on her own, we'll help. But I don't think she'll need it. This isn't her first. Any later and we would've missed the whole thing."

The baby slipped out onto the straw. Tears streaked Rebecca's cheeks.

"Is it a colt or a filly?" Rebecca had to blink to check. The little horse tipped its head up off the straw and wobbled around to look at her. *It's a boy.* "A colt."

She sniffed and scooted back to the fence by Leander. Clark stood by her, close enough for her to feel his warmth. She liked his closeness. It made her feel safe—a feeling that wasn't her normal.

Sheba found her baby and nuzzled him. "I could get used to watching that." Clark seemed as proud as if he'd done the work himself.

"I never grow tired of the sight. Jules used to come to the barn when a baby was coming, any baby. Goats, pigs, sheep, didn't matter. She always came. Can't watch one without thinking of her. Funny how the memories work. She named the babies. She named Sheba. You want to name this little man, Rebecca?"

Leander had included her in his memories of his wife. She felt warm and special. Was it really only this morning that she'd finished walking? Her tired legs and mounting tears told her yes. The watered dry places deep inside her said she'd been here for years. Rebecca bit her lip and nodded.

They all three stayed in a comfortable quiet, as they watched the little horse stagger to his feet—legs splayed out. He teetered and lurched and eventually nursed.

She looked at Leander and said it. "Samson."

"Samson is a good name. You'll have your hands full over the next few years as you show him how things are done. Think you can manage?"

Samson flicked his tail and almost tipped over. "I'll try."

Clark added, "I should haul in more water. Look how much she's drinking." He left the barn with a water pail in each hand.

When he was gone, the hair on the back of her neck tingled and Naantam's warning to watch, smell, and listen came in a rush.

She looked around. Her eyes stopped on the barn door, but the darkness outside was too thick to see in. She wouldn't be able to tell if there was someone watching. She was ready to leave Samson and Sheba alone.

Clark took on the watering of all the barn animals. "I'll check on them throughout the night, and if all is well in the morning, I plan on going back toward town and meeting up with Eddie. I'm sure he could use the help with all the animals."

Leander furrowed his brow. "This has been quite a day. I'm bushed. I may not see you in the morning, but I'm looking forward to the activity and the bustle the animals will bring when Clark gets back—chickens and pigs. More drafts." He shook his head at the wonder of it. Pain tinged all his features.

Rebecca wished she could do more than assisting him back to the house. She helped Leander to his feet and gathered his chair. She still felt that shiver of alertness and it grew worse when she crossed the yard ahead of Leander on her way back to the cabin.

Was someone out there? Was someone watching? She walked faster even though the wood chair banged her shins.

She felt me. I saw the wary look in her eyes. "It's me, Rebecca. I'm here." Joe wouldn't let Naantam run him off from what was rightfully his. And he wouldn't let this new fellow, Clark, edge him out either. He could stand there watching her all night after seeing the glowing happiness she showed the new colt. He could only imagine what it would be like to have her look at him that way. He was so close. None of them saw him on the other side of the barn wall, looking through a knothole. He could have reached out and touched her, if the barn wall wasn't another barrier between them.

He should've spoken when she'd come outside carrying Leander's chair. He should've let her know he was there. He didn't. Watching was better. This way, he could have all his thoughts to himself and not worry about what Leander saw in his eyes. He could see through slits in the barn wall, just fine. Her chocolate eyes softened as she watched the new horse find its way to its mother's side. He would never forget.

She should look at me like that. I'll make her. And by then the farm would be his. He'd be the one watching a new foal being born. He would be the one who encouraged her to name it. He would be the one to reach out and stroke her hand when she was nervous.

With this new guy hovering, he was going

to have to come out of hiding. And his old plan to take out Naantam and Leander would need adjusting. Tomorrow Clark would have a schooling on charm.

CHAPTER THIRTEEN

The next morning, Rebecca was up, dressed, and in the barn before the sun rose. Leander was still asleep. After she checked on Sheba and Samson, she went to tend the other animals, but all the work had already been done. Clark must have done it before he left to meet Eddie. She was leaning on the fence watching Samson when she heard steps behind her.

"I thought you left already. He's walking strong—" She turned and cut herself off with a squeak. It wasn't Clark who stood there.

Whoever it was, he nodded and smiled. "Nice to meet you. I'm Joe. Reuben's brother."

Joe looked nothing like Reuben. His hair was black, and slick oil held every hair in place. He smelled like he was ready for church and he stood *way* too close. "Oh sorry. I thought you were Clark." She stepped sideways to make space. He followed.

"Samson's showing everyone how strong he is already."

"Did Reuben send you? I bet he did."

"You're right. I'm here for chores. He's not coming. I offered to take his morning rounds today, but I can see you've managed. Thank you." He gave a mock bow. Not a single piece of his perfectly combed hair moved. "If you keep that up, you'll take away our leverage for trading chores for grazing with Leander."

"Sorry." He was crowding her again. Nothing inside her felt safe like it had in Clark's warm closeness. She tried to step back again, but the fencing blocked her in. She made herself stay there and looked away from him back at the horses.

"Strong-looking little fella. Picked a good name."

She couldn't reply. Her legs felt locked stiff. He was here to feed the animals, nothing more. *Wait.* "How do you know his name?"

"You said it when I came up?"

Rebecca bit her tongue, but she frowned. She *hadn't* said it. She hadn't been speaking aloud to the colt, only watching him.

Joe must have seen her doubt. "No? Maybe Leander told me when I stopped in and said good morning before I came down here. It fits him." Joe moved away.

She breathed. She accommodated his conversation as he walked around and inspected all the chores Clark had already done.

"I'll drop some more hay down for you before I leave. She'll eat more than usual after all the work of yesterday." Joe climbed the ladder to the hayloft.

She froze and listened to his boots clump on the wood as he retrieved the pitchfork. Space away from him was what she wanted, but even with him up in the loft and her down here, she couldn't make herself relax. Great fluffs of hay fell from the top floor down through the open hole and landed in a pile ready for use.

One of the three chickens clucked and complained at having her egg-laying choice of the day disturbed. The hen ran, flapping her wings from the corner, like a coyote was chasing her. She flew off the top loft and ran out the door. Rebecca wanted to join her. She stepped to the door. It made her closer to Joe when he came down the ladder, but she could feel the morning breeze ruffle her skirts from the doorway. And it put her nearly outside. If she ran, he couldn't corner her.

When he was back down, Joe came too close, again. She was expecting it. She would have loved to pop him in the eye like Cora Mae did Archie, but that would tip her hand. She didn't think Joe could tell she was uncomfortable. She tried not to show her discomfort as she stepped out of the barn. He was their neighbor, and he was trying to be nice.

But still she wanted out of the barn with him. Once outside, she spied Naantam inspecting her garden in the dawning light. She yelled, "Naantam, the baby! He's here!"

Joe jumped beside her. She was glad he wasn't settled either.

She flagged her arm at Naantam to come and see. She wondered if he would even come. She'd only known him for a day, and she'd never asked him to do anything before. She wilted with relief on the inside when Naantam made strong steps toward her. He walked tall like Cora Mae's father did—like he was in charge and knew it.

She wished to have him, or someone, between herself and Joe. When she was about to take her first step toward the Indian, Joe placed his hand on her forearm. She pulled it back.

She thought he would be mad at her for it, but when she met his gaze, he was locked on Naantam with a flat look. He clenched his jaw and said, "Looks like you have company. I'll let you go. Thanks for doing all my work. I'll stop by in a couple days to see how Samson is doing." He left the barn and retraced his steps back down the trail Reuben had used. Funny, he didn't ride a horse like Reuben.

Naantam came to her side. His straight, black brows pressed together tight as he watched Joe's back. The Indian stood as close as Joe had, but Rebecca felt safe. "Come see." Rebecca walked in front, hoping he would follow. She enjoyed introducing Samson to him.

He drew a knife. She eyed her path to the door and watched to see what Naantam would do with the knife. Rebecca wondered if farm living would always be one fear to the next. In fast movements, he cut a small clump of hair off Samson's fluffy mane and left the barn, leaving Rebecca with questions. He went into the bushes in the same place he had the day before.

Had it only been yesterday that she helped him smoke the venison? She should probably check on the meat and gather more firewood. The smokehouse still had wisps of smoke coming out of it, so Naantam must have fed the fire through the night. She'd have to do that.

Her stomach growled. Firewood was another chore that needed to be tended. She had better make a list and pick what should be done first. She would work on it after breakfast. She headed back to the cabin and was surprised when she heard Leander's sleepy breathing mix with her father's snores—neither were up—neither had been up at all yet today.

Did Joe lie to her about talking to Leander? If he lied, how did he learn Samson's name?

She didn't like Joe but felt guilty for feeling that way. She put herself to work in the kitchen and gave herself a scold. *He has done nothing wrong. He has done nothing to me.*

But . . . how *did* he find out Samson's name?

And perhaps more importantly—how was she going to butcher a cow?

Rebecca had venison steaks on, eggs gathered and scrambled, and a small basket of raspberries on the table before Pa and Leander were awake enough to join her. She straightened her blankets and tidied her cot, not being quiet. Pa was soon rolling over and waking.

The last time these two men talked they told her about baby Isaac. How much more was there to glean? If she could get them talking before Eddie and Clark came back with the livestock, that would be great. She didn't know when she would have them to herself after that, and she didn't know how she was going to get them to talk about Mother.

She waited until both men were at the table and Leander was settled and eating before she started. "Yesterday was a blur. I can't stop thinking about Sheba and Samson. I can hardly believe what happened in one day."

Leander answered, "I slept like a rock. Haven't been able to sleep well through the pain in quite some time. And I think Eddie will be back before long. He prefers to wake with the chickens."

Rebecca knew the conversation would be all about the farm and the animals once they came back. She went to the fireplace and poked the ashes back to life and added a small piece of wood. When she stood she fingered the framed cross-stitch.

"Jules made that. She liked doing all manner of hand work. There are some pieces in her trunk in my room. We'll have to drag them out sometime.

Your mother's too. She left hers here. There was no way to take it on the trip back East."

Words flowed like Beaver Creek out of Pa—more than he usually used in a week. "It was a rough go. A trapper led us out over the Rockies. I wasn't sure we'd make it. Luckily more folks had taken the trip ahead of us and marked the trees about the snowline. I wouldn't want to do that again. If I'd known it would be that hard, I wouldn't have taken Ophelia and you. You were so little."

She went back and sat down, too stunned to respond. It was like he kept every event of his life, or at least his life with Mother, bottled up and corked like his jugs. What else happened that made him talk like he was confessing sins?

They'd walked the Trail once already—all three of them? And there were the trunks. Two of them. Two holding separate pieces of her history. She was trying to figure out a way to stop right then and there and go to Leander's room to discover their depths when the sound of what could only be a wagon pulled by drafts carrying chickens and a couple hogs rolled into the yard.

She went outside to meet it, leaving her plate of food untouched and her questions unanswered. Leander followed behind her.

Clark called down, "We made it *almost* without incident."

"You don't have to tell them about the incidents.

They weren't there. They can imagine things going as slick as a greased pig." Eddie climbed down and went to the head of the draft horses. He scratched their foreheads and talked to them like they were old friends. "We really picked up a deal. Widow Jenson is in a pinch, and she needs the income to set up her new boardinghouse business. We got this pair for a song, and they aren't even worn down. And Clark got his sows."

Clark jumped down from the wagon. "She didn't even ask me to pay for them. She asked me to provide one pig a year for five years running, so she knows she and her children won't starve. I can manage that. She thinks they'll farrow in less than a fortnight and both had good sized litters last time around."

"They look like Chester Whites. Good breed of hogs," Leander said.

"Yes, a good mothering pair. I'll have to find a boar that's new to them both, and any gilts I keep."

Rebecca smiled to see Clark so excited about his new adventure. He petted and patted each sow multiple times as he gave his speech. She found his joy endearing and catchy. She would find things to learn and tell Leander, Clark, and Eddie all about it too.

"I never had the pig barn up to capacity. I had twenty pigs growing out in it once, but it could hold more."

Clark looked over at her. "Rebecca, there's a

crate in here for you. We had a time keeping the girls out of it at first." He pointed to the pigs. "I had to move it and strap a branch or two over it to keep it secure. Ma would have my hide if her prize blackberry preserves went to hogs."

"Your mother sent me a crate of things?"

"She felt sorry for you having to feed four men with a limited larder. She gave us both a tongue lashing ahead of time, if we didn't help you get ahead of things." Clark seemed to be enjoying everything about the moment. He reached back and grabbed something. "She sent a box of apples along with seeds and a metal craft of milk with the cream still on it."

"If we didn't shake it into butter for you on the way," Eddie teased.

"Cream and butter. Apples. Such bounty. If I get back to town, I'm going to insist on meeting your mother. She deserves more than a hug."

"I'm sure there will be more trips back and forth to think about. Keep a list of the things you need or would like, so we can keep from getting a switching. Mother means what she says."

Clark chomped down the rest of the apple he was eating, broke the core into two pieces and fed half to each of his new sows. He turned to one of two crates of chickens. "You ready for these?" One crate was filled with skinny pullets, the other with full-sized hens, both annoyed and complaining.

"With the few hens that you have here, if you leave them in the crates inside your coop for a day or two, with food and water of course, they will get along easier. Hen-pecked is a thing." Eddie was unhooking the drafts as he gave her the information.

"Hen-pecked is a real thing? Sure is! Trust me, I know." Clark placed a wide board on the back of the wagon to make a ramp for the pigs to walk down. He untied the first and kept the lead rope short. He fussed and clucked to the first pig until he had her safely down off the wagon.

Rebecca wanted to laugh at his over care. "You know about chickens, Clark?"

"Not chickens. I know about being hen-pecked. Amongst other things, I have five sisters and a queen mother. Believe me, I know." He tied the first pig off to the wagon and repeated the process of unloading the second. He practically romanced the second pig with his consoling words. He was so focused.

It felt good to be a part of changing things. She looked around for Pa. He was missing it all. He was sitting alone at the table eating his venison steak.

Things were definitely changing. She wanted to keep up with it. She would become a farmer. What was she going to use the milk, cream, eggs, and apples for? "I'm going to take the chickens to their coop. Clark, can you help me when you're done moving your pigs?" She felt shy saying his name and asking for his help. But he stopped preening over his sow long enough to catch her eye.

Then he smiled, and his joy was like the sun bursting through the clouds. He made it seem like it was just for her. "I can do that."

Rebecca almost forgot what she'd asked. So far, talking to him was as easy as talking to her sister-family.

"I'll find a big scrap bucket for you to keep for me in the house. These girls are going to love you."

Again, with the bright smile. Rebecca might have stayed to see it longer, but one of the hens was pecking at her fingernails through the cage rails. She had a coop to settle before they got there.

Several days turned to a week, and each person found their own routine. Clark woke early, but not as early as Eddie. Eddie went to bed earlier than everyone and slept like the dead until the rooster crowed.

Which it did—or rather, *they* did. All four of them. That was one of the chores for today. There were three young roosters in with the pullets and one great rooster in with the mature hens. That was three too many.

Clark climbed from the loft after dressing for

the day. He stretched and checked on his girls. They were looking much bigger than they had even the day before, but no signs of farrowing yet.

Leander would be helping them today. He gave a stern lecture to both himself and Rebecca for how unsure they were around the rifles. According to him, that would be remedied today. Clark wasn't complaining. He didn't mind any extra moments or extra excuses he was given to be close to Rebecca.

If he had a lick of drawing ability, he might be able to draw her face with how much time he spent memorizing it, studying her expressions.

Clark made quick work of the barn chores, and then he fed Rebecca's chickens. He even filled and carried a couple water cans for her garden and topped off the wood pile by the door. Anything to make her load lighter. He smiled the whole time.

Then he went inside for breakfast.

"You're awful cheerful this morning. How are the girls?" she asked. "Piglets yet?"

Eddie came inside and dried his fresh-washed hands before he sat down beside him. Clark checked his disappointment. He was hoping for more time with Rebecca.

Eddie asked, "You still lovestruck?"

Clark swallowed hard. Why would his friend say that in front of her? That was more than a joke or a sucker punch, that was making things uncomfortable.

He playfully punched Clark's shoulder. "With your pigs?" Eddie shook the last of the wet drops from his hands into Clark's face.

Relief poured through Clark's soul. The feeling of being exposed was more telling than any of his joy had been. He was invested more with Rebecca than she would know. *For now.*

Thankfully, she seemed oblivious as she bustled around the stove. "I put some farmer cheese in with the eggs. Leander showed me how to make it. And I made a stack of buttermilk biscuits."

"I was feeling spoiled before. This is luxury."

Otis came in from outside and ignored all of them. Leander came in from his bedroom and sat. His slow movement seemed normal to Clark. He was learning to watch and see if he overdid it and needed more rest. He caught Rebecca giving Leander the same once over. When her eyes found his, he smiled. They understood each other.

Leander said, "Naantam came by last night when you were all down with Samson and Sheba. He said he will take you both out archery hunting soon. I don't know when. I never know when with him, but he keeps his word, so be ready. And learning to use a bow and arrow is no excuse to not refresh your shooting skills today. Otis, do you want to help with either shooting or with butchering the cows?"

"I was going to water my corn today. I'm ready, and I need to get to it if I want it to grow in time."

Clark could tell Rebecca didn't like her pa's answer and hadn't any of the times he got out of the farm work by working on his corn crop.

He understood. His parents were like that with him these days. They cared, but their disappointment was as thick as these buttermilk biscuits.

When he was in town to help Eddie, he stopped in on his mother for a brief moment. Her tears were heavy. He needed to work hard. If he was a success on the farm and on paper, then maybe they would change how they viewed him.

Father respected numbers. Numbers never fudged the truth. He needed to find a boar and a few more sows, and he needed to earn his keep here on the farm. Maybe he would get everything done and help her pa with his corn. Maybe that would please Rebecca.

Maybe he would plant a field of feed corn for his own gains. There was room on Leander's farm. He wished he owned his own land and was making these designs for his own place. "Please pass the butter." He reached to take the small bowl when Rebecca handed it to him.

Their fingers touched, and Clark had to tell his heart to settle down. He was so far ahead of Rebecca, he would ruin things if he rushed. He thanked her and then asked, "Eddie, do you know of any other pigs I can purchase? I'd like to build up my stock, and I think there is time to get one more round of piglets before winter comes or at least early spring, if I act now."

Eddie took his time answering between bites.

When the meal was over and everything cleared, Leander gave Rebecca and Clark both different caliber rifles. "It's time for a shooting lesson." He also brought out a handgun as he led Rebecca and Clark out to a place beyond the pond that gave them a mountainside to shoot into.

For the next hour, they bent over the guns to inspect whatever Leander showed. Rebecca was so close to him that he thought he would burst into flames and catch the tree beside them on fire. What was he going to do about how he felt about her? He needed a small beginning. Wasn't there a scripture about that? Hadn't his mother quoted it as some point? *Don't despise small beginnings.*

Leander gave them the goal of shooting a limb off a dead tree thirty paces in front of them. Hard at first, easier as they practiced. He needed something simple to begin with Rebecca.

He lifted the long barrel, ignored how close she was to him, and squeezed the trigger—eyes open.

"You hit it! You get the prize." She handed him a leaf used to hold a handful of ripe blackberries. "You made that look easy, and I know perfectly well it's not."

He handed the rifle to Leander, and she handed

the berries to him. "Did you get the prize too?"

"I didn't hit the branch." She was looking down to the target. Confused.

He reached out and wiped a blackberry seed from the corner of her lips. "Did you get some of my prize?"

She smiled. "Tastes good. Someone needed to test them." She was teasing him.

That was its own beginning. He could tell by the way she stepped back, it was more than she was used to. She left his side and pretty much hid on the other side of Leander. But he could handle that. His fingers still felt warm from touching her lip.

Eddie would make so much fun of him, if he could see how besotted he was.

CHAPTER FOURTEEN

The shooting lessons continued over the next few days, one of the cows had been butchered and smoked, the garden was green with new growth, and Rebecca was feeling contentment in each direction she turned, with each thing she learned.

She was outside weeding around the base of the row of blueberries that were close to the house one afternoon when a neighbor and fellow farmer arrived, delivering the mail to the neighborhood. He pulled three letters bound with twine out of his dusty mail bag for her. She knew they were from Cora Mae, Rose, and Heather before she even looked at them, but how could they be here so fast?

Rebecca fingered the twine. "Thanks." There was no way her first letter made it back already, even though she'd been here nearly a month. Her sisters must have talked to Mrs. Mabel and figured out where to write.

Twine was wrapped three times, keeping the letters in a bunch. "Did you really need to use that much string?" She imagined Cora Mae binding them together. Rebecca blindly walked back to the cabin and up the steps—all chores forgotten. She couldn't find a single project worth doing when the letters sat there in her hand, ready to talk to her. She tucked them under her arm and knocked on Leander's doorframe.

"Here."

She poked her head into his sanctuary. Leander did his best not to overdo his back, but he still needed to spend long hours propped up in bed or sitting in his special stump chairs. Today he was lying on top of his covers, fully dressed, with a book open in his lap.

Before she could say anything, he said, "Something good must've happened. You have the smile on your face that you save for baby chicks and Samson."

Rebecca beamed and held up the bundle of letters.

"Ah, news. There's nothing better. Have fun. Naantam told me the blackberries below the pond are ready, if you want to go down there and savor your news."

"I'll do that. Cobbler sounds good."

"No hurries." Leander plucked his feather bookmark off the pillow next to him and marked his page. "I can't keep my eyes open. A nap is in order."

Rebecca pulled the bedroom door closed behind her. She hoped he would sleep and give his body even more time to mend. She'd grown to love their evenings together. He shared his books with her, with them all. But now it was time to hear from home. *Home?*

She wanted to be alone with her letters. She left the house and galloped full-speed past the garden and the cow barn, slipping through the slats on the split-rail fence after checking to see if Baron the Bull was about. The bull was nowhere to be seen, so she ran through the tall, sun-golden grass that stood to her chest.

She crushed her way through the blades and slid between the slats of the split-rail bull fence on the other side of the pasture, and ran on until the land beneath her feet turned to a hill. When she was sufficiently alone, she sat down—the grass creating a familiar, towering wall around her. Grasshoppers sang. She untied the bundle of letters and plucked the top one off the pile to read first.

> Sweet Rebecca,
>
> All three of us are together. We haven't received a letter from you, yet. Mrs. Mabel gave us your uncle Leander's address. We should have thought of that ourselves. Hope you are well. We're all lying on a quilt outside in the backyard of the sewing circle. Cora Mae even brought Victoria for the occasion. She is reminding us of our pact. As if I'd forget. However, I'm not sure why she insisted we bring the blanket, she hasn't sat on it yet. Rose is trying to get her to settle

down while I write. She is pacing back and forth, working herself into a lather. I'm sure she'll tell you herself, but I don't see what is so terrible about her father inviting Archie Millikin's over for dinner. Sounds sweet to me.

Things are getting worse with Mama. Doc wants her to stay at his office for a while. He's hoping to try a few things that might help her hurt less, but he has to watch her close. I don't know what I'll do without her. Pa still hasn't come home since you left. I hope he's not hurt.

While Mama is at the doctor's, I'll be staying at Mrs. Mabel's, like you did. I'm hoping she'll share her cinnamon roll recipe with me.

Write soon,
Heather

Rebecca sniffed and wiped her eyes on the back of her sleeve. She didn't want to think about the hard things in Heather's words until after she'd read the other two letters. She was too far away to help, and even if she was there, she wouldn't be able to help much. She knew what it was like to keep going even though afraid. She'd done that almost all her life. But things were finally starting to feel different. She looked at the wall of grass in the farm's direction. She pictured her garden and the animals and the cabin. She was glad she'd kept walking all those miles. This was better than what she had before in so many ways.

I'm not trying to take something from you. I'm trying to give something to you.

The phrase came back to her, thick and solid—comforting. She could lean on it with her heart. "Thank you. Thank the Good Lord." She imitated one of Mrs. Mabel's favorite quotes. It felt good to say it out loud.

She opened the second letter.

> Rose here,
>
> I have little news. Things stay the same for me. I thought I'd fill you in on a little town news. Do you remember that town meeting that Cecil got himself invited to that time you were in the mercantile? Well, last week he was in a pucker because Cora Mae's father showed up at it too. He spent the rest of the day flapping on about how "This town will come to a crossroads. It will have to choose between a good leader with a solid family and reputable name, or a grizzle-faced bully." He called Mr. Reynolds a bully. When I went to bed that night, I had to bury my face in the pillows so I could finally laugh it off.
>
> I wish I could tell Cora Mae he said

that. She would tell her father. Then Cecil's fanny would be in the fire. But I'm sure that would come back on me. I've grown even taller since you left. Cecil doesn't like looking me in the eye. He started watching my food even closer than before. He put a lock on the pantry. What am I supposed to do? I try to stay low, literally. He always seems to behave better if I let him look down at me. The low shelves of the mercantile have never been so tidy.

I wish I could start my own store. If I had my own, I'd have a meal delivered from the cafe every night like the blacksmith does. It's hard to feel hungry all the time. I don't mean to make you feel sad for me. Cora Mae helps. She takes me to lunch every time I run to the post office for Cecil. That happens at least twice a week. I make sure the idea comes to him right when he's sitting down to a hot cup of coffee and his favorite newspaper.

Cora Mae always stops whatever she's doing and eats with me. Even if she's already full. If I ever own a mercantile, you can be sure I'll send you seeds and books and whatever you need out there in the wilds. That's my gumption, even though it's really a fairy-tale story I tell myself when Cecil gets under my skin.

Oh, and one last piece of town news. When I was heading to the post office, I saw Mr. Reynolds entering Mr. Orville Briggs's home. That is Cecil's uncle and Fitch's father, remember? He's the one who really owns the mercantile. I can't help wondering if Mr. Reynolds will act on Cora Mae's gumption. Were you even here when she had her idea? She thinks her father should buy the mercantile out from under Cecil and let Fitch and me run the place. Can you imagine?

Cora Mae hasn't stopped bellowing about Archie long enough to ponder it. I'd really enjoy working here if I didn't have to deal with Cecil.

Oh, and Cecil and Amelia are going to be parents. Cecil as a father?

Got to go. Cora Mae is walking the grass down to the dirt. Archie Millikin has been at her again. We get no peace from him these days.

Did the rosebush make it?

—Rose

Rebecca opened Cora Mae's letter. She smiled at all the ink splashes that dotted the page. She was still in a temper when she wrote it, for sure.

Archie Millikin is a Prig with a capital P. He had the audacity to tell me that no matter how much of a fit I threw, I would eventually be his. His. HIS! He may say he knows just what to do to tame me, but it will never happen. Even if he has Father duped into thinking he is as priceless as a new patent. I will not be sold and shackled to a pimple-faced schoolboy. I don't trust him. He thinks cruel and is always scheming, and that will never go away no matter how much money he earns for Father.

You might as well know he kissed me again. All Rose does is laugh about it. It makes me so mad, I could bite a hole in my pillow. And at my birthday party, of all things. What kind of weasel does that? I told Father, and all he did was give me that look that says he knows what's best for me, even if I don't know it myself. I didn't talk to Father for a full week. But then he said I reminded him of Mother— that was the cruelest thing he could have said—again Archie's fault.

Mother couldn't hack it in Meramec. She was dainty and delicate, and she ran back to England. I've never met her, and I don't want to. And I don't care if Father says I'm making a tempest in a teapot.

I will be heard. I will come up with something. I'm not sure what. If you have any ideas, send them in your letter.

The biggest ink splatter of all was at the bottom of the page where Cora Mae's name was supposed to be. Rebecca chuckled even though her eyes were full of unshed tears. She was so glad to have the letters. She imagined her fiery friend jumping back up from her letter to pace off her pent-up angst. "Oh, Cora Mae, what are we going to do with you? I wish I could bring you here."

Rebecca sat there with the wall of grass shielding her from the outside world and imagined what it would be like to have Rose, Heather, and Cora Mae all there. She dreamed of Rose working in her own store, Heather baking the dailies for her, and Cora Mae running around town like an irritated chicken.

Rebecca laughed, gathered her letters, and meandered to the closest cluster of blackberry bushes as she replayed each letter through her mind. She thought about what she would write back to them.

She made her way back to the split-rail fence, but Baron the Bull was guarding his space, ears on alert, head high. The ring in his nose had a coating of cow slime on it. Rebecca retraced her path and moved toward the trickling sound of the creek.

She hadn't yet explored this stretch of creek

between her home and Reuben and Joe's place. At the water's edge, she followed a deer path up the hill and around some boulders. When the creek took a bend away from Leander's property, she stayed with the path that paralleled what looked like a dry creek that came from the direction of the pond.

She remembered Reuben telling her that the stream ran underground. She could hear rushing water underneath her. She put her letters in her pocket and climbed an embankment of rocks covered in ferns and berry vines. When she crested the top, she was shaded by thick cedar trees and out of breath.

Standing in front of a black mass of boulders covered in sod, moss, and stickers, the muffled sound of the water grew louder. The boulders created a dark cave that seemed like a warm invitation—for a bear. Rebecca listened to the water trickle for a long while before she mustered the nerve to step between the rocks and see if she could see the stream.

"Mr. Bear. If you're in here, don't mind me. I just want to see where the water is coming from." Her heart pumped. She imagined running as fast as she could with a bear lumbering behind her. She'd run straight to Baron the Bull's pen and let them sort it out while she ran away.

She ducked under a rock covered in hanging moss and waited for her eyes to adjust to the darkness. The smell of wet earth surrounded her. A few shafts of light pierced farther back, showing her how large the space was. She came fully inside and stood to her full height with space above her head.

On the back wall of the cave, water poured out of the ground above her and fell onto the rock floor before disappearing into the crevices. Everything inside the dank space was moist, dripping, and cool.

Careful not to soak the letters in her pocket, she reached out and rinsed her hands in the flowing stream. The rock walls blocked the sound of wind, birds, and bugs—just the sound of the water met her ears. Two boulders sat at almost the same height beside the mini waterfall. They were the driest surface in the room, so she made one her chair.

This place was perfect. *Beauty hidden.* She wondered if Leander knew about it. She unlaced her boot and took off her stocking, then tucked her letters in her boot to stay dry. Satisfied, she stuck her foot out toward the cascading water.

It was chilly at first, but she soon had both feet wet and was trying to keep the water from splashing her work dress. She gave the room a more thorough look, making sure there weren't any openings for animals before she took the pins out of her hair and pulled her dress over her head.

She felt scandalous when she stepped out

of her drawers, knowing it was full daylight outside. She washed herself head-to-toe and felt so refreshed she didn't care.

Cold water gave her the shivers. Waves of panic made her flinch and check the door more than once. On one of those flailing moments, she saw something white poking out of a smooth hole in the rock. She laughed when she found an old, crusted bar of soap that still smelled like lavender. "Jules was here?"

She used the piece of old soap and made plans to bathe here again.

It would always be cold. More so in the winter. But worth it. Her baths in the cabin were awkward. She had to wait until Leander wasn't using his own bedroom before she could drag the tub in there for privacy, and she had to do it at night—she didn't trust the old curtains to block out the windows.

After she was as dry as she could be without a towel, she dressed. When she left, she paid attention to the trail out of this secret cave. She stayed on the deer path so she wouldn't leave any sign of its location. Her three letters safe in her pocket, she jogged the rest of the way back to the cabin. She'd been gone longer than she intended to be.

As soon as she was inside, she put her letters in her empty crock. She kept it under Pa's cot at the foot of her makeshift pallet.

"Rebecca?"

Rebecca pulled her damp hair back and was at Leander's door, ready to help with whatever he needed. She was surprised to see someone kneeling at the end of the bed—but that wasn't right. It wasn't a person. It was a full set of stiff buckskin breeches and a three-quarter length buckskin dress over the top. She stepped forward and fingered the beading across the shoulders and chest. "This is lovely."

Leander smiled. "From Naantam, of course. For you."

"For me?" She sucked in an awed breath. "Look, he put the tuft of Samson's hair on the end of this strand. How beautiful. And special."

"I think so too, but Naantam said they were work clothes. He brought you those too." A bow and a full quiver sat in the seat she usually used when Leander read. "It appears he's planning to teach you to hunt soon. From what I gather, he has a bow for Clark as well, but it's not finished yet."

Three letters, a secret place, this beautiful outfit, and her very own bow? This day was too full of blessings for her to know what to do with it all.

CHAPTER FIFTEEN

Rebecca held the buckskin up to her front to see if the size matched her.

Leander reached to finger the heavy material. "Naantam will come for you soon. Maybe in the morning before light."

"I'll be ready." She would learn to hunt tomorrow.

"Never really thought about it before, but you're tiny like my Jules. That trunk over there, that I told you about before, holds all her stuff. You should make use of anything you can."

Rebecca froze. This was it. He would repeat his offer for her mother's trunk next. She didn't feel free to bring it up to him. She wished to see what was inside both trunks, sure they held more connection to her roots and history than she'd ever known. She was torn between focusing on that and treasuring the beautiful beadwork on her buckskins.

Leander stared out the window, lost in memory—obviously good memories by the faint smile, but he didn't say anything else. The evening sun and trees made shadows on his face. She held still until he seemed to come to himself.

"You would've loved my Jules. She had a cheery way of looking at everything. She would've talked you into a corner the first time she met you. She would've been thrilled to have another woman on the property. You really must take what you can use out of there. She was generous like that."

Rebecca tucked a wet strand of hair back into the tussled pile on her head.

Leander must have noticed. "I almost forgot about the spring. Jules loved to slip away. She said she'd never take a soaking bath as long as she lived after she found it."

"I found a soap cake."

"Hers. She had a wooden crate to sit on and another to keep her clothes dry while she bathed. Once, it was frozen over and the falls were icicles."

Rebecca smiled. How was she supposed to ask about her mother's trunk when he was filled with such sweet memories of Jules? She would wait. This was her place for a long while, she hoped. The secrets would eventually be told.

Shouts from outside drew them both to the window—Leander sucked in painful deep gasps. Rebecca's soul hurt with how close she'd come to hearing more about her mother—yet didn't.

"Hey. Hey! Hey!" Pa's shouting had her tossing her buckskins onto the bed and running to the door.

She was down the front porch steps and around the corner of the building in time to see Pa running as fast as his stiff skin would let him.

He made it to the base of the apple tree and climbed it just in time. Baron the Bull shook and scraped his head and neck onto the ground—knocking the knee-high cornstalks over and trampling them.

Rebecca pressed her back against the cabin so the bull wouldn't turn on her. Clark came running from the barn, making a wide arch to keep out of Baron's path of vision himself.

Baron ripped and tore and shredded the stalks in a wide path.

"Go on. Git! Git out of my stock!" Pa yelled.

It seemed like the animal knew what was important to him.

Pa plucked a couple apples from the tree he was hiding in and threw them one at a time, punctuating his hollers. The half-ripe fruit pinged off the bull. Baron barely noticed until Pa pegged him in the face. Then the animal's head came up and his shoulders flexed. He bawled a warning and stalked around the base of the tree, kicking and thrashing in the cornrows.

"You better stay up there, Otis!" Leander called from the window. "Let him blow himself out. He'll head back in when he gets hungry."

"Go on, you big ox. Git back. Git! He-yah!" Pa yelled as he flung a couple more ill-aimed apples that did nothing but annoy. Dirt flung ten feet in the air with each shoveling foot Baron scraped.

Rebecca didn't think she'd moved, but she

must have, because the hulking bull saw her and strutted two steps toward her. Rebecca flew to the porch and didn't look back until she was inside the door. Clark came bursting in right behind her.

"Ha. Ha. Ha," Leander laughed. "He got you both quick-stepping for sure."

They all heard Pa hollering and cussing and Baron bellowed back.

"I wouldn't antagonize him too much, Otis. That tree isn't all that big around!" Clark added.

Pa's curse words burned Rebecca's ears, but only made Leander and Clark laugh harder.

"We'll save some dinner. I think we're having steak and new potatoes." Leander laughed again and walked stiffly to his seat, the creak of his whalebone stays ignored by all. "Will you fetch my book? I'll do the reading, since I won't be much help in the cooking. Let's get that steak on to fry and see who it tortures the most, Otis or the bull."

"I'll get your book," Clark offered.

While Leander read, Clark wrote himself notes on a piece of paper, and Rebecca sliced onions into the hot pan with the steaks sizzling. Then she trimmed out an apple pie. It would just be the four of them—Eddie had gone home the day before to manage his own place.

She was surprised when Leander went back to the conversation they were having before they were interrupted, since Clark was there. "I meant what I said when I offered you Jules's trunk. Does my heart good to think of her stuff being lived in and used. Maybe after you go hunting with Naantam tomorrow, you can drag it out and see the contents. I'm not sure I could tell you what's in there anymore."

"Hunting?" Clark was on that almost as fast as he would be on the steak she was frying.

Rebecca turned to smile at him. "Yes. Did you see the buckskins on Leander's bed? Naantam brought them. The handiwork is amazing. I haven't tried them on yet."

One last steak was cooling and the apple pie was hot on their plates when Pa stormed into the house. Rebecca had the buckskins out and was looking at the detail work when he came stomping in. "He nearly cleaned out all the corn I done planted. And I used all the seed I brung and some of yours too, Leander. There's not enough left for more than a few jugs."

Rebecca was sure he was exaggerating in his frustration, but she asked, "You brought your own corn seed?"

"Yep, two of my best socks filled plum-to-the-ticker. Barely had room to tie 'em off. A man's gotta think ahead. Wasn't enough though. I found a sack in the barn loft by the hay and other tools. 'Tween the two, I had something close."

Leander dropped his fork onto his tin plate. The rattle made both Rebecca and Pa stop. "You planted the bag with the double leather tie?"

"Don't know. I used the one from upstairs in the barn. Darn near killed myself trying to carry it down and hang on to the ladder with this tight leg of mine. I didn't want to throw it down and have it bust open for the chickens and hogs."

"That was the stock for next spring."

Rebecca was the first to understand. "That was the last of the seed corn?"

"I didn't make a backup stash this year. Because of my back." Leander placed his hand on the stiffness at his waist that held his back in place.

Rebecca looked at Pa, who seemed unperturbed as he hacked hunks of meat off his steak and shoved them into his mouth faster than he had time to chew them.

"So, what is out in the field and in the garden is all we have?" Clark asked.

"Yes. What escaped Baron, that is."

Pa had eyes only for his food. She said the only thing she knew would get his attention. "That means there isn't enough corn to eat, to save for stock, *and* to use for whiskey?"

The thud of Pa's silverware dropping on the plate pinged around the room.

"Every plant that is standing has to be stored or it will take years for us to catch up. Sorry Otis," Leander said. "Let's hope and pray there isn't an early frost or too much rain. We were getting a late start as it was. We need that crop."

Pa cussed and was looked ready to abandon his steak. He was about to turn ugly. Rebecca saw the familiar signs of his temper rising.

Just then, the door opened. Reuben poked his head in. "Sorry to disturb your supper, but I thought you should know Baron was out in the garden. He's back in his pen now. He was standing at the trough, happy enough to eat his dinner. He worked up an appetite. I repaired the split rail as best I could. I'll come back and split a fresh post in the morning. Can't imagine why he rushed the fence. Never seen him do that before. He roughed up the garden some." Reuben didn't wait for anyone to say anything. He went back to the barn.

Rebecca let the men talk out all the reasons why the bull would have rushed the fence and what they would change to make it so he wouldn't do it again.

How fast things could change. They'd changed fast for Ma and Pa. They'd changed fast for Leander. When she thought of the seed corn being ruined and the farm having a setback, everything in her wanted to stand up and fight.

She hadn't felt that when she was digging through the ash of the shanty. But it was different here. Her roots were beginning to grow and settle. She couldn't go back even if Pa never changed. She really wanted to see inside her mother's trunk. She wanted to know.

She fingered the tight beadwork on the chest of the buckskin and thought about the words in her letters, and the soap and spring. She looked up to find Clark watching her. His smile was soft this time. Different than the one that felt like sunshine bursting through the clouds. He wasn't afraid to let her catch him watching. She wasn't afraid to catch him. That scared her more than the lost seed corn or not learning about her past.

He said, "This apple pie is wonderful. If there is enough, I may help myself to seconds. Need to keep my strength up for hunting with Naantam."

"Yes. Hunting. I'm a little nervous." She had so many things to write to her sisters about. She smiled back and listened while he tried to reassure her about the unknowns of hunting with Naantam.

She would find out if she could hunt soon enough.

Joe watched the bull riot in the field for long enough to be satisfied and then slipped back home unnoticed. When Reuben came in, Joe feigned sleep in the chair. He could sneak out from here later better than from his bedroom. The front door squeaked as loud as Bessy the pig. He'd have to remember that. Maybe he would get a chance to spy on Rebecca, when he was there after dark. If she stayed up late enough, and worked by candlelight, then he had a little view through the window of heaven on earth. Thinking of Leander's smooth-skinned niece made him want to smile.

But sleeping men didn't smile, so he held it back.

Reuben's dog growled at him. Joe couldn't flinch.

His plans had begun. Leander's two pigs were asleep for the night, but they would be out in the garden at first light, nose deep in green tomatoes and bush beans by sunrise. And none would be the wiser. They would all have to share his garden. He and Reuben would be their heroes. He would be near her. She would come to him for help and that would grow into more. He would make it grow into more.

He could picture himself now, sitting at Leander's table eating a full spread of food with Rebecca's brown eyes blinking at him with gratitude as she passed him dishes of food provided by him. Darkness enclosed him, and Reuben's snores pulled at his ears. It was time. He did smile then.

He ambled out of his chair and gruffly hushed the dog when it gave a warning bark. After making sure Reuben stayed asleep, Joe left and closed the door behind him.

The dog barked again. He froze. "Worthless beast. I'll carve you up, if you ruin my plans." The dog growled behind the door. Reuben hushed him and went back to snoring.

Joe slipped down the trail, ready to see the damage the bull inflicted on the cornfield and then he would double check they hadn't seen and repaired where he released the pigs. "Here piggy-piggy."

That night, Rebecca dressed in her new buckskin clothes and slept with her hair in a single braid down her back, so she would be ready as soon as Naantam came. The buckskin cloth was solid and soft. The strong, weathered odor gave her strange dreams. She woke several times in the night wishing morning would hurry and come. Naantam didn't come the first night or the second. She still slept in the buckskins. On the third night, she drifted off and woke with Naantam in the cabin, standing over her sleeping pallet. Her heart hitched, and she sat up fast.

His head tipped to the side. His black braid hung down beside her. Naantam picked up her bow and quiver, left the cabin, and headed toward the barn instead of the timber behind the pond.

She was up and by his side without being fully awake. Too sleep-dazed to figure him out, she just went along with him.

He tapped her shoulder and pointed to the pig's fencing. Clark's two very pregnant pigs had obviously been out of their pen, foraging under the oak trees—content with the acorns, they worked the ground there and didn't travel but a handful of feet from her precious garden. Naantam had herded them back in and tied the fence post back in place with a leather lead.

Clark was fixing a portion of the fence right next to where Reuben had repaired it the other day. Had Reuben somehow missed this railing? Or a better question still, how did Baron knock any of them down to begin with? Those fences should hold for years.

Once the rail was in place, Clark checked the pigs to be sure they were secure enough while she looked around for signs of a windstorm or some other explanation.

Her garden stood charming and cheery, knee-high greenery waving a greeting. The rough brown furrows the hogs burrowed were so close to her tender plants and growing food. Suddenly, she had a little sympathy for her father's ruined corn.

"A near miss," Clark said softly. "Eddie keeps telling me that farming has pitfalls as big as the successes, and I wasn't sure if I believed him. But this is as close to a near miss as you get. Pigs out in the garden, the bull in the corn."

"All the work could be gone in minutes. I'm not sure I want to think about that."

Clark reached out and gave her arm a comforting squeeze. She responded by adding, "I'm glad all your pigs are safe. That loss would be hard to take also."

"Agreed. I don't think we'll have a hard time staying focused today. It's going to take all our wits to keep up with him." Clark pointed at Naantam's back. He was halfway across the field.

She followed in Naantam's agile, silent steps, very aware of how different she felt moving in the buckskins than she did in her calico work dress. Naantam sped up. She kept up. Now she needed to learn to hunt and not be distracted by what had come over the animals to make them crazy, or what Clark was thinking as he walked the trail behind her.

This was important. If something went wrong with their crops—as it was, they didn't have enough on hand to feed them all for the whole winter—and if something happened and Clark and Eddie had to go back to town, she would need to become the main provider. She had to learn this. She should be good, or at least competent. *I can do this*.

Somehow hunting, trying something new, made her miss Cora Mae and the others. Tears squeezed in her throat. She held them in check. Naantam was sure to misunderstand them, and Clark too. They might think she was afraid or too soft-hearted. Naantam might even give up on teaching her, if he saw them. She made herself think of something other than her friends.

Maybe, instead of being afraid of loss, she should encourage Leander to add to his herd. The more they had, the more they had to barter with. With each step through the forest, the idea sank into place. It seemed easy to see. Leander said he had sheep and goats at one time. They hadn't gotten those back yet. If she increased the herds, the meats, she increased the income. She would always fight to keep Leander's dreams. It would be more work, but she was up to it. She had more to give. This was her home too.

Before she could think it through, Naantam thrust her bow into her chest. He put his finger to his lips, silencing and stopping her and Clark and then he slid an arrow out of the quiver and slipped it into her hand—never taking his eyes off a rabbit frozen in place, hiding in plain sight.

She pulled back on the arrow, unsure of the proper hold. *Well, sisters, today I have gumption enough for all three of us. Sink or swim.* She held her breath and let the arrow fly.

Clark had never seen anyone he knew, besides Naantam, dressed in buckskins—and certainly not a lady. She was breathtaking. It was a good thing Naantam urged Rebecca to walk in front of him. He tried to imagine each one of his sisters in a pair.

It wasn't happening.

And thinking of his sisters wasn't the same at all as seeing Rebecca with her long braid down her back, quietly walking in the same tracks Naantam took.

Naantam had his buckskins on as well. His were well used and molded to his exact shape—impressive in their own right, but not the same at all.

Clark followed behind them both, getting nothing accomplished except staring and trying to be as quiet as possible.

He nearly bumped into Rebecca when Naantam pulled them up and thrust the bow and arrow into Rebecca's hand. He saw the rabbit. He had no thought for the rabbit. When Rebecca pulled the bow back, he was mesmerized, and in an instant he didn't care one jot what his father thought of his piggery business.

Well, he cared, but it was no longer his main motivation to be successful, just to put it under his father's chin. No. He needed to be successful enough to buy his own land and have his own cabin and barns, so he had a place to bring Rebecca home to, if he could convince her to come. Would she take him seriously? It didn't matter yet. He couldn't get close to her until he had a place and a plan. But she was the future he wanted.

She released the arrow and wasn't just successful in lancing the rabbit's heart. She slayed Clark too.

CHAPTER SIXTEEN

"Dag blame it!" Joe said to himself. How did he find himself out here working on split-rail fences? Baron didn't get it done. They'd caught Leander's pigs before they ruined anything—he'd never made so many plans and had them all come to ruin before. He was usually successful on his first try. He wanted to riot like Baron the Bull and tear everything to shreds. Leander didn't deserve all he had. None of this was fair.

Jeb responded to his tense touch and dragged a downed tree to the chop site. Drops of sweat dripped off the end of his nose. He'd been working for hours. Reuben worked up ahead of him, swinging his mallet in well-timed intervals. Rebecca adjusted the glut and wedge on the log to save Reuben time. There was a pile of thirty or so fence posts spread out beside them.

Joe's irritation burned. What was the point of working as hard as Reuben, if Rebecca wasn't alongside him—if he didn't have this farm? Joe slowed the horse. At the rate the two were working in front of him, they'd have three more rails split by the time he reached their side.

He pulled his feet out of the stirrups and continued to ride his horse in an almost side-to-side gait it was so slow. Rebecca's buckskin-clad backside was occasionally aimed in his direction—her movements relaxed and efficient. "Can't complain about the view."

He watched her and waited to see the point she noticed his presence—felt him watching. Would she smile or would she stiffen? *She's perfect for me, Mother.* He liked talking to Mother about her in his head. Mother was the only one who understood. *She's my own Diana—goddess of the hunt. What would you have me try next, Mother?* He wasn't a quitter, that was for sure.

His horse nickered loud enough to draw attention.

Reuben looked up first, wiped the sweat from his eyes, and went back to swinging his mallet. She froze. She didn't blink. She didn't smile.

He didn't break the moment.

A smart man sized up his quarry.

Mother taught him that. Reuben's chopping covered his whispers, "Know your opponent before you play the game. It's never a risk, if you're sure of the outcome." Mother stepped away from her own advice once—just once—and proved her point as nothing else could.

Rebecca was about to look away.

Joe kicked the horse. "Here's another one, Rebecca." He pulled the limbed log to her side. He walked Jeb as close as he safely could beside her and then dismounted so close he bumped into her. His skin flashed fire. Good thing he was already sweating. She wouldn't notice his heat.

"Oh sorry, I didn't think you were . . ." She hesitated.

He looked down at her, savoring her fine brown eyes. He smiled so she wouldn't bolt. She stepped past him, agile as a cat—his cat. She dragged a split-fence post with her.

Maybe all this work wasn't a waste. He got to touch her. He turned to remount his horse and dutifully head back to the pile of fallen timber. He'd do it for her.

"Naantam!" Rebecca called out.

Joe flinched.

She went right over to the Indian who had just appeared. "I didn't think you would come today since we hunted yesterday. I set a snare this morning, I think Clark did too. Maybe we'll catch dinner for us all by tonight."

Joe's hot skin was instantly cold. Was the Indian always gonna step in on him?

Naantam carried a basket heaped with something on his hip. Joe walked Jeb back to the group as fast as he could stride, without a new split-rail, not letting the Indian's black-eyed gaze worry him.

Naantam saw more than was healthy for any man. *I won't be afraid of you.* He bit the inside of his cheek. Joe should've killed him in the landslide alongside Leander. The savage was ruining Joe's visit with Rebecca. *Today is mine.*

He'd make it his. And tonight, he would sit and smoke a cloud until he could think of a plan to be rid of Naantam at the same time he kept the farm and Rebecca. A plan that had no chance of coming to naught.

Joe locked his shoulders back. Their gazes met and held—dueling for dominance. When Rebecca looked between them, Joe conceded . . . but he didn't surrender. She needed to think of him as gentle.

Surrender usually meant defeat. Today wasn't about surrender, it was about the petite brunette behind him. She was what mattered. And she knew nothing, and it needed to stay that way.

He dismounted again and came close, Naantam offering him a plum. Surprised by his generosity, Joe reached for the offered fruit. When his hand was on the same level as Naantam's, the Indian struck like a snake—knife blade out, he cut the plum's purple flesh in one liquid movement, leaving two halves.

Joe pulled back, and then Naantam clamped his blade between his bared, white teeth, leaving a half of the fruit in each of his open palms.

Their eye contact lingered. Coal-black eyes burned through him. Reuben's hammering and splitting of wood sounded behind them. Joe conceded again—hoping his hand didn't shake when he reached for half a plum offered. Naantam growled, the same as Reuben's dog.

Joe wouldn't be afraid. Not here in front of Rebecca. He took both pieces and made a show of taking deliberate bites of each, smiling at Rebecca the whole time. Rebecca quit watching them both and went to tie the tow rope to another log. Naantam dried his knife on his buckskin and drew it slowly across his arm, cutting a thin strip of flesh. Red blood billowed, pooled, and dripped in fat drops at their feet. Naantam smiled right at him.

"You're crazy."

Rebecca came back to them. "What's in the basket?" She took the basket Naantam set at Joe's feet. The cut on his arm out of sight.

"Plums," Joe answered. All jovial kindness. Rebecca smiled at them both—at him. She put the basket on her hip and walked away. Joe was close enough to smell her soap.

He turned to crow a smile at the Indian. Naantam, close enough to slit his throat, held another plum in two halves—blade between his teeth. Naantam threw them at his chest.

Joe jerked away from one and caught the other, glad Rebecca missed the whole exchange. "Mangy cur." He chucked the fruit he caught and rubbed his sticky hand on the horse blanket before he climbed into the saddle, turned his back on the crazy man, and rode away. He'd drag the next log to the farthest point Rebecca wanted. He needed to be away from Naantam. He wasn't surrendering—he was pleasing his woman. *His woman*. And if that batty old Indian left while he was across the field, he'd sing a hymn of praise and offer a prayer for inspiration on what he should do next. He was tired of sitting and watching and working in the darkness.

A week later after the fence rails were all split and in their place, Rebecca was up early tending the garden. She tugged a couple carrots that Naantam had planted before they came to the cabin and rubbed them free of dirt. She crunched into one and gave the other to Leander, who was sitting in his special garden chair, made by Clark, admiring their new split-rail fence.

She used a sharp knife Leander gave her to harvest squash, beets, turnips, and a few early onions. The late planting was coming along nicely. Bees drank from yellow, red, and orange blooms. Color and life in every direction. She was as warm inside as the sun on her back.

Her rosebush, with its handful of new leaves, was setting its first bud. It was settled. She was settled. She'd worked hard, learned new things, and lived, surprised at how good it felt to do so.

Her hands were covered with dirt.

Rebecca sat back on her heels and took it all in. The birds sang from every corner of the trees. Pa was watering each of his cornstalks by hand, pressured to save all the seed corn and have at least a little left over to make drink. It would surely take him half a day.

Eddie was the source of new ideas of how things should be set up to improve the function of the farm. He made trips from town to the farm, back and forth. It seemed Clark was learning as much as she was. Even now, he was busy tying new sticks into her garden fence to patch a hole. A couple visits from pesky rabbits needed to be stopped.

Leander interrupted the birds. "It's hard to believe how much has changed having you all here. I didn't think I could dream again after the accident. I downsized and I really never thought I would see the place looking so alive again."

A rooster crowed his agreement.

Rebecca put her muddy hands in her lap and gave Leander her full attention. "Is there anything else you'd like to see on the farm again?" she asked.

"I've been thinking about that. The animals ebb and flow like the water levels of the creek. Some seasons will be fat and some thin. I even love all that. I chose this place, Jules and I did. I wouldn't have it any other way. But as much as I see my future here, I can't see that it will always be mine to care for and run."

Now Leander really had her attention. Was he finally going to explain the inheritance part of the letter? Pa must know what he meant. If Pa didn't, why would Leander put it in the letter? She watched Clark hesitate in his rhythm of string, tie, and repair. Was he listening the way she was?

"This place has more to give than what I can steward. I want to be here, along for the ride, but it's time to look at my part realistically. Eddie is my nephew. I'm going to talk about plans to build me a smaller cabin. He's outgrown his father's land. I know he values the connections and opportunities afforded by living in town, but he is managing both in these last weeks and that doesn't seem manageable for very long. It's too much work. I can see his vision for things around here. I'd like it if he could stay. He's only begun to make this place flourish. I want to see that happen." Leander was quiet and pensive after he said his piece.

Rebecca looked at Clark. He was already looking at her. Their gazes met and held. The things Leander was saying would change everything. She didn't want to break the connection with Clark and face that.

Leander continued. "Eddie doesn't have a lady now, but at some point, that will happen. I want to make it easier for him to have that too, to give him what I wish I had for Jules at the beginning. Jules had to build alongside of me instead of coming into a home already settled. It was hard on her." Old sorrow seemed to make him sag in the chair.

Rebecca was silent—careful with his grief. Was Eddie to inherit this farm? If Eddie was to be the owner of this place, where did that leave her and Pa? Why had Leander asked them to come all this way? He didn't seem the cruel sort. Had all her dreams of putting down roots and making this place home been for naught? She should be glad to know straight up what the future was for her. But what next?

Leander took a deep breath and looked around the garden, field, and cabin. "Eddie will be great with this place. I don't think he's even thought it could be his. He's never said so anyway."

Clark made eye contact with her again. "He's never said it to me either, and I think he will love it out here. And I think you're right, he is outgrowing his folks' property. He has more plans than their land can handle. I could only wish for such an opportunity."

She saw more than his kindness this time. He longed for something greater too. She could feel it. She let herself keep looking at him when he went back to tying her garden fence.

Her garden fence? *My garden?* She looked around and valued all the work that went into bringing the space into green life, but what was it for in the long haul? It wasn't hers, it was Eddie's. She may be Leander's niece, and she could see herself contributing to his family, helping and caring for him and his home, but with Eddie she would be nothing more than a worker—or worse, she would overstay her welcome.

She'd done the worker thing with Pa for years already. She wouldn't go back. But this news placed her a step backward from her dreams. This couldn't be the home she dreamed of. Deep pressure crawled up from her belly and lodged in her throat.

She set the knife down and collected the basket of food. If she walked away now, she would spare Leander her tears. His inheritance plans changed all hers. What was she going to do?

All the roots she'd carefully tended were uprooted in one conversation. She mustered a smile for Leander and patted his shoulder as she walked by him, heading to her charming rose. She set her basket down beside the plant, found the shovel, and dug up her rose. This wasn't the place for roots. She put it back in the canister she used on the Trail.

She wouldn't plant it again until she found her permanent place, even if that meant working hard, saving enough money to walk all the way back to Cora Mae, Rose, and Heather. Their sister pact was the only thing she could count on. It was all that she had that was hers alone.

Tears slid down her cheeks. She swiped them away with her sleeve, clearing her sight. Tears wouldn't solve anything. She put the crock with her uprooted rose on the wood washstand and washed the dirt from her hands and let the cool water sober her.

Where was home now? All the joy she'd felt that morning was snuffed. She couldn't find a foothold.

She went inside and kept her hands busy cutting and drying peas and saving seed. She was preserving things for a future she couldn't be a part of. The next time she settled into a place, she needed her own independence. Independence required income. *I can work on that. I can find a way to bring in my own money.*

She could save and pay her way back to Meramec. It would take time. She wished she could run back to them today, but walking for months required planning. Rose, Heather, and Cora Mae were her safe place. She chopped until she could finally swallow the lump in her throat.

Boots on the steps echoed seconds before Clark opened the door. He didn't come all the way in. He leaned on the doorframe. He was close. If she reached out her arm, she could rest her hand on his shoulder. He would know she'd been crying.

"Eddie arrived just after you left the garden. He and Leander are talking now, I'm sure he is sharing his good news." He gave her a kind smile.

Rebecca nodded, afraid to trust her voice.

He went on. "Eddie said he has a lead on a few more pigs for me. I'm going to head back to town when he goes and take the wagon with the sides on, and I was wondering if you wanted to go with us as well?"

The look in his eyes seemed to offer kindness and a break from this sobering news. She couldn't think about why he would do that now, though. He was still talking.

"If we all went, I think we could get Reuben to pull the chores for a couple days. You could meet Eddie's mother and maybe my mother and sisters. Is there anything you need from town that would give you reason to join us?"

Clark didn't say anything about how it was for him to hear Leander's announcement. Was he concerned at all about how things would be with Eddie stepping into ownership? Did it change his pig business? Maybe he wasn't concerned. They'd been friends for a long time, him and Eddie. Maybe he felt free to keep on as he did now.

She certainly didn't. She needed a business of her own. The only thing she could think of was what they'd been missing and appreciating when Eddie's mother sent it. "Yes."

She said it a little too loud. The idea surprised her. "Do you think Widow Jenson would make the same deal with me with her milking cows as she did with you and your pigs?"

If she could save for two or three milk cows. She could have a way of earning money. But she had no money to start with, just willingness to do the hard work.

"She has a milk cow. It can't hurt to ask."

She tried not to stare too long at his kind eyes. She wanted to explain her need for an income, but she couldn't. It would break the tight control she had on the runaway wagon of her emotions. Having a taste of home and having it ripped away was worse than not having it at all.

He seemed to warm to her idea. "Cows? A dairy." He nodded as he tried the idea on. "Maybe Widow Jenson is ready to be done with hers. Eddie has one of hers with his cows, already. I don't know if he's planning on keeping her or not. I remember him saying Widow Jenson also had one in the back of the boardinghouse. Maybe she would make a deal with you about milk, butter, and cheese delivery like she did with me and bringing her pork. The timing seems just right."

"I will go with you both."

"I'll ask Eddie if we can keep our animals on his farm, about the milk cow at his barn, and find out when we leave." He pulled back from where he leaned on the door post, about to leave. But he added, "I can't wait for my family to meet you." He didn't wait for her to respond before he pulled the cabin door closed behind him.

She looked over her shoulder at the bedraggled rose back in its crock. She wished she could apologize and make it a promise of a better home in the future. But there were no promises to make, except that she would change. She couldn't go backward to the way life was before her sister-family and before working alongside Leander, Clark, and Eddie. She craved home and family. She would have to make her own. The only way she could see that happening was if she imagined living alongside the sisters of her heart.

I wonder why Mother chose Meramec. She could understand the driving pull for more. Maybe Mother was looking for home as well. But that couldn't be. Ophelia had family here. She had her brother, her husband, Rebecca and this was where she had Isaac memories. *No.* Mother must've run away from family. She'd always imagined Pa was the one running, but maybe it wasn't him. Maybe there was more to it. She sighed.

Why would she run from what Rebecca wanted most? Still so many questions without answers.

She shook her head and went to the oversized larder to see what vessels would work for holding milk.

Boots on the steps sounded again, and the door opened. Clark was smiling wide, his white teeth flashing through a scruffy beard he'd grown out while becoming a pig farmer.

She crossed over to him.

He said, "We leave day after tomorrow. Eddie

thinks the trip to town, the visits, and rounding up the new animals will take more time than we think. He says we might need to plan for staying out overnight, maybe two. And he said the cow is yours, if you promise to share the milk and cheese with him. He would be relieved to not milk twice a day with all the added farm needs. He asked me to see if you would want to take over milking his dairy cow as well. He will let her dry up if you can't or don't want to."

"That's nice of him. I can do that. He would be doing me a favor. Use the milk from his cow here for us and use the rest to possibly help Widow Jenson and sell?"

"Yes." Clark reached out and squeezed her shoulder, offering her comfort.

Rebecca was comforted, but there was no way she was going to put the tingling feelings that jumped through her belly like crickets into words right then.

He was about to leave, but he turned back. "Oh. You should pack your buckskins. If my sisters saw you in them, they would faint dead away. And that would be the best thing ever." He laughed at his own joke as he left.

His joy was catchy.

The logjam of tears was cleared. She had two cows to milk and two days to prepare for them— two days to think how she would use all that milk. Determination swiped away her fears. She would earn her way. She would get back to Cora Mae, Heather, and Rose.

Would Pa want to go back? She didn't think so—his corn was forming, his plans for a whiskey still were coming together. That was his home. Maybe while she was in town, she could learn of a caravan working their way back across the Trail.

She went through the motions of her day with plans to pour out her heart in a letter home. "Yes. A letter home."

Why didn't that feel good to say?

CHAPTER SEVENTEEN

Clark went back to repairing Rebecca's garden fence. Leander was telling Eddie about all the things that would need to change or become Eddie's to care for.

Leander said, "I was thinking a small, one-man cabin could be tucked over there in the tree line. Close enough to look over the pond, but far enough from the creek and this house to be comfortable."

Clark listened with half an ear while Leander and Eddie made plans together. Clark could tell his friend was ready-as-ever to step into his inheritance, taking care of Leander included. Why wouldn't he be?

Clark was glad he'd decided to build a pig business. At least one thing was going in the right direction. Father would crow, if he could see how unstable his plans were.

But down inside, Clark was still smiling. Sure, there was pressure, and the need for land of his own was great, but he would find a way through—Rebecca was his motivation. There was no one supervising his success or his failures. His life was his own and he was glad of it, proud of it even.

Clark wouldn't stop until he was settled and

solvent. And he would increase his stock as much as he could while he was here, before Eddie needed the space for his own doings. And if he had to move off before then, he would find someone else he could help, like he had helped Leander. He couldn't worry about what wasn't now.

The cabin in the woods the two men were talking about building would take them through next spring and probably into next summer. There was enough for them all to do between now and then. Eddie would slowly move his farm from Oregon City out here to Eagle Creek. That alone would require him to be away from one farm or the other often. Clark could help with that. But then eventually, Eddie would be gone from this farm less and less. Clark would need to be ready by then.

He wanted to stop fixing Rebecca's fence and run into town and buy up all the pigs so he could begin, but impatience wouldn't lead to sound decisions. He would use the reasoning tool that had been instilled and refined by hours of Father's hovering over business ventures to reflect and make his decisions with wisdom.

He would need to keep track and make sure the work he did around this farm, and Eddie's parents' place, was fair trade for room and board of his piggery. Next spring would come fast and hopefully bring many healthy piglets.

The words his father flung at him about making his independence by standing on the back of someone else's success, even Eddie's, needed to be proven false.

He'd heard enough of Leander and Eddie's plans. He ignored them and kept his fingers busy repairing Rebecca's fence. He'd watched her face out of the corner of his eye when Leander was sharing his new dreams. He felt her world fall. He recognized it, because it was close to his own thoughts. But how was he supposed to help her, if he had nothing to offer? It would be cruel to even bring up how he felt about her, if all he had to offer could be taken in one conversation. He wished he could know what she was thinking, how this news affected her. Maybe she would share on their trip to town.

She would meet his mother. Wouldn't that surprise Mother? He'd never brought a girl home for dinner. This wasn't exactly that, but he could almost anticipate what Mother's face would look like. Maybe it would slow down the matchmaking schemes.

He tied another branch into place, creating a healthy barrier to the garden, while he made a mental list of what he needed to do to get ready for the new pigs. Then he made a mental list of what he would need to do to be prepared for more beyond that, if his savings went that far. He understood buying more animals came with risks, but so did growing too slow. He'd seen the paperwork of many businesses over the years. Money changed everything. He needed more of it.

It was the only way he could gain enough to offer Rebecca. His fingers slowed. His heart tugged. That was truly what he wanted. Sure, he wanted to be successful and independent especially in the eyes of his folks . . . but *her*. He drew the next branch into place to tie, but he simply held it there and closed his eyes and pictured her as she just was in the kitchen, chopping vegetables with tear-streaked cheeks.

It hurt him not to be able to collect her to his chest and reassure her. Even now, he still wanted to scoop Rebecca up and run with her until all the unknowns were known. He had no right to do that now. He could offer no security. He could offer no true protection.

He finished tying the fence piece he was working on and interrupted the other men's talk of a tree-lined orchard and more fenced pasture Leander and Eddie were having. "I'm going to prepare the wagon for more pigs and Rebecca's milk cow, maybe cows. I should make sure the barn is ready for all of them, too."

Eddie said, "I'm planning to separate a couple steers from my pa's and bring them here too. It's going to take all of us to prepare and get these animals safely here."

"I'll talk to Reuben about cutting trees for

the cabin," Leander said. "I can do that work."

Each man left to do the next thing, Clark went to find paper to make his lists, adding more as he went, including checking the assayer's for any nearby listings. He knew there wouldn't be any. This land had been settled and claimed long ago with all the newcomers staking close to town. But if he couldn't live on the same farm as Rebecca after next spring, he could try to live within courting distance.

He smiled. *Courting.* All the more reason to work hard. He whistled. Now he was even more interested in what Mother would think of Rebecca—and more importantly, what Rebecca would think about his family.

The trip into town went fast. Clark stepped down off the wagon and turned to help Rebecca. His hands felt large on her thin waist. Eddie, Rebecca, and he sat hip-to-hip on the bench of Leander's biggest wagon. He could still feel the warmth of her leg against his from where they were pressed close. Not that Eddie couldn't feel the same thing.

Eddie spoke to them both from his side of the wagon. "We'll have to walk on the way back. The animals will need to be led. Rebecca, do you know how to drive a wagon?"

"I do. I helped a woman on the Trail for a couple weeks."

"That's helpful." Eddie went on, but Clark looked at Rebecca. She seemed far off in memories, and if the sag of her shoulders told the story, sad memories or hard memories. He wished they had privacy enough for him to ask. The only memories that would draw that response from him were from the day Gwen got hurt.

He would consider telling her about that, if he thought it would help her.

He watched her tuck her skirts into place and finger her hair. He squeezed her arm to reassure her. "My house is over there, and that is my father's business. I worked there until just before I came out to the farm."

"It's hard to think of you as a banker."

"He was." Eddie came alongside them. The three made their way to Clark's house. "His days of lily-white, callus-free hands, and clean, city-folk clothes are behind him." Eddie elbowed Rebecca. "Clark's work pants still had a crease in them the day I met you. I haven't seen clothes so new since Lester Mills was laid out in his coffin. His wife said she hoped cleaning the outside would help him get a better chance at gettin' into heaven. He was a cattle thief and no good. Nope. For Clark, even a few weeks ago, there was not a whisker in sight. Now look at him."

Clark worked hard to keep from smoothing his new beard while Rebecca did look at him. Why had he grown a beard? He didn't really like it. It itched. It was easier to get to work each morning without shaving, but why had he kept it? When he went back to the farm, he would shave.

"At least you won't have to deal with your mama's schemes, for once. She doesn't know you're coming, and who would want you now that you've fallen from your only-son-pedestal—joining the ranks with the rest of us drudges? She'd have to be a better businessman than your banking-father to sell you off to a pretty face. Especially now that you're a poor farmer boy with only two pregnant pigs, no land, and the only prospects being dirt, pig dung, and more hard work. And there's nothing she can do about that face." He elbowed Rebecca again.

Rebecca was looking at Clark as if she should feel pity for him until the last line, then she smiled. Eddie was playing, and knowing him, he was probably trying to distract her from the pressure even he could feel building in her. But Eddie was poking at a blister—making it funny didn't take the pinch out of the honest statement of his situation.

And to do it when he was nearly entering his father's home wasn't helpful. "Do I dare ask about my face? My mother might take exception to what you say next. Oh, look at that, you're out of time. We're here."

Clark opened the door and put a hand to Rebecca's waist to nudge her in ahead of him. He tried not to notice how well she fit beside him. As soon as they were inside, he called, "Mother, I'm here. And I brought company."

Rebecca was glad Eddie bantered with Clark. Her hands were trembling. She didn't need anything from Mrs. Sutherland, but it didn't seem to matter, her tummy churned. She wasn't looking for approval. Her nerves couldn't be about Clark—meeting his mother and all. She barely knew him. Maybe it was because this woman was close enough in age to be her own mother, and she'd never been around that. Mrs. Mabel was much older, and the ladies of that age at the sewing bee were too busy with their own grown children and friends to pay her any mind.

Rebecca didn't know what she expected Clark's mother to be like, but she wasn't expecting the petite woman with her hair covered in a lace cap. "Clark. I didn't expect you." She came in and gave Clark a side squeeze. "And who is this?" She reached for Rebecca's hand.

Eddie added, "Hello, Mrs. Sutherland. Smells good in here as always."

"Am I to suppose it was an accident you boys stopped by at lunch time? On bread baking day? You know I always have a pot of soup going." As she sparred, she never took her eyes off Rebecca. "I know better." She wiped her hand in the air to dismiss the chatter. "Welcome to my home. If you'll follow me, I can get you a warm bowl of soup while my son fills me in on who you are and what has him home in the middle of the day, in the middle of the week. New business going well?"

Rebecca watched the smile disappear off Clark's face but didn't understand why. She turned toward the kitchen, and they all followed Clark's mother like the pigs followed slop.

Rebecca didn't wait for Clark to answer his mother. "My name is Rebecca Packwood. My pa and I are staying at my uncle Leander's farm. We're helping him out with the chores. And your bread smells wonderful."

"It is wonderful. Oh, I'm not boasting, I just begged the recipe from Widow Jenson. My husband ate at her boardinghouse with a colleague last week, and he went on and on, until I had to pry the recipe out of her. She said I can share it as much as I'd like, if you want me to write it up for you."

"That would be wonderful."

Rebecca could see resemblance from mother to son in the way her hands moved to fill enough bowls and slice thick hunks of bread with butter spread for each of them. She talked to the boys all the while. She didn't miss a thread with Rebecca. "So, Leander is your uncle? And you said your pa was with you?"

"Yes. My pa, Otis Packwood, and I walked

from Meramec, Missouri. We arrived the same day your son came to the farm." Rebecca gushed. Nothing stayed in her head. She wanted to say whatever this woman wanted to hear. Why did it matter so much? She made eye contact with Clark. His eyes were already on her, just like in the garden. That made her skin hot and her stomach jumpier. She put her back to him, so she could listen to what his mother was saying.

"Mr. Packwood, do tell now. I've known Otis for years. Glad to know he's in town. I met him just after I married. That's when I met your mother as well. I should have known you were Ophelia's girl right off."

"You knew my mother?" Rebecca's skittery feelings bolted. Maybe this was why this moment felt so different—so important. *She knew Ma.* Maybe she would have answers to questions she didn't even know to ask.

Mrs. Sutherland turned to her son. "Otis came around Cape Hope with your father, Ophelia and Albert, and Leander and Jules. I made friends with them all when they were in California, before her and Otis took up, when you were a little one. I tried to talk her into staying. She said she had to leave behind the bad memories and make a new start with Otis for you."

Rebecca felt the smile freeze and drop. Did she say Albert . . . before Otis? Wasn't that the same thing Leander had said? *What is she talking about?* She wanted information about Mother and she got it. So much it choked. She coughed as she swallowed the soup in her mouth.

Rebecca put her spoon in the bowl, ignoring the delicious steaming meal. She went with a safe question, surprised when her voice sounded almost normal. "You have memories of my mother?" She wanted to scream, "And who is Albert?" But that wouldn't help.

"Yes." She dished her own soup and bread, taking her sweet time, cleaning crumbs and spilled soup before she sat across from Rebecca. "I spent many an evening sewing, having Bible study and such with your mother. Your mother and I were fast friends. I miss her dearly. I spent the week with her when she lost your brother, before Albert left. That was such a hard time. I suppose you were too young to remember that—not even two?"

It felt like Rebecca's heart cramped. Then it made a run for it. Her ears and neck went hot, and she saw dancing white dots for a flash before her sight cleared. This woman had more than answers. Her memories were more than she'd ever get from Pa. She talked, where Pa and Leander kept secrets. "I don't remember that or much about my mother."

A pressure pulled at her elbow. She looked down at her arm, feeling slow and groggy like she woke from a long nap. Clark's hand was there.

Was he offering her his strength? She couldn't think. "Ma liked cherry pie. I look like her." The offerings were meager. Things this woman already knew. She knew that better than Rebecca did, and she'd already spoken of it.

As long as Rebecca could remember, she'd wanted information about her mother. Now that it was happening, all she wanted to do was get out of this house, get out of this conversation, and nurse the wound pooling deep within her—keep it from pushing to the surface and springing out. She had no words. She stared at Mrs. Sutherland.

"This is good. Thank you, ma'am." Eddie wasn't paying much attention to anything but the food in front of him . . . or was he?

Mrs. Sutherland didn't acknowledge his compliment. She was focused on Rebecca. "Several years ago, I wrote back East to his family. There are still so many unknowns. They hadn't heard anything new. Albert passed on his return. No one knows the hows or the whys, just that he was gone—dead. I'm sorry. It really is better for you. Albert was . . ." She paused and started again, "Otis is so kind—he was so good to your mother. She needed to go. To start fresh. I tried to talk her into staying. I couldn't help myself, I cherished her and wanted her here."

Rebecca shook her head. Still no words.

Under the table, Clark reached for her arm and rubbed small circles with his thumb on the back of her elbow. He cleared his throat. "Let me tell you about my new business, Mother."

Clark launched into stories about his new pigs, but Rebecca couldn't concentrate on his words. *Otis—Pa—was kind? Albert passed and it was better for me? Back East? Family?* So many questions.

Mrs. Sutherland nodded along to her son's story, but when he paused, she leaned toward Rebecca and whispered, "Whenever you want, I can tell you all I remember about your mother. I would enjoy doing so."

All Rebecca could do was nod. She felt like her head was beneath the spring water too long. Her breath pulled shallow in her chest.

"I can bring her home, here, anytime she likes, Mother."

Home. Clark had a home. Rebecca nearly sobbed.

"Good. You do that. It might get you out of disgrace with me." Mrs. Sutherland offered a warm, teasing smile. "All right, now that I know about the pigs, tell me why you're in town."

She let Clark and Eddie talk all about their ventures. Rebecca sat as quiet as Pa. But Pa wasn't her pa. *Albert?* If he was the secret, Pa and Leander better get ready to give her more than secrets and stories. She wouldn't be quiet once they got back to the farm.

CHAPTER EIGHTEEN

Joe followed the three into town and watched until they came out of the banker's house. He'd spent too much time skulking in the shadows. If he was going to charm Rebecca, he needed to be around her.

This was his chance. And they only needed to hint of going in the same direction as him, to find he would join their party, and they would think it was their idea.

Even from his place, leaning against the log wall of his favorite tavern, he could tell something was wrong with Rebecca. What had they done to her in that house? More important, how could he comfort her? How many times had he seen Mother make her play in a melancholy moment, just like this?

Rebecca didn't see him. She didn't even look up.

When the group of three was crossing beside him, he stepped forward. "Hello, neighbors."

Rebecca came to a stop. The men followed suit.

"I didn't realize you were coming to town on the same day. I should have offered to run errands for the lot of us. You here for nails, or something for your fencing? Your new projects look great." Would they tell him their plans?

"We're bringing back hogs and cattle," Clark answered.

Was he guarded or distracted by Rebecca's low mood? Joe assessed. "More pigs? Cattle too? Are you driving them back up the hill? I could stick around and help." Joe made a small step to face Rebecca more fully without drawing bristles from the others.

He could sense she felt his closeness. She focused on him and spoke fast, "I'm planning on leading a dairy cow or two back to the farm as well."

That's right, darling. Give me something to work with. "If you're leading them, that'll take a while. I can tie my horse to the wagon and drive the wagon for you. Many hands and all?" He opened his hands wide to include both men without moving away from Rebecca.

He could see them thinking, deciding his character. He'd already come up with a plausible reason why he was in town. Why he could delay to match their pace, and what he could bring that would benefit them. He laid it on, slow and smooth, like cold maple syrup.

"I have the mail bag for our area. The boardinghouse is making me a picnic big enough to feed Reuben and me for a few days, to get a break from cooking, and the blacksmith won't be done with the welding fix I brought him for Reuben until next week. Reuben isn't expecting my help until tomorrow." *As if Reuben ever requested or expected my help.*

He didn't see them doing anything other than accepting his offer of service. Clark and Eddie shared a look between them.

He nearly cheered when Eddie didn't refuse, but said, "We're headed to the boardinghouse now."

If they didn't refuse him, Joe would treat it as an invitation. He turned and stepped down the boardwalk. "Widow Jenson had a full parlor. Her cooking is the best in town. The smartest thing she did was open up her meals to more than her boarders."

Joe watched Rebecca out of the corner of his eye. She was not paying attention in the least. Something had her distracted, which was good for him. She'd been as skittish as a wild horse around him when they were working on fencing. The more normal it was for him to be around her, the better his chances of getting her alone.

He pulled the thick, wood handle of the boardinghouse and let them all in ahead of himself.

They all stood in the doorway and watched two women cleaning up after a lot of meals. Widow Jenson didn't even look up. "Be with you in a moment. We're clearing fresh places. Plenty of food left." She dumped dirty tins, used cloth napkins, and empty coffee cups into the large crate she held propped on her hip.

When she finally turned, she focused on him. "I'm sorry. I didn't think you'd be back so fast. I haven't put your basket together yet."

Joe removed his hat and smoothed a hand over his hair. He'd made sure he looked clean and pressed while they were inside the banker's home. He said, "I'm in no rush. Please double what I requested. I'm traveling back with these folks." There it was. He invited himself and before they could reject him, he added, "I think they are here for business with you."

Widow Jenson set her dirty dish tub down on the table in front of her. She was wiping her hands on a rag she kept in her apron pocket as she came toward them. Joe didn't wait. He was invited, and to stay too close now would only irritate. "I'll head to the livery and bring my horse to your wagon. You brought the large one, I'm assuming? Is it at the livery?"

Eddie nodded. "I'd like to have more help with the animals. The wagon is in the back of the Sutherland home. I'll drive it to my folks' place when we are done here. If you join us there and help drive the wagon home, it really would help. We were planning on an overnight."

Joe barely checked a smile. Overnight meant more time. He didn't want to say anything to tip the wheelbarrow. He nodded and left, allowing himself to take a deep breath as he brushed past Rebecca. She smelled like honeysuckle and innocence. Hat still in hand, he left the boardinghouse. He would need the time they were gathering the animals to think about how he could make them *need* his help. He would play the hero.

The boardinghouse had a welcoming smell of good food and clean linen, but her head spun with all Mrs. Sutherland revealed. Rebecca wanted out of the silent shell. Pa wasn't her father? Did that change her plans to go back to Meramec? No. Her sisters were the only home she had left. She needed to step toward them, and that started here, now. By securing an income to save for her trip to Missouri.

She straightened her shoulders and summoned a smile for the widow. "Mrs. Jenson, hello. Eddie has told us so much about you. I'm sorry for your loss."

Clark was right beside her ready to shake the woman's hand as well. "Thank you for trusting me with your hogs. Once they've farrowed and the piglets are grown, plan on how you'd like the meat prepared and delivered."

"If this room keeps filling like it did today, then we'll need to talk about more meat than what my family eats, that's for sure. There is a nice sized root cellar off the kitchen. Storage won't be a problem."

Eddie chimed in, "Rebecca is taking over my

milking your cow, as well. We'll have to move her out to Leander's farm. I have a building project that's going to take all my time. Does that sound like something you'd be okay with?"

The tall, thin woman bustled about the big room full of tables covered with dirty dishes. The mealtime was over.

"This is getting better and better. Now, while you come in and sit down, tell me you can grow my garden goods, and enough chickens and chicken eggs, to keep me going and I'll have to kiss you. Would you like a cinnamon roll while we work out the details?" She assumed the answer was yes and served them each one, with a dollop of melting butter over the top.

Rebecca added, "I can expand my garden, and we're already expanding the chickens."

"Best news I've heard all day. I have a milk cow out back with her yearling as well. We're milk sharing with her and the calf at the moment, but she is ready to wean and give us the whole portion. Her calf is a little heifer. Would you like to see her?" She made to show them and then stopped to keep talking. "It will be some time before the calf can come into milk, but she can be part of the deal, too, if you're willing to bring milk to town for me a couple times a week. I can use all the milk you can bring in. I have a few cans you can use to carry it. I just don't want to milk on top of everything else I have to do in here. You know the routine—washing udders and dirty milk pails is not the way I like to start and end each of my days."

"It's lots of work," Rebecca said.

"But a place like this can't go without milk, butter, cream, and eventually cheese deliveries—I'll trade like I'm doing with the pigs. Once you've reached the value of the stock, then we'll talk payment. That gives me time to build a clientele and continue to settle the boardinghouse before I have to pay regular."

"I'd like that. I'm not sure I'll be here when the heifer is old enough to milk, but I'd be grateful to do deliveries for as long as I can."

Clark snapped his head up in her direction. "You're not going to be here?"

Rebecca didn't answer his questions; the drowning feeling came back in a flood. Why did she feel so sad? Going home to Cora Mae, Heather, and Rose was the only thing that made sense.

Eddie asked, "You going to make it?"

Rebecca turned to face him. She didn't know how to answer that, and then she realized he was talking to Widow Jenson.

He continued, "Lots of change for you and your young'uns this year. If there is anything else we can help with, let us know."

"You have been a great help. I'm glad I decided to move to town. We're too busy keeping up to miss the farm." The black band tied around her upper arm didn't detract from her subtle beauty.

The widow was almost as pretty as Cora Mae with her smooth skin and dark eyes. She took her time shaking both Clark and Eddie's hands. The hint of sorrow crinkling the corners of her eyes added to her appeal.

Rebecca took in everything about her. The long look the woman gave Clark made her insides clench, shocking her almost as much as Mrs. Sutherland's words. Something inside her woke up. She saw Clark. Each act of attentive care he'd offered since he'd splashed into the pond came to her memory. She didn't want to share him or her memories with the widow, but what was she to do with that revelation if she wasn't going to stay here? Was she so desperate for a sense of home that she would do or believe anything? Was she setting herself up to be as vulnerable as a hen outside the coop with raccoons about?

How many changes could one day bring? The smell of the cinnamon roll helped her. It reminded her of Mrs. Mabel's care—stable and warm. She needed that, all the new information and feelings terrified her. She put a hand to her stomach and closed her eyes. She couldn't watch the other woman's sad eyes invite Clark.

I'm not trying to take something from you. I'm trying to give something to you.

The subtle, peaceful words had her eyes open

and looking around. She scanned the room with its white-washed walls and delicate, tatted-edged curtains.

She'd heard the words before. She'd been settled by them before. She avoided looking at the others and watched the melting butter drip off the cinnamon roll onto her plate. She now owned cows. She needed supplies to milk. The rest of the information could wait—maybe wait forever.

Pa's silence. *Otis's silence.* He wasn't really her father—a thought which did nothing to settle her. She felt like she was spinning in all directions at once. *Pa is the pa I know.* Pa was a broken man, but he was alive and he'd loved her mother. *And he kept me with him . . . when I wasn't even his.* She sighed. And everyone stopped to look at her. "Do you have a milk stool and milking supplies to go with the cows?"

"Let me show you what I've got." Widow Jenson led them to a lean-to attached to the side of the large house.

Over an hour later, Rebecca walked down the street leading the milk cow with her baby trailing behind toward Eddie's house where two other cows awaited her. Clark walked beside her, notably silent, while Eddie drove the wagon alongside.

She wondered why Clark was silent, but if it had anything to do with her announcement that she was leaving, she couldn't handle his feelings about it. She couldn't handle her own feelings about it. She focused on the cows.

Later that night, on the trail home in the middle of the woods, Rebecca watched the clouds drift past the moon and leave nothing but stars in their path. Sleeping overnight outside was familiar. She found a pinch of comfort in it and made notes of what she needed to gather for her trip home.

After running through the list in her mind, she couldn't believe she was still awake. She, they all, had worked double hard to load the new pigs into the wagon, secure a couple crates of chickens to the side, cut Eddie's cattle from his father's herd, and tie her three milk cows and one yearling to the back of the wagon.

Nothing had gone terribly wrong, but each step took more work than normal. She'd heard Eddie thank Joe for coming along. She should be glad for his help too, since he went out of his way to meet her needs. He secured all her milking supplies on the wagon so the pigs wouldn't smash them, and he'd taken care of her new chickens. But that didn't make her want to get close enough to thank him. Every time she turned around, he was in her space. And with everything else about her life feeling upside down and backward, it didn't help.

Joe was sleeping under the wagon, the farthest away from her. She was relieved and let her shoulders sag into her bedroll. She strained to hear his heavy breathing over the happy crickets, assuring herself he was still over there. Eddie's deep snore sounded alongside the pigs. That made her smile. He was on the other side of the campfire. Clark on the other side of him.

She rolled on her side and, as quiet as she could, put a couple more pieces of wood on the fire. Smoke and sparks raced up into the darkness as the heat increased. One of the cows mooed.

She heard Clark change positions in his bedroll. "You still awake?" His whisper was low.

She froze in the darkness.

"Are you feeling good about your milking business? Things are really coming together for you. Did I hear Eddie's mother say she had a lead on another milking pair? Four at once. That seems like so much."

"Yes, she said she'd fill me in next week when I take my first load of milk to the boardinghouse. She also said she thinks the people who own the cow have an old milkman's cart that needs some repairs that I can eventually buy." The darkness grew quiet for a long stretch. Talking to Clark felt nice . . . as long as he didn't ask probing questions. As soothing as watching the flames dance. She searched her mind for more to say.

He beat her to it. "All your cows and all my pigs. We owe Widow Jenson a service for all she's doing to give us a head start on our fledgling businesses. We're going to be swimming in piglets and milk soon."

Rebecca's tired mind wandered. She couldn't help but picture his bare chest and drawers from their first meeting. She smiled in the darkness.

He said, "I could tell you were surprised when Leander shared about giving the farm over to Eddie."

The dirt crunched under her when she twisted to look over in the direction of Clark's voice. Eddie was right next to him. He could be listening. He must've guessed her thoughts.

"Don't worry. Eddie can't hear me. Watch this." She could see Clark's hand and arm in the flickering flame light. He picked up a fist-sized rock and carefully balanced it right on Eddie's forehead.

"Clark." She put a hand over her mouth to quiet herself.

"I could do worse. When we were kids, his father was irritated because he'd left a fence open and some of the animals got out and he had to chase them for hours in the dark. When he came into the room where we were, he picked Eddie up by the ankles and hung him upside down to roust him, but then had to give up, because he slept right through it." He pushed the rock off. It tumbled down the side of Eddie's face. He only snorted and snored louder than the pigs. "Were you surprised at Leander's news?"

She smiled and took her time. Glad for the darkness, so he couldn't read too much into her face. "I was very surprised. I'm not sure why Uncle Leander wrote for us to come all the way from Missouri, if Eddie was only miles from him."

"I can see sense in it. Leander wouldn't want Eddie to give up his life to come and tend him. The only reason he changed his mind, is because Eddie came out on his own and you can see how much Eddie loves the land. And Eddie loved it, thinking it would never be his. Probably a pride thing, but I get it. Does it change anything for you or your . . . pa?"

Was he being careful of his words because he really didn't know the answer or did he hesitate because he'd learned, as recently as she did, that Pa wasn't her father? And that she wasn't planning on staying since that conversation in the garden.

"I have friends back in Meramec. I miss them dearly. I came here with Pa because I didn't know if I'd ever see him again if he went off on his own. He needed help pushing the cart. His scars limit his movements. But I don't know what's here for me now." She stalled. Not knowing what else to say . . . what else to think.

She liked talking to him in the dark. Did she dare speak openly? Surely talking it over with him would be better than writing to Cora Mae,

Heather, and Rose. It would be such a long time before she heard back from them. "I've loved living here, learning to hunt and to farm, planting my rose." She choked on the words.

"Me too," Clark said. "I'm so glad to have a place to learn about the animals—the pigs. Have you always planned to go back to Missouri? I didn't know you were going back, until you said it to Widow Jenson."

"It surprised me when Uncle Leander said he was giving the farm over. I was stunned." She repeated herself, trying to understand how she felt.

"And you were stunned tonight when my mother told you all those things about your folks?"

It was true. She was quiet.

"Did you know those things?" His words came slow.

She thought he was being careful of her feelings again. "Nope."

"If you had a place of your own? Land? Would you stay here and do this?"

She had to think about that. Her first answer was simple. "Yes." But it came with no hope of it happening. "That's not possible, but yes. I'll find a caravan to join. I still have a couple months to get back this year. I have a couple weeks to save for and gather supplies or trade for supplies by then."

"I need land too." He rolled over to settle for the night. The cows shifted, and Eddie and the pigs snored on. "I wish you didn't have to go." His words were whispers in the darkness.

She collected his words to her heart like she collected a special rock to her pocket. Warmed, she fell asleep with a smile on her face.

Joe, pretending to sleep, heard every word. She was leaving. She would stay, if the farm belonged to her. He *could* make that happen. He *would* make that happen. She would be his. He would have it all. They would all envy him.

CHAPTER NINETEEN

After they finished caravanning the animals back to the farm. Life slipped into a normal balance. Rebecca rose extra early to accommodate her new milking routine. Even in the cabin, she put on a sweater to beat the chill. She was determined to put action to her plans to leave. She grabbed her garden basket and knife and slipped out of the house as quietly as she could, leaving Pa and Leander sleeping. She hadn't brought up the fact that she knew about Albert. What did she really need to know, if she wasn't going to stay, besides he'd run off and likely died?

She would milk after the sun came up. Now was for her garden. She made her way there. Dew sparkled on all her plants. She would plant more of everything that could grow before a late October early November frost for the boardinghouse, even if it wouldn't harvest until after she was gone. She chose to focus on leaving, since it hurt too much to think about not getting to stay.

She went to work harvesting the garlic to dry for the winter. When she was done with that, she moved to planting crops that could hold their own all the way over winter, so their stores would stay full and they would have more to provide the boardinghouse's needs. Eddie's farm would prosper.

Before the sun crested the trees, Clark came out of the barn, stretched off his night's sleep, and came over to her.

Rebecca wasn't sure if his company added to the tightness in her chest or if she felt more relaxed. She was aware of his every move down to the bunch and pull of his shirt around his shoulder muscles as he added wood to the smokehouse fire.

When he was done, he leaned on the fence, watching her, watching the morning. She was glad he let the comfortable silence be broken only by the waking birds. He couldn't know his whispered words, from the night on the trail back from town, were loud in her ears.

She moved her way around the garden pulling weeds, pulling spent plants, and turning the soil for new seeds. When she started digging, he came through the gate and joined her.

"I can help, but I still don't know a carrot from a parsnip."

She smiled. "I harvested the garlic Naantam had planted." She pointed to her pile and where they came from. "We can replant that area. There is still time for some things. I planted those two rows of potatoes to store when they are harvested later. Some things we planted late, so they are still coming on, won't be ready to harvest until the end of summer, just before I leave."

She added that for them both. "But these potatoes volunteered from Leander's old garden. He must've grown them here before. If we dig them now, the potatoes will be smaller, and not store well, but they taste real good with spring onions and a fresh garlic."

He began to help her harvest them by digging a section of soil, bigger than necessary, to keep from spearing the potatoes.

She piled uprooted plants and gathered the potatoes separately, savoring the time spent working alongside him, denying the warm thoughts of a future that could do nothing but disappoint.

"Leander said potato plants will poison the pigs."

"I'm glad you said so. I didn't know. I'll put these on the pile over there. They will turn back to dirt over the winter. Look at how many potatoes there are." Her basket was full of spuds of different sizes.

"Food. Always a good way to begin the day."

Rebecca knelt and sifted the soil in her hand. So easy and normal. It felt like her whole being took a settling breath, but it wasn't real. It couldn't last. This place wasn't hers to fall in love with. None of this was for her roots.

"Once we're done here, I plan to plant a second round of carrots and beets for Eddie or you to harvest after I'm gone. They can store in the ground even if the frost comes." She said it out loud a second time. It felt like a pinch to her skin, on the inside. It brought her to attention.

Clark didn't look up at her. He gathered up the useless vines from beside her and brushed her shoulder as he came by. Tingles bounced around on the inside of her. She was sure Cora Mae didn't feel that before she punched Archie.

She studied him without his knowing as he stepped his way carefully across the growing space. She cared, but she still had to leave . . . yet that didn't mean she couldn't enjoy the moment. She kept an eye on him as she took in the beautiful morning, and before he returned, she had herself back to work, hands busy.

He came and checked her basket of potatoes. They rolled around in the bottom.

"They're going to taste good. Do you want to learn the difference between a parsnip and a carrot?"

His face lit up. He was so easy to please. Was it her or the learning that warmed him? He brought her basket close. When he set it down, she could reach out and touch him. Surprised at how much she wanted to, she took her time showing him the difference between carrots and parsnips well established in their beds. And then included him in the new planting. "Here are carrot seeds. I'll show you the parsnips seeds next. They look very different." He reached his hand out to catch what she poured from hers.

He lifted his cupped hand to keep the breeze from carrying away the seeds. Their hands touched. That had happened before, but this time both froze, at least it seemed like it to Rebecca. She saw a small smile about his lips.

A thump clattered beside her. Rebecca squeaked as a burlap sack came to a stop by her ankle. She nearly spilled the carrot seeds. Clark reached for her hand to settle her and turned to see what was happening.

Naantam stood at the same place of fencing Clark had claimed earlier. His long black hair was tied back. Naantam stared at Clark for a long, cold second. He nodded once before he turned and left as fast as he came. Rebecca watched him go, long enough to slow her beating heart, long enough to wonder why Naantam's stare wasn't the same challenge compared to the one he gave Joe, long enough to miss the feeling of Clark's hand touching hers. She almost wanted to cry. Why did she have to leave?

She refused to think on it.

"What is in the bag?" Clark asked as he knelt to plant his carrot seeds in a straight row.

She opened it. "Oh good. He's brought me these before. Some kind of tuber, I don't know what to call them, but they're good. He brought them cooked the first time and made me taste one. I was so sure he was going to poison me. Look." She held a chain of small, potato-like bulbs for him to see. "They are strung together by their roots."

"It's funny what we are afraid of when we don't understand," he said without making eye contact.

"That's true." She was afraid of a lot of things she didn't understand, like what the secret her mother made Pa and Leander swear too was. Did it have anything to do with Albert?

Clark said, "Naantam came around a time or two when I was here in the summer, when we were younger, but he only brought food to Leander. He didn't give us a second glance. We were sure afraid of him and never stopped looking for him. Eddie and I tried to walk like him after he left."

"Walk like him?"

"Yes, like this." He straightened to his full height, rolled his shoulders back and held his head high. "More impressive than a soldier." Clark walked over and retrieved and filled the water bucket with the same tall walk. Then he brought it back to water the carrot seeds.

She grinned like a fool. He almost caught her. She quickly dropped back down and sprinkled the carrot seeds she'd had in her hand until they were cascaded all over the turned soil. Water sloshed when he set the pail down by her. He scooped a handful and washed his face.

Drops splashed the back of her neck and shoulders. She flinched and laughed. It felt good to laugh.

"Sorry." He laughed with her.

"You're supposed to be watering the seeds, not me." She shivered as she used her own cupped hands to carefully water the seeds.

"I know, but the seeds don't make a cute little noise." He scooped and poured water over the seeds like her. "You could always get me back. Eddie always does." His grin was so big, a dimple appeared in his cheek.

She was half-tempted to try to get him back. But that would lead to feeling more loss when she hit the Trail. Now, she was more content to enjoy the sense of being free and safe. He shadowed her and her milking chores the entire day. Then she helped him feed his pigs.

The next morning, Rebecca pulled the steaming buttermilk biscuits out of the oven and put them in a basket with a towel covering. She loved it when the cabin was warm and smelled so cozy. She stood stirring the thickening gravy, thinking about their new guests.

The cabin was quiet except for the popping of the fire in the fireplace. Leander slept. Pa and two of his precious jugs were gone. The third jug was still there, so she figured he was tending customers and would be back. "Who knows when?" she mumbled to herself.

She heard jovial murmuring before the sound of Clark and Eddie's boots on the porch. She rushed to open the door so she could shush them. She wanted to let Leander sleep long if possible. He'd been going too hard keeping up with Eddie and the cabin plans the last two days. Her fault for not slowing him down. Would Eddie notice that sort of thing when she was gone? Would he share the burden of Leander's pain?

A rush of cold air hit her in the face when the door opened. "This is ridiculous. Give me my kit," Eddie said.

"Why? Are you in a hurry? Got somewhere to go—someone to see?" Mischief emanated from Clark.

She tried to catch up with the banter. She looked back and forth between the two and did a double-take. "Eddie!" She giggled and covered her mouth.

"What?"

She stood back to let them file into the cabin, but her eyes locked on the fresh pink cheek of the redhead. One cheek. The other side of his face was still covered in the thick, auburn beard she'd seen yesterday.

"Told you he sleeps heavy."

"But why?" She tried to show Eddie compassion, but she was still laughing.

"My question exactly. Why, Clark?"

"I was awake this morning and shaving my own face when I had a thought."

Rebecca uncovered her mouth and let the smile she was blocking free. Clark shared it.

"And what did your one thought for the day tell you?" Eddie's frustration and tolerance were as thick as her gravy.

She crossed to stir it.

When Clark remained silent, Rebecca turned and saw him watching her. She put her back to him and faced the stove so he wouldn't see her face heat. It made her feel like a bird flushed from its nest, jittery and watchful, and if she was honest with herself, more curious than ever. *But I'm leaving.*

"That's it. I stood there with only one thought."

Eddie groaned, rolled his eyes, and stole a warm biscuit. "Apparently, thought is wasted on you."

Rebecca laughed even more when he took a bite and exaggerated his chews. His half unshaved face a sight to behold as it bobbed up and down without its matching counterpart.

Clark winked at her. Warmth flooded her chest and her stomach tickled. *That wink.* He'd probably wink at Widow Jenson, if she was here too. He couldn't mean anything by it.

"Cow pie. That's the one thought I had, my friend. The one thought I had when I was standing there shaving my face and you were sleeping as sound as a dirt clod was cow pie. Rebecca reminded me of paybacks. We are now officially even."

Rebecca lifted her hands. "I had no part of this, Eddie."

"Even. We're even? Huh! Now that you've had your fun acting out your own traveling troupe performance, where is my kit?"

Clark laughed, and Eddie gave a begrudging smile.

"It's in the chicken feed bin." He turned to Rebecca. "Turns out the hinged lid used to keep things out is also good for keeping things hidden."

Eddie grabbed a second biscuit and headed out the door. "Even? That cow-pie incident was years ago, and I'm sure you deserved it, like you do now. We'll see about even. I never forget."

"No, you don't, you have a mind like a steel trap, but you definitely don't sleep with one eye open."

Eddie was heading back to the barn when Rebecca said, "I'll keep breakfast warm for you." She moved the pot of hot gravy to the table, and by the time she had the plates set and was ready to sit, she found herself alone across the table from Clark, unless you counted Pa sleeping on his cot in the corner.

"Mmm, this is good. Thank you. You know, it took almost an hour to accomplish that. I worked up a fine appetite."

"He slept through it all?"

"Yup. I knew he would. The summer we stayed here, I set off a string of fireworks in a tin can right under his cot and he simply turned over.

Once the rooster crows, he's awake and he has more hard work in him than a healthy draft horse, but when his head touches the pillow . . ."

He shook his head like it was sad news. "It is like the other night around the campfire." He smiled at her. She couldn't look away. "Did a fine job shaving him—not even a nick—if I do say so myself. Suppose I could use barbering as a fallback plan, if pigs don't pay."

She took a bite of warm biscuit and heard Leander begin to move behind his bedroom door.

Clark pitched his voice a bit lower. "Father owns a bank in town. He's talked my brother-in-law into working permanently for him there, but it won't work on me."

This sharing felt different to her. Like he needed her to know. "You don't like banking?"

"I don't mind it. I'm good with numbers and look forward to using what I learned with the piggery. It's just that Father doesn't share the workload very well. He meddles and takes over. I like the fresh air and freedom I have here, even if I don't have my own place yet. It's hard working with Father. Like fixing a beautiful breakfast, like this one, and never being allowed to eat it." He shook his head and took another bite.

They ate in silence for a moment. Rebecca glanced at his face only when she thought he was focused on his next bite. He must've shaved his own face smooth that morning too, before he worked on Eddie. She liked it. She met his gaze.

"Getting away from the bank was my main reason for coming here. Pigs came second. Eddie helped with that. Between that and my mother and sisters playing matchmaker with every lady over twelve and under ninety in town, I had to get a break. And then I bumped into you."

They both smiled at each other, then he said, "There was a bush between us."

"My rose." *My home.*

"My sisters spit-washed me and stuffed me into my Sunday best. That was enough sacrifice for one day. I wasn't about to let them parade me in front of God knows how many simpering misses that would turn into a puddle at my feet with just one glance." He gushed and grinned, obviously knowing how he sounded.

"A puddle? At one glance?" She teased at his dramatics, but she believed it. She saw how Widow Jenson looked at him.

"You have no idea." He lowered his voice again. "But I can't run from you."

She paused mid-bite. What did he mean? He must be teasing. He hadn't stopped teasing since she met him. And especially so this morning. Eddie was proof of that. But why did it feel like he was accusing her of running away? Was going back to her sister-friends running away?

She couldn't wonder about a future wedding and a husband—like Clark was doing. The disappointment when it didn't happen would break her heart. Cora Mae, Rose, and Heather along with Leander, Eddie, Naantam—they'd all staked a claim on her heart. Clark made her mouth go dry. She brushed off Joe—content to call him a neighbor. "You can't run from me?" She hated the insecure squeak in her voice. It sounded weak.

"Nope."

"Why not?" She wiped her mouth and sat back—leery of his next words.

"Because." He leaned close and whispered loud. "You have an enormous gun and you can shoot better than me. I'm scared to run from you. Plus, you cook good, so I wouldn't want to run from you." He winked at her again, sweeping away the ache in her soul as he ate more. She relaxed and laughed.

"I got it!" he gloated.

She startled.

"I got you to laugh again. I heard it when Eddie was wrangling all the animals on the trail and needed a repeat. And I couldn't have you chuckle at Eddie's lame jokes and his even lamer face, and not get more than a pretty little smile for myself." He crammed an overly large piece of biscuit into his mouth and looked quite proud.

Just then, Eddie came back in with a wet, smooth face and sat next to her. "Thanks for the meal, Rebecca. After I eat, I'm headed to the barn. I have several wagonloads of things to cart back here from town over the next few weeks. I'll have to eat fast and run. I think one draft I'm bringing in has a bruised foot. I hope that's all it is. I might get a poultice recipe to wrap his ankle once he gets here. I might need your help with that. Lots to do. Thanks for the meal."

"Chicken?" Clark stabbed a piece of biscuit off Eddie's plate as he taunted his friend.

"Me, chicken? Why?"

"You sat next to her and not me. *Brok, brok.*"

"That wasn't fear. That was me practicing what the Good Book says—turn the other cheek. I'd be an idiot, *like you,* if I tempted a fool twice on the same day." Eddie stood and left.

Rebecca laughed, again. His dry humor made her miss Rose. She wondered if they would ever meet. Probably not, if she went back to Missouri. Why would they? Rose would get along great with these two. She'd have to write a letter soon and tell her more about them. She still hadn't written to tell them she was coming back, and she wouldn't tell them this time. Why was that? She checked a sigh. She missed their chatter and almost choked when she found Clark watching her.

"What?" she asked. The warmth she saw in his eyes heated her skin, and the strange tickle was back in her stomach. His eyes were kind and warm. What was she going to do? Did she *have* to do anything? He'd go outside soon and fuss with his animals and she would be alone with Leander and Pa for most of the day. Why did that make her a little sad? Why did that make her wish for yesterday, when they were working together around the farm?

Just then she heard a cow bawling off in the distance. "Is that one of my cows? It's too far away, isn't it?"

"We better go check." Clark opened the door for her. And they both went out to see what was going on.

CHAPTER TWENTY

As soon as they stepped outside, they could hear the cow bawling down by the pond. "That doesn't sound good," Clark said.

"No. It doesn't," Rebecca said.

Rebecca had three dairy cows to keep up with. She named them on the long walk home—Gertie, Bella, and Daisy.

Eddie stepped out from the barn and yelled, "That's one of your cows, Rebecca. She was just here with the others when I came down from the loft. She got down there fast. She'll be up to her udders in the mud."

"I'll get her," she called back to Eddie.

Wanting to prove himself useful, Clark yelled to Eddie. "I can help her. We can handle this. Go ahead with your plans."

"I still have an hour or two of work before I head out. Take Sheba. If you can't get her out, holler." Eddie disappeared back into the barn.

"That's a good idea. I'll need a bucket of grain and some rope." Rebecca went to the barn, trying not to read too much into how grateful she was that Clark was going to help her.

"Let me get the grain and the rope. You get Sheba. You've spent more time with her. She knows you better." Clark ran ahead of her to the barn.

He was back with the bucket and the rope at the same time she had Sheba coming. He asked, "How did your cow get out? We were over those fences so many times when we divided the field, and after the pigs and Baron escaped. Leander always says about the fences, 'Hog low, horse high.' Nothing about a dairy cow in that sentence."

She let herself laugh, since she knew that was what he was going for. Sheba walked behind her along the path.

"Ah. See, that wasn't so bad. Laughter is good medicine. You should keep me around to be your medicine man."

"I'll keep you around as long as you always help with my cows, splitting firewood, cutting more split-rail fence posts, and anything else that's really hard."

She was trying to banter, but was silenced when he responded with a fast, "Deal." He went on, "I heard Leander and Eddie talking. Eddie is preparing to build Leander's small cabin over the next year. He isn't planning to move onto this place until after that. That's good news." He shook the bucket of food for the cow to hear.

"Why is that good news?"

"It means you have more time to save. You could gather for a whole year instead of a few weeks, before you went back. I bet you could save up enough that you could buy a cow back in Missouri to start a business there."

The idea had merit. Was he trying to give her a reason to stay a year for her sake or for his? She did need to have a possible job when she got back home. *Home.* It always came back to that. Where was home? She still didn't know what to do about Pa not being her pa. On the inside, her soul cried louder than the cow bawled. "I'll think about it."

"Your pa was there when they were talking. He's planning on building a small place of his own, like the one you had before, over there in those trees." He pointed to the tree line beyond the pond. "Maybe that was why Leander didn't offer the farm to you. Maybe he thought you would stay with your pa in his new place."

That could be why. But why didn't they tell her. Why did Pa never tell her anything? "I didn't know Leander owned out that far. I wonder why he hasn't used it for pasture?"

"Maybe he has plans for the timber. Maybe Eddie does."

She studied the trees and the way the land fell. She could see why Pa would pick that location. He was nearly hidden from the farm there. *Oh no.* She didn't like the reminder of all the times she packed sour mash for him. She would not go back to living like that. She would most certainly go back to Meramec, but could she save for a year first? Learn for a year, first? Maybe?

Sheba nearly trotted with her dinner-plate sized

feet behind her. When they came around the corner to the pond, the cow lowed so loud she couldn't think on her plans anymore. She needed to help. "Look at her."

"What was she trying to do? Swim across? No wonder she's complaining." He shook the bucket again.

"Good thing we brought Sheba." She patted the big black horse's side. They were close enough to see the whites of the milk cow's cupid eyes and hear her panting breaths.

"What's the plan?" Clark asked as if she knew.

This was her animal—her business. She would be the one to figure this out. "First, you're gonna wanna take off your new boots."

This time Clark laughed. The sound was good and solid. She felt herself lean into it.

When his bare toes peeked out from his denims, he gave her a wry grin, "First time a lady asked me that. Anything else?"

He was boldly flirting with her. Was it because she made him take his boots off or because she said she'd think about staying for a year? *What could happen in a year?* She let his flirting pass. She tied the extra lead rope securely to the horse and handed him the other end. "Take this out and string it around Gertie's neck. Be careful. She has a mean kick."

"Hopefully, I'll be dealing with her head and not her backside." He stepped down to the water and was knee deep in the same muck. "Why doesn't she get her water from the shallow end like sane animals do?"

"What's the fun in that? Be careful. She leans into me when she's upset."

By the time he had Gertie's head secured, Clark's was covered in brown mud. Rebecca was on the bank as clean as when she arrived. She felt the light wind tease the hairs that framed her face. She acted like she knew what she was doing. She'd told him what to do and then patiently waited while he figured out how to do it without getting stepped on by the cranky cow. If she left here, she would be on her own all the way back to Meramec, and then she would start over—again. And how she would make her way was unknown. But she would have Rose, Cora Mae, and Heather.

"Look at that. We work well together."

Together. She didn't say anything to him in response. "Back," she called to Sheba and put an added pressure on the horse's front shoulder. She did as told. The cow set her front legs to resist the pull and her neck stretched to length. "Go to her back end and carefully pull her tail to the side. Eddie said that's what you do when they get stubborn. It will make her want to go forward."

What would make Rebecca go forward? Which way was forward? Was she being stubborn? *Lord, I don't know anymore. I need your help.* "Back."

She pushed on the draft horse. It felt good to pray—comforting like Mrs. Mabel.

"That works." Tail in hand, Clark ran in the water toward her, splashing muck up his thighs. "After we're done, I should take her head and talk sense to her before we let her go. Even though she might bite me."

Rebecca laughed. Her most genuine laugh since she came to stay with Leander. The cow was coming. Sheba was still walking backward.

"What? I wasn't even trying to be funny that time."

She settled herself down to a chuckle, "Cows can't bite. They don't have top teeth. Slow and steady, now. Keep her coming all the way up the bank and onto the green grass, or you'll have to work her tail again." They were almost done. The cow was covered in muck.

Clark flicked his hands and sprayed glops of mud before he bent and washed his hands in the murky pond. "They don't have enough teeth? Suppose I won't live that greenhorn move down for a while."

"Don't let her bite you now." She would enjoy being around Clark for another year, if she could tease him like this.

Clark stepped forward with the cow, stumbled, and knelt in the shallow water before he jumped back up to assist. Muck and mire covered his hands, arms, and smeared across his chest, but he turned Gertie's tail until she was clear of the pond and the bank.

"We did it," he said. And Rebecca said she'd think about it. *Thank you, Lord for giving me the idea and the words to say.* A lot could happen in a year. He could make a lot happen in a year... or she could leave in a year.

Clark kept working until Rebecca pulled Sheba to a halt in the green grass. Satisfaction made him feel alive, capable, and strong. Unlike working with his father, he saw this project through, mistakes, muck, and all. Right enough to see Gertie safely on the green.

Gertie folded her weary legs under her and lay down so she could rest and keep an eye on them. She still bawled as if her life was over, complaining even when Rebecca placed the bucket of grain right in front of her mouth.

"We did it. We saved Gertie." He closed the distance between them. Her eyebrows raised, but she didn't look afraid or skittish.

He swooped in and gave her a comrade's hug—shoulder-to-shoulder, like he would his favorite sister. As soon as he held her, everything in him knew she was *not* his sister. He didn't want to stand down.

"You're muddy."

"What's a little mud? It's today's badge of honor. The price of a job well done. I wonder how many more such adventures we're gonna have?" Consumed by how wonderful it felt to hold her, he slowed his movements, hoping she wouldn't balk. He turned her to his chest for a real hug. All thoughts of mud left his mind. He wanted her to stay there forever.

Her tiny hands move to the small of his back and patted him, he squeezed his eyes tight. *Thank you, Lord.*

When the warmth in his body sparked white-hot, he released her, but stayed close. She wiped off the mud on the front of her without looking up at him. "I should have worn my buckskins."

He liked it when she wore her buckskins, but his mind was still on the hope of having a year more with her. More time. Hope. He drew her chin with the tip of his dirty finger. "Rebecca, I'm glad you might stay for the extra year. A lot can change in a year."

The light reflected off the start of her tears. It took his breath the same as if Eddie landed a punch in his gut. "Rebecca?"

She sniffed and looked over at Gertie, who stood up and was trying to shake herself free of muck. "Thank you for rescuing her." She was talking about the cow? Was she implying more?

He watched for even the slightest sign of encouragement. "Rebecca?" Why had he rushed her? Why had he put his own desires above her needs? He didn't even know her well enough to know what her needs were.

Her lips creased into a tiny smile. She blinked away the start of tears. "Sorry. Don't worry about me." She squeezed the hand he used to tip her chin. Gertie bellowed a protest and broke the spell. "I hear you. You don't have to yell anymore. Let's get you back to the barn." She turned from him.

Clark was frustrated with the cow.

She spoke to the cow, "You'll be fine now. Besides the mud, you're no worse for wear. Come on now, let's clean you up."

She untied the lead from Sheba and held both ropes in her grip, talking to the animals while she made her way back. He picked up the feed bucket.

His chest squeezed. She was perfect—a wild beauty.

When she brushed the black neck of the massive horse, a sweet glow passed over her face, and all vestiges of tears was gone.

It was slow going with the tired cow, but a slug's pace was his choice. He came up beside her. Glad to know Gertie couldn't bite him.

She seemed so settled. Almost like she drew her strength and serenity straight from the animals. "We'll have to repair where she escaped from. It seems strange. Baron got out, the pigs, and now her? You'd wonder if we had any fences at all."

He listened to the sound of her gentle voice. She was the one he wanted; impatience tugged. "That does seem strange. Leander and Eddie have both tried to brace me for the hard part of a farmer's life—for days animals get sick or injured or worse and days that you have to deal with things like a cow getting out. I'll check all the fences when we get back." He studied her, trying to memorize her delicate features.

He wanted to take care of her. He needed to be able to do that before he offered. Would a year be enough time?

He would *make* it enough time.

She said, "The pigs look ready to farrow any day."

"I'll be watching them close. One was using the extra straw I put in there to make a nest. Since I'll be down there, I can help you set up your milk stanchions and get you settled."

"Leander suggested I make my stanchion in the barn—because it rains so much. There are several things for me to make for the boardinghouse, but I'll need to harvest some rennet to make hard cheese."

He could tell she liked to talk about her new business as much as he liked to talk about his. The mud on his hands and arms began to dry and itched. The same mud his hug placed down the front of her dress. Heat flamed him again. He needed to get away before he did something even more forward than stealing a hug. She still hadn't said she would stay for sure. What would he do if she left in a few weeks?

He forced his gaze elsewhere. "I want to get started right away, so I think I'll go back and wash all this off. I'll meet you out at the fence or back at the barn."

He handed her Gertie's now empty feed bucket, their fingers brushing. Clark froze to prolong the touch—watching her big, brown eyes to see if she, too, felt like a teakettle at full boil.

Her eyes warmed for a fleeting second, then it was gone, and she was pulling away. "I'll see you back at the cabin."

His heart tripped.

She clicked her tongue for Sheba, leaving him to cool off on his own as he gazed after her. He watched her until she went into the open barn door. "Whose eyes are begging to be loved now? You're a fool, Clark, just like all those gals your sisters picked for you . . ." He stayed there a moment longer. "I'm a fool sure enough. A fool with excellent taste. A fool who, hopefully, has a year to figure things out." He whistled his way back to the pond.

The next time they sat for a meal, he would sit by her, and he would suggest they all hold hands for prayer. Families should *always* hold hands for prayer.

CHAPTER TWENTY-ONE

Several hours later, Clark was proud of the milking station he'd built with a feedbox and a sturdy counter he'd also built to put Rebecca's full milk pails on, to keep them out of the way.

Rebecca worked alongside him, putting her stool and pails in the order she wanted. He thought the more Rebecca enjoyed her life here, the harder it would be for her to leave. "I wonder if Eddie has an extra mouser. A cat or two would be good additions, don't you think? With all the grain and slop we're working with, mice and rats won't be far behind."

"I like that idea." She scraped out the remnants of the grain they fed to Gertie. Water had made it stick to the bottom of the bucket. She went over to his pigs and used a stick to dislodge the mess. "Your other pig isn't here."

He stopped what he was doing and came over.

"She's down there. In the stall, lying down. I think it's time." She turned a glowing smile on him.

If he wasn't already gone on her, this would have been the moment. "Let me see." *Lord, please don't let her leave.*

He quietly worked his way along the side of the pen and looked over the rail. "There's two babies.

We have piglets." The sow groused at him and acted like she would get up to drive him away.

He came back to Rebecca, caught up her arms and danced a jig. "Piglets! I did it."

She laughed and went along with his bouncing movements. "*She* did it."

They both settled, and then Rebecca slipped over to peek. "Another one is coming. Oh, it's here."

He let his shoulder press against hers in the crowded space. They stayed there until two more were born and the afternoon light turned golden around them. He savored every second of her presence.

"I should get back and make supper."

"Yes. We should let her be. I wonder when the other mama will farrow."

They were coming out of the barn when Joe came riding up on horseback. "Clark. Clark!"

They both stopped.

"I have a message for you from your mother. From town. Your father is terrible sick. Your mother asked you to come to her. She needs your help."

"What is it?"

"Was he in an accident?" Rebecca asked.

"I'm not sure. Your mother was beside herself. He's laid up. I wouldn't delay. Be prepared to stay for a long while."

"A long while?" Clark turned to Rebecca. "That

doesn't sound good. But what about the pigs?"

"I'm sure Eddie can watch over them. This sow didn't need much help. I can make sure they are fed and watered, too. You should go pack. I'll fix supper so you can eat before you go."

"I have a lot to do before I can leave. Did you say I would need to stay for a long while?" Clark called to Joe, to be sure.

Joe had come closer, dismounted, and was only feet from Rebecca. "Your father has been down for a couple days, and your mother was in a fit to send for you. It was providence that I came across her path when I did. She was preparing to send a messenger, and I was already coming this way, because I was bringing you this, Rebecca. A friend of mine harvested more rennet than they needed. It's in the crock." He handed her a beautiful basket with the rennet container inside. "You can keep the basket, they said. This is to help your dairy along." He lingered over the exchange.

Clark saw it for what it was. Joe was making an advance.

Rebecca didn't seem to notice. "I was just talking about this a few hours ago. I can pay you back after I make my first run to town."

Clark chimed in, "If I'm heading to town tonight, I can take milk, eggs, and whatever else you're sending to the boardinghouse."

"You don't have to. You should focus on getting to your father. Your family needs you. Besides, I don't have enough to share yet." Rebecca came away from Joe and to Clark's side and then turned to ask, "Mrs. Sutherland didn't say what ailed him?"

Joe shook his head.

Clark looked at Joe. His mother was always good with her words—and used way too many of them. Why wouldn't she tell Joe what was going on? Was it such terrible news it needed to be protected? What would happen if Father didn't make it? Clark put a lock on that thought.

He would wait until he was there before he tried to answer that question. What if Father couldn't run the bank anymore? His mother and sisters needed an income. He would have to go back to the bank. *So much for putting a lock on my thoughts.*

Rebecca put a hand to his shoulder. "We don't know enough yet, wait to decide until we know."

Could she read him so easy. He shook off the morose ideas. *We. She said we.* If the worse happened, he would step up for his family, for his mother, for Gwen. It was the right thing to do. If Rebecca was to be by his side, the Lord would have to work that out. All he could do now was prepare to leave the farm—to leave Rebecca—for who knew how long.

Rebecca fixed them all a meal. Joe stayed for it and sat so close to her that she could hear his breathing. Clark ran around and prepared everything for him to be gone for a while. He packed one of the saddle-trained draft horses.

Rebecca couldn't believe how sad she was to think of him having to go. It was like the joy was leaving the farm.

After the meal was over and Joe left and everyone else was about their business, she collected her bow and quiver and headed out the door.

She'd practiced a little each day, with Clark, ever since Naantam gave it to her. It seemed easier than carrying the shotgun around when she wanted to go to the spring.

With the dirty laundry in a basket under one arm and her bow in the other, she went to the barn first. Clark was shuffling things up in the loft where he and Eddie made their beds. She checked on the mama pig. Nine piglets happily suckled while the sow snored. All that time working and waiting, and Clark had to walk away from his reward. She couldn't stay there and watch him leave. It was too hard.

She herself would leave soon enough. After all the work of beginning a successful dairy, she too, would walk away, leaving it to someone else.

Rebecca went to the spring in the last of the daylight, planning to be gone until Clark was gone. It was a moonless night. By the time she was done washing the dirty laundry, she wouldn't be able to see her own hands. She didn't care.

She wanted to cry and feel sorry for herself and she wouldn't be able to do that with Leander going on about the new piglets and Pa telling her all about the copper that was getting made for his new still. And Clark was leaving. It took her breath away more than the cold water.

The trickle of the spring splashing on the rocks was a comfort. She stripped and washed. The freezing water kept her moving through her ablutions. When she was done washing, gooseprickles stiffened her cold, damp skin. She twisted her toweling over her hair and lingered as she redressed in the dark.

She could think here. Her best ideas for improving the farm came in this dank, quiet place when the scent of lavender hung in the air. Was it because she was finally alone and left to her thoughts, or did it have something to do with the chilly water? She pulled the toweling off her head and ran the boar-bristle brush through her thick mass in the cave's darkness.

She pressed her thumb into a thick callus in her palm before she pulled another stroke through her hair. She'd earned the callus in the last weeks. She would earn more. How long would Clark be away? Why did that make her so sad?

She would tend his pigs, for weeks if need be. She would work hard to be a place holder for his dreams and his agreement with Widow Jenson. That would take her past the time she was planning on leaving for Meramec, if she went this year and didn't stay until late next spring.

She liked that idea. She would stay and help Clark fight for his dream, for her dream. Tears of pride and ownership clogged her throat. She wanted to stay. Why did Leander have to give the farm to Eddie now?

That's not fair. It was the right thing for them both. Why did it seem like she got the rug pulled from under her feet right when her desires were within reach? No, that wasn't true either. She didn't have dreams for anything other than family and home until she came here. What should she do about Albert? Would Pa be upset she knew? Would Leander?

"Oh what a confusing mess." Her words bounced off the cave walls.

She dressed in the plain gown that Mrs. Mabel made for her and tied Jules's apron Leander said she could have over the top—the blending of both her worlds. She wished she could feel cherished—like a loved child. That was how things were supposed to be with her and Pa, despite Albert. She knew Pa loved her in his own way. Why else would he stick with her through all the years? Most days he was so caught up in his own pain, he didn't even bother to check to see if she was well before he disappeared into the hills to make his numbing drink. Well, she could understand why he wanted to be numb.

She plaited her long, wet hair—still enjoying the soap scent.

Would she ever have someone love her the way Leander loved Jules? She pictured Clark and grunted. *No room for fancy dreams.* Not even here in the quiet.

Thanks to Pa, she was as rugged as shoe leather—she would get through this. Something would happen to sort it all out or she would find a way through or a way back to her sister-family. Until then, she would take care of Clark's pigs and make butter and cheese.

She tucked the soap back into the hole and hung the towel to dry from the root that pushed through a crack in the rock wall. Stockings on, she tied her shoes and collected her nightgown and a few things she'd washed for Pa and Leander into her basket.

Joe gave her the basket earlier. It was perfect for her projects, but she didn't know how she felt about accepting it from him. Had she even thanked him? Next time she saw him, she would have to. She shivered, but whether it was from the cold or from picturing herself close to Joe, she didn't know.

Happy with her clean clothes, she pulled her quiver strap in place over her head and across her shoulders and picked up her bow. Never fully dressed without it these days, she walked outside.

The dark night was thick and dense. Not a star

in the sky. With the basket on her hip, Rebecca reached one hand out in front to protect her face from random branches. She needed to get back to the cabin. A pan of dried apples simmered in water preparing for a pie. Hoping Clark was already gone, she wanted to make it before Leander read to them, his evening routine.

A branch snapped next to her.

She turned in the dark.

Heavy hands shoved her from behind.

Dropping the basket and bow, she stretched both arms into the darkness and collided with dirt. A knee pressed into her back with the weight of a man behind it, snapping her bow underneath her.

Before she had time to think or do anything, a gloved hand clutched her upper arms and forced her to roll onto her back. Her apron and dress bunched, leaving her boots and stockings exposed. When she was about to scream, a gloved hand clamped her mouth. The trapped scream cramped her belly and scratched her throat with little sound.

A man's weight pressed her into the earth and stole all the air from her lungs. She kicked but was no match for his solid weight. She clawed and scratched at his hands. He caught her wrists in one hand. She had to get away. Unless she screamed, no one would come. *Clark, Naantam.* She struggled, kicked, and tried to gather enough air to scream, but the only sound was the guttural laugh of a man enjoying her struggle.

Hot breath on her neck held the licorice scent of fennel. She swung her head and collided her skull into his brow. He loosened his grip on her wrists enough for her to get one hand free. She swung at his solid back and nearly choked when he kissed her roughly.

She flailed and fought.

The fletching of her arrow scraped the wrist of her trapped hand where he pressed it. She quit hitting his back with her loose hand and felt for the shaft of the arrow while she tossed her head back and forth to escape his onslaught. She pulled an arrow out until she felt the hard stone of the arrowhead drag across the back of her hand.

He pressed his head down on her chest and neck to hold her as his free hand groped down her body and fussed with his belt. Was this happening? Her thoughts so free and clear a moment ago felt stiff and still, frozen.

The sound of his buckle clanking broke the ice.

She turned her free wrist and, with the arrowhead in hand, pressed all her strength into the point, scraping down the back of his shirt sleeve until she met warm skin. And then she shifted her weight off the ground and dug the biting point into the back of his hand. He dragged his hand away. The arrowhead stayed in her grip even though the arrow broke under the pressure. She pressed more.

He roared and pulled back, but his hand was pinned. She felt like a fox besting a bear by being faster and smarter. Could she get away? Warm blood slicked her hands. She bore down harder while he pulled back even more. *Hope.* She twisted her weight under him until all she was, all she would ever be, pushed the arrow in. If she could stake him to the forest floor, she would.

His groan turned to a bellow, and when he pulled his hand away for the third time, she swung the top of her head into his face, connecting hard against his nose and brow bone. Then she scrambled up and ran, faster than she'd ever run before. Her heart thundered and her skin coursed with what felt like lightning. She raced the trail in the black-as-a-bat darkness as if the fires of hell were licking at her heels.

Vomit rolled up her throat—she swallowed it and choked. She scrubbed his kiss off her mouth but didn't slow. She ran and ran until she climbed the three steps to the cabin and barged in. The door banged hard, shaking the window glass. Pa dropped his jug and swore. She bolted through the living room and into Leander's room, startling Leander when she flew past him and hid in the corner of his room farthest from the door.

CHAPTER TWENTY-TWO

She was shaking. Every bit of her quivered. Leander limped over to the door and dropped the bar of wood into place behind them all, locking the cabin tight. Before he made his way to turn up the lamp, someone banged on the closed door.

Rebecca screamed.

"Who is it?" Leander's voice was deep and gruff like a dog with his hackles up.

"What happened? I heard crying," Clark called through the door.

She clamped her hand over her mouth to stop her sob. He hadn't left yet.

Pa's voice grumbled, "Let him in before he shouts the house down."

She let out the breath she held. Leander looked at her and the door before he opened it. Was he checking to see if she was afraid of Clark? That was crazy. She nodded to let him in. He lifted the lock. If terror wasn't still racing in waves through all her limbs, she would find a way to be grateful to Leander, but she couldn't breathe.

Clark darted over to her. She couldn't stop herself from cowering back and shielding her face with bloodied hand. She ran here to find safety, but this place wasn't any better. She gave all she had to finding a place to call home, but there was no place safe. Even if she went back to live with Cora Mae, Heather, and Rose, something would happen to uproot her or her sisters, sooner or later. Hadn't the same thing happened to her mother? But if she let the pursuit of home go, what did she have left?

She wanted to look at each man in turn and scream, "You aren't my pa! You gave away my home! And you're leaving! Don't any of you want me?" Self-pity was as ugly as the blood on her hand. She didn't know what to try for anymore. She slumped farther into the corner.

Clark knelt in front of her. She didn't look at him. He stiffened, but she couldn't soften. He didn't wait for her to meet his eyes or say anything, he pulled her up to stand and hugged her until her sobs broke free.

Her muddy quiver and a few battered arrows hung crooked at her back.

"You're here," Clark whispered. "You're safe. We're here. We've got you."

Leander came close and stroked her arm, soothing her like she was a wild horse on the verge of bolting. She hid behind the clumps of her hair stuck to her cheeks.

Clark continued to hold her. Slowly she heard his heartbeat over her own. Leander brought the lantern over and pushed it high to inspect every part of her face, head, and neck. Pa moved off his bed and came to sit on Leander's. Watching it all, he said nothing.

The calm of the moment lasted until she felt the throb of a bruise from where the man had dug his knee into her back. Rebecca squirmed in Clark's arms. She turned to the wood dresser Leander told her he'd made for Jules as a fifth-anniversary present.

She clutched it for the strength to stand on her own.

Leander continued to use the lamp to inspect each part of her before he set the light on the floor. Pain dotted his forehead with beads of sweat. She wanted to object—to keep him from hurting himself—but no words would come, and it didn't matter how much he hurt, she knew he would stay right there until he knew she was unharmed.

Clark reached to tuck a strand of her tousled hair behind her ear. She flinched, but focusing on his fingers blocked out her quaking-terror.

"Rebecca?" Leander asked the unaskable in one word. She tried to pretend everything was normal—like nothing happened, but it had. She stood from the dresser. How could this place be home now? Pa reached from his place on the bed and patted her hand. No words—never the words.

Clark examined her until he found the blood on her hand. He smeared and swiped at it until he knew it didn't come from any place on her. "Wolf?"

She jumped at the sound of his voice so close to her ear.

He'd tempered his scowl, but a blind woman would know he was ready to exact revenge with his bare hands.

"Sorry. Was it a wolf? I've heard there are more of them than usual this summer," he said.

With the smallest of head shakes and another sob, she looked around the room. She pushed past him, she pushed past them all. Their eyes said they cared, but they weren't safe either. She lurched forward and grabbed the clean chamber pot from under Leander's bed. She emptied her stomach, but even after there was nothing left, retches clutched her guts over and over. Leander's tears spilled into his beard as he rubbed her back. Pa continued to watch.

Clark took the chamber pot when she was through, then he filled the wash basin with cool water and handed her a wet cloth. She reached for it, and a tear in the shoulder of her dress flopped back and exposed cold skin. Clark saw.

It scorched her heart with spinning memories. She was back by the spring, in the dirt, pinned.

"Who?" Clark demanded.

She jumped. *Who?* It all played through her mind again. How could she not know the answer? The man was right there . . . on her. Leander came close and pulled her in a hug. His creaking stays settled her. "You're safe now."

Clark added, "You made it home. We'll figure this out together."

Her sobs quieted, but tears still fell. He said she'd made it home. She laughed low and hysterical. "Did I? Do I even have a home?" She pulled back from Leander, talking to Clark. "You are going back to your father and don't know if you'll be back, Leander gave this home, my only home, to Eddie—so I can't stay here forever. And Pa isn't my pa, Albert is." She said the last part quietly, unable to look at Pa.

She was forced to look up when he asked, "You know about Albert?" His face was white. The red, puckered burn scars stood out more pronounced on his pale skin. He turned to Leander. "I didn't tell her. I kept the promise."

She spun away from them all and went to the table. "What promise is that, Pa? The one Ma made you both make—that made you willing to walk the Oregon Trail? You do all that, yet you keep it a secret from me? Why?" It was easier to face these men that were here than the man in the dark. She didn't hold back, "The same promise you wrote about, Uncle Leander, but never explained?" She could feel herself pouring out like spilled perfume. Only nothing she said smelled sweet.

She would tell her sister-friends of this moment. She wanted them to be proud. She squared her shoulders the way Cora Mae would, mustered the quiet strength of Heather, and spoke simply like Rose. "He attacked me. I fought. My bow broke." All well and good, but she had no roots. She would be like Jules's rose. She would slowly fade and dry up.

Clark came to her and turned her to face him. He wasn't gentle. He spoke firmly. "You're safe! You fought and won! Do you hear me?" He gave her a little shake.

Rebecca cried as she searched his face. He kept talking. The scared-rabbit twitching inside her lessened when he did.

Pa got up and came over and patted her hand. "Albert left. I love Ophelia. I love you."

Her knees buckled. Clark held her fast as Pa found his jug and lifted it for a long pull. Pa said no more before he lay down.

"I'm sorry, Pa. I love you too." She didn't know if he heard or not. But it was true. She would say it more. He was broken. He'd been poured out a long time ago, but that didn't mean she couldn't give what she had. That felt right. She could water instead of expecting to be watered. Sobs rose again. Pa was unruffled. Like a chicken roosting as soon as it was dark, his drink had him settled and snoring in seconds.

But he was her pa. She said she came with him across the Trail to learn of her history and her family, without realizing she was with her history and her family. Messy and broken, but hers. She wasn't as alone as she felt.

Clark spoke, "Your pa is out. He won't wake tonight. The door is locked. I want to get on the road, so I can get help to find this man."

"I have my gun." Leander left to get something from his room.

Clark stayed with her. "Do you need something to eat before I leave?"

She shook her head.

"I didn't think so. I can't imagine you want to eat, right?" He went back to holding her. "I don't want to leave you, but I have nothing to offer—no land, no home, and I must go to my folks."

She didn't fight it. She stepped into him, trembling under his arms. *No home.* There it was again. A choice to water or be watered. "I'm finding my home." She tried to reassure him, "You need to go and take care of yours."

Leander came back with two books. "I think you need to shore up."

She tipped her head back from Clark's chest and gave Leander a quizzical look.

"When Jules and I added the root cellar here, below the house, we dug deep. The sides would slide and cave in at first until we stacked river rock in there to hold the weak spots. Something happened to you tonight. Something real and something that scared you. Do you want to talk about it?"

She said, "No."

"Shoring up is what Jules called it. You need

to dig deep. You need to strengthen the walls and shore up—make your way through whatever happened. Am I right?"

"Yes." She sniffed and swiped the tears that flooded her face. And she stood a little taller—only coming to the middle of Clark's chest. Clark didn't say anything, but he rubbed circles on her lower back. She didn't want him to let go, but Leander was right. She needed to find her peace—her place—her home. One that couldn't be uprooted so easily.

"Bring her here, Clark." His voice was gruff and stern to cover his emotions. He strode them straight over to the mantel of the fireplace. He flipped the lid of a wood ammunition box. "Here." Careful with the blade pointing away, he shoved an Arkansas toothpick into her hands—the blade as long as her forearm. "I'll have this, and Clark can carry my Colt." He showed her the wide-bladed Bowie knife. He passed the Colt to Clark, Clark tucked it into his waistband with one hand. He didn't let her go.

"You see that?" Leander waited for her to look at the bolted door. "The thick logs would stop anyone, but then they have the window. Right?"

"Yes," she answered.

Clark stiffened. His grip tightened at her waist and took her breath.

"That first year Jules and I heard so many things about bushwhackers, rogue-trappers, outlaws, and Indians, it's a wonder I ever got her to agree to come. This is why she agreed." Leander disappeared inside the larder.

Clark turned her to follow him into the tiny space. The smell of potatoes and burlap mixed with apples made her look around. She'd been in here hundreds of times as she'd cooked for them. Why was he digging around the wall? And then she saw it. There was a door. "It closes?"

"Yes, this is the original homestead. We built the rest over the next three years. Spent our first winter in here. And it was a cold-white one. Not complaining." He chuckled.

"It was a great winter for Jules and me." He grinned, pulled the door free, and then grunted with the familiar pinch of pain. He was overdoing it. He should most certainly be in bed all day tomorrow.

Tomorrow. What would there be for her tomorrow? Did what happened change everything?

Clark let her go and pulled a sack of flour by the top corner until it shifted away from where it blocked the swinging door. "This thing is built like a fort," Clark said.

"Because it was one. Or at least that's the conclusion Jules and I came up with. See that cut in the logs up there? It shifts open to let in air. Or if necessary, you can use it to shoot from. Easy to shoot out, nearly impossible to shoot in. You know how thick the walls are, right?"

"You couldn't even burn it out—not even this time of the year." Clark moved things before Leander hurt himself more.

They worked together to remove everything off what she thought was a bottom shelf. When uncovered, she could see plainly it was a built-in bed.

"Clark, bring her pallet in here. You can bolt yourself in—give yourself a chance to shore up."

Clark rolled her bedding and carried it back to the vault-like space. Pa never stopped snoring. Leander brought her folded buckskins in and laid them on a shelf too.

The space was small. The air didn't move, cushioning the sounds. Thick walls allowed her to take her first deep breath since she was jumped.

Clark must've been able to tell. He folded a lock of her hair behind her ear. "You were attacked by a man, right?"

She nodded.

"I don't want to go. I want to stay here with you, but I still must go to Mother. I'm going to head to the sheriff too. Do you remember anything to tell him?"

She shook her head. Then she remembered. She remembered the smell of his breath, but that wouldn't help. *The arrow.* "I got away by gouging the back of his hand."

"So the blood is from his hand?"

She nodded.

"That will do. I'll give him the information and see if he knows of any other troubles in the area. And I'll be back as soon as I can, or I'll send help. Keep her safe, Leander." Both men talked around her for a moment before he left.

She wished she could call him back. She felt safe around him.

She was still standing there watching the door from her place inside the larder, wishing for him to never have to leave and for a future that she knew couldn't become a reality, because her dreams never came true in the past.

Leander shoved the two books to her chest and went out and came back to the tight space with the lantern. He set it on a small water barrel.

His face blanched. He stood still, gritting his teeth, squinting for a time. "Here now. You got your bed, a table, chair. You have anything you need to eat at your fingertips. And with the knife I gave you, you're set. And these—one is my Jules's Bible and the other is your mother's diary. She wrote all about her life and you in there. I don't know if she wrote about the promise, but I'm hoping she wrote enough for you to understand what your pa and I agreed to. Stay in here. Read them both. Catch your breath."

She stayed put, books clutched to her chest. He was right. She needed to be still and listen to the silence until all the screaming inside her quieted.

She wiped at the blood on the back of her hand and before she could think twice, she bolted past Leander, out of the larder and grabbed the wash pitcher and bowl, before she hustled back into her room.

"That's my girl. Jules came in here with that"—he pointed to the Bible in her arms—"to shore up after losing each of the babies. She said this made things on the inside of her stronger than they were before." He touched the dried rose that poked out of the top. "If I was thinking, I'd have given you more of her things long ago. You still haven't gone through her trunks to see if you can find anything you can use. I kept your mother's from you. I'm sorry about that. I thought you would leave after you learned about her. I know understanding her was why you came in the first place, but I really needed your help. I'm really sorry for keeping that from you. After you read that, ask your questions—when you feel better. Your pa had the right of it, a lot needs to be said."

He was trying so hard. And he hurt. He reached out to her. "Otis is more of a pa than Albert ever was—take my word for it until you can read your mother's words. I am family. I didn't think through how Eddie's taking over here would affect you. We'll figure that out too." He kissed her forehead and turned to leave her.

The attack pulled at her, threatened to uproot her, like she had uprooted her rose, but it led to all this. Pa loved her. Leander wanted her, and even if Clark had to stay in town, she was connected here. If she left, part of her would tear.

"I'll be right outside if you need anything. And I'm sure the sheriff will make his way here sometime tomorrow. This room is right-perfect for you. Should've done this as soon as you made this your home—too much time as a bachelor to notice the important things. Take as much time as you need. This will be your room as long as you're here—until we build."

He took a long look around at her new little haven and when he was satisfied, he gazed at her. His concern was thicker than the butter on the counter—so unsure.

A stampede of oxen ran across her middle. It was time to water back. She could tend his roots. She offered him a small smile. "These will help." She clutched the Bible and journal. "You should go lie down—your back."

"My back will hurt tomorrow, same as yesterday. I'll sit out here and guard. You settle in and try to get some sleep. If you can't sleep, just rest yourself. You've been through somethin'."

Tears came again, fast. She blinked.

Leander said, "We'll talk later. We need something more to go on to catch him. If you remember anything, write it down."

"Thank you." She waved the Bible and clutched it like armor. Only then did Leander slowly close the door. "The lamp will last all night if you turn it as low as possible."

Rebecca slid the heavy wood bolt into its place. The exact twin of the one on the front door. Silence cocooned her.

She sat on her new bed and pressed her back as far into the corner as she could fit. Nothing about her felt the same as when she'd hid in the corner of Leander's bedroom. Her whole world had changed.

She sat listening for a long time, thinking of nothing, feeling nothing. Soon the silence wasn't enough. She lifted her mother's journal and set it on the small table. There would be time to savor that later—maybe she would take it to the spring.

The spring. She shuddered. She remembered his weight on her, and her lack of strength when pitted against his. The licorice scent of fennel mixed with his sweat. *I can't.* Would the attacker steal her lovely spring from her too? *No.*

She ran her fingers over the ornate lettering covering the Bible's firm leather. How was she supposed to shore up, like Jules? Was she supposed to think about what happened or ignore it?

She slid sideways until she was lying on the bed, curled, with the thick logs pressed roughly at her back. She held still, wishing and hoping sleep would claim her and give her an escape. But every fiber of her was still alert and ready.

Who attacked her? Was he still out there? Had he studied and planned? Would he do it again?

She squeezed the Bible into her belly until the edges gouged, her thumb still exploring the raised design. Was time passing? She couldn't tell without windows. Even with the lamp burning low, the room was dark. She felt even darker.

CHAPTER TWENTY-THREE

The late July night was so dark. Not a star in the sky. Clark had to ride slow. Random night sounds made him reach for the Colt Leander gave him. He was as skittish as a bobcat and he was going in the opposite direction of his heart. How was he supposed to build his future with her if he was trapped in town? *Lord, help me.* Even if he had to let go of the piggery and support his family business, could he ask her to move into town? She fit out there on the farm. Her cows were out there on the farm.

He'd left her. He'd left his heart, on the worst day of her life, behind a bolted door, and he couldn't do anything about it. Father was taking him away from his desires, again. This time he had even less choice—the honorable thing to do was to care for Father, Mother, and his sisters.

He wiped his hand over his face, trying to keep his shoulders from sagging like his dreams.

He'd pushed as hard as he could—baby piglets proved it. Yet here he was back at the beginning, pinned between loyalty to family and his own dreams with no way to bridge the two.

At last he reached Oregon City and made his way to the street that had always been home, his gaze finding his parents' house. The only light on was Gwen's. *It must be worse than I thought.* He rode the horse right to the back door, looped the reins on the porch rail, and went in.

The house was silent. Was the rest of the family all right? Was it contagious? He went through the kitchen and into the parlor. He struck a match and lit a candle before he darted to his parents' bedroom door. He hadn't gone to their room in the night in years, but this was different. He knocked. "Father? Mother?"

He cracked the door and lifted the light to see the bed. Mother sat up and Father lay back with his mouth open, snoring. "How is he?"

He came in and walked to the opposite side of the bed to get a better light cast over Father. "What did the doctor have to say? Are you well?"

Father's eyes opened. A halo of confusion clouded his face. "Clark?"

"I can take on the bank, if that helps you. Is that what you need?"

Father sat up. "What's the matter at the bank? Do you know something?"

Mother slid out of the bed. Her nightgown fell into place, her braid dropped to her shoulder as she lit her own candle. "What's wrong now? Are you well?" She came to him and lifted the light to see his face.

"I came."

"I can see that, but why?"

"And what does that have to do with my bank?" Father made to stand and winced.

"Stay abed, dear. It took forever to get you settled." Mother set down her candle and fussed with the quilts that hung heavy over his father's bare ankles. He couldn't remember the last time he'd seen Father's ankles.

"Stop your fussin'. I can handle myself. Hand me the cane. That's all I need."

She did.

It was Clark's turn to be confused. This was nothing like he expected. And why did Father need a cane?

"Did something happen, brother?" Gwen came in behind them. She used her shoulder to push the door so her good hand, balancing the candle, was free.

"I came when I heard," he answered.

"Heard what?" Mother asked.

"And why couldn't it wait until morning?" Father added.

"Joe said you sent for me, Mother. That Father was terribly ill."

"Well, Joe got it wrong. I said he was terrible sore."

Clark thought about it for a bit. Did Joe really get it that wrong? "You said sore, not sick? You sure?"

"The only thing I'm sure about, is that I want to

go back to sleep, and you're keeping me up," his father said.

"A terrible pain is more like." Gwen came forward. "Now that we're all awake, Father, do you need anything to make yourself more comfortable?"

"Not you too. I never understood, until now, how we tormented you with attention. That's why the hair, isn't it?" Father looked Gwen in the face.

Clark wouldn't have believed it if he hadn't seen it with his own eyes. Maybe Father had a fever and was out of his mind.

Understanding had Gwen and Father grinning at each other in the shadows.

Gwen nodded. "I'm sorry you hurt your ankle to realize it, but I'm not sorry you realized it. It's suffocating."

"Like these quilts." Father flung the blankets back and then winced.

Mother looked quite bewildered. She didn't move to help Father. Her gaze stayed glued to Clark. "You thought I called for you, and you came. You stopped what you were doing to come help us—to help Father at the bank? Did you hear that?" She turned to her husband of decades. "You said he was selfish and spoiled. That doesn't sound like selfish and spoiled to me."

"He was, he is. You are, Clark."

"Because he wants to follow his own dreams

and make his own way without other people breathing down his neck and telling him what would be best for everyone according to how they see it?" Gwen's words were caustic. She was so close to father's face there was no way he couldn't catch her double meaning.

Harrumph.

Clark rubbed a hand over the back of this neck. "So, you aren't sick?"

"I fell off the boardwalk and hurt my ankle."

"Do you need help at the bank?"

His sister answered. "Max has things well in hand. He comes over after the bank closes and tells Father about every little transaction. It's working beautifully."

Father held Gwen's gaze and then added, "Careful, Gwen, I heard you. No need to turn shrewish. Take your tea with me later this afternoon. I'm sure we have much to discuss." He lay back in his bed with a swollen, purpling ankle left free of the quilts.

"Only if you're up to it, Papa." Gwen leaned over him and kissed his forehead.

Clark wasn't sure if he was more relieved or irritated that there was nothing more than a passing injury here. "I don't know how this misunderstanding came to be, and I'm too exhausted to figure it out now."

Mother said, "Settle down. One hard-to-manage Sutherland man at a time, please. Come around for breakfast—no—make that afternoon tea, if you're still in town." Clark's mother climbed back into her own side of the bed.

Harrumph. Father grimaced again.

Gwen squeezed Clark's shoulder and made eye contact with him before she left the room.

Father said, "Go and chase your dreams, Clark. We seem to be managing fine without you. It seems the bank can manage just fine without me too."

And like that, he could see clear. Something lit and popped like dry kindling on the inside of him. Father wasn't trying to force him into banking to bend *Clark* to his plans. His father feared losing what *he'd* worked for. He was afraid of losing the business and his reputation.

"I would come if you needed me, Father. I love my new business. I'm not sure it will ever prosper as much as your endeavors have prospered you, but it's mine. And I will always have favor in town, because I'm a Sutherland. Sutherlands are kind, generous, hardworking, people of integrity, because *you* are. People like that will always be needed."

Harrumph. "Appreciated. Wish I didn't have to fall off the boardwalk in front of half the town to hear it from you. Now go to bed. Your room upstairs is still in order—or go to Eddie's. Close the door on your way out."

He wished his father didn't have to fall off the

boardwalk to say what he'd said either. All the wasted time.

Harrumph. Clark imitated his father. But was it wasted? He was free from the office work, he now had his parents' blessing, and a room to stay in when he came to town, and he met Rebecca. "Rebecca," he said. *The sheriff. He needed to go.*

He left his father's room and the house before Mother started asking questions that would take too long to answer. Across town, he roused the sheriff, filled him in, and was back on the trail home to Rebecca before the sun rose.

He wished he could kick the draft horse into a canter, but the darkness made his progress slow—and gave him plenty of time to think.

Blackness spread like spilled ink from the places on her skin the stranger had touched and kissed. Denying another shudder, the only change in her surroundings was the sound of Leander's heavy snore on the other side of the thick door. It settled her more than anything.

If he could sleep, then surely the danger had truly passed. The dry rose crinkled. *From Jules's rosebush that died?* She couldn't see in the dark. She moved the book and felt with both hands, but as she did, she felt the crusted blood of her attacker on the back of her hand. *Oh, God!*

She flung herself off the bed, dropped the Bible on the small, circle table with the night lamp, and felt the shelves until she found the stack of empty flour sacks used as wash clothes. She dunked one and scrubbed until both her hands were pink and raw. A splash of water dropped onto the cover of Jules's Bible. "Oh, no." She grabbed another flour sack, drying her soaked hands before she sat on the log-round stool and carefully dabbed the cover.

The low light spread its warm glow over her movements. She opened to adjust the dried rose, turning the page so she could see. It marked Psalm Thirty which was read so many times the ink was blurred and worn thin—even wrinkled. Her handwritten note, beautifully slanted, fit between the lines.

> Weeping may endure for a night but joy comes in the morning. You have turned my mourning into joyful dancing. You have taken away my clothes of mourning and clothed me with joy, that I might sing praises to you and not be silent. O Lord my God, I will give you thanks forever. And I will see you soon my precious babies.
>
> Janice Morton
> Roland Morton
> Evelyn Morton
> Richard Morton

"Tears. Jules's tears." The crinkled paper made sense. The other woman found comfort here. She'd shored up here. Rebecca could do the same. Could she follow the path Jules left or would the dirt path between her hidden spring and the cabin forever haunt her? Fear twisted and balled in her belly.

"Jules lost babies. Four of them." Her own tears spilled as she traced the old ink names. "What have I lost? What have I really lost? I got away." *This is my home.* Even if Clark must stay in town. She could thrive here, with Pa and Leander. She could write to her sisters about that. She could learn about Ma here. She didn't have to leave. Leander would tell her about the secret promise soon—even if it was hard. Would she let some stranger in the night take it all from her?

She had a choice. She would either shrivel and die like Jules's rose, or she would thrive like the one Rose gave her.

She didn't have Mrs. Mabel here, smelling like cinnamon and sugar, saying she would help her find her way. Leander tried his best. He'd given her a safe place—a place to grieve and think and decide. But it was up to her.

Pulling her quilt off the bed, she wrapped herself in it and turned the light a little higher so she could find all the places Jules left notes in the Bible. Maybe there was more help here. Maybe she could find her way out of the darkness that had nothing to do with the nighttime.

Hours later, shoulders hunched and neck sore, she still read. She'd found a favorite.

The LORD is my rock, my fortress, and my deliverer; my God is my rock, in whom I take refuge, my shield and the horn of my salvation, my stronghold.

The words poured into her cool and fast, like the spring she showered in. *The Lord My Rock.* Her rock? If He was her Rock, then He was the strong one. Love stole her breath. She could hide in Him. She read the verse over and over until it felt like a familiar path, like a rock in her pocket.

She unhooked her boots and slipped out of them and her stockings and continued to read long into the night. Denying sleep. Denying the memories. Like a rain barrel, she collected the comforts from the book—from her Rock—whether they were type-set print or written in Jules's delicate, looping hand. "You are my stronghold." Her words echoed in the tight space, bouncing off the thick walls.

Leander shifted on the other side of the door. She flinched and gulped hard against the zinger of fear that tried to become a scream.

"No." She put her hand up to stop the fear. *I'm stronger than this.* She was the one who ran for help when her pa was burned. She was the one who walked the Trail, pushing that blasted cart. She was the one who learned to farm, garden, and hunt. She would adapt. She would plant herself right here in these words.

She stood. The blanket fell to the floor. She

paced, hands balled into fists. She would not write to her sisters and tell of her defeat. She would share with them, but not until she fought and won.

She needed more than the words on the page and hiding in this room. She stripped out of her clothes and dressed in her buckskins. She would fight now and sleep later. She tucked the pointed blade that Leander gave her into the waist of her pants.

Boots on, she pulled the lock back on the door and tried to get out without disturbing Leander. It was still dark outside, but morning would come.

Leander woke. "Rebecca?"

"I'm good. You did a good thing. I needed to shore up as you said, but now I need to go to the barn, do normal, be normal. You should go to your bed. It's almost dawn." Could she do it? Could she go to the barn and behave as if nothing had hurt her?

"Are you sure? Nothing tried to get in last night. You are safe in here."

"I know I'm safe in here. This is my home." She said it and she meant it. *Home. I found it.* Tears welled. "I need to shore up out there. I have the knife. And I'll only be down at the barn. I'm sure Clark would appreciate if I checked on his pigs. Let's get you to bed. You overdid it." She helped him to his feet. Pa snored on his cot in the corner. She pulled a quilt over his shoulders before she helped Leander stand.

He listed to one side, sucking pain in through his teeth. He went to the wall and pulled the shotgun off the shelf and handed it to her. "If he comes again . . . kill him for me." He squeezed her hand and walked to his bed.

Rebecca smiled, content at having instilled him with at least enough confidence to keep him from worrying.

"I will." Rebecca left the cabin.

Once on her own, cold sweat beaded her forehead. Light was on the horizon, but it would be hours before full sun. She clutched the barrel of the gun tight enough her knuckles turned white. Then she lit the lantern and turned the flame as high as it would go.

Joe pulled a cotton stocking off the clothesline, sure to stay out of the line of sight of the old farmhouse, and tied it around his wounded hand.

He pressed his fingers into the thick sock. She was stronger than she looked. He licked his lips, remembering her sweet taste, ignoring his failure.

He liked to rehearse a thing. Practice. Plan. Know his every step, and his escape—like Mother taught. Since the overnight camping trip home, he'd thought of little else. She needed to be broken in order for him to win.

But he was coming to spy on her at a distance and then she was there. Right in front of him. Close enough to touch in the dark, she slipped out in front of him, in the same place he'd seen her several times. He knew her routine.

This was a hands-on job. He smiled. *More than hands on.* He was in it this time, not pulling the strings from a distance, like with Leander.

But she got away.

She bested me.

Not planned.

He growled. "I made her afraid." Would that be enough? Only part of the plan? She would be afraid, that was in his favor. Leander would still realize he couldn't protect her—and that Clark and Eddie couldn't always be around. He'd timed it all so well. Maneuvering them.

He never anticipated her getting away before he was done. He wanted to steal all that mattered to any single young woman. He wanted to soil her, so she would be more inclined to marry a man willing to look past it. Clark wouldn't do that. The whole town knew the Sutherland charm was a yoke of morality strung like a noose around father, son, and all those sisters.

Clark would have left. Would he leave now? Joe ran his escape path—the one he'd planned for, skirting Baron the Bull's pen, staying in the shadow. He hadn't planned on being marked. He pressed the bloody place seeping through the sock until it hurt—sharpened his senses.

He would be delayed. He couldn't go back to his place until his hand healed. Reuben would ask questions—too much risk. Maybe he would watch again and finish his goal another night. If she was ruined, all his plans would fall together. It was the fastest way to be welcomed to the farm—as a saving hero. She would never find out. He would be the one who took her innocence. He would never tell her, and he would never forget.

He pulled the heavy blanket over his shoulder for protection from the cool evening breeze and leaned against the closest tree, listening for fresh movements, for Naantam, before he walked back to the farm. He would watch and wait his next move. The farmer would miss the blanket, but there was no way they would put this together with the attack.

Silent, he waited for the dark to cloak him. The darkness that was his closest friend—his sweetest confidant.

His plans had been interrupted, but they could be rectified. This wasn't the same as when Naantam intervened. He could turn it. He'd felt her fear. He could grow that seed—and then harvest it when he stole her virtue.

Had anything else gone amiss? He needed to show caution. His mind was so full of all that had changed, he didn't need to leave a simple detail unnoticed. As he walked, he felt his clothing. Had anything ripped? Had she claimed a piece of his clothing . . . that could identify him?

He felt around until he was reassured. *No.*

Had he left any of himself behind? Made any marks in the soil that would give him away?

He found a place to think and watch. The more information he gathered, the better his chances of finishing what he'd started. "Patience."

He was sitting there when she came out of the cabin and ran to the barn. He smiled at the palpable fear surrounding her movements. He'd created that. He was still sitting there when Clark came back and when Eddie rode home.

He'd bide his time. Nothing could be done with the two new fellows around. He could outsmart them and outwait them. He could control his passions. "You might still be here, Mother, if you had a grip on your passions all those years ago. How I wish you'd held yourself in check. I'd love for you to see her. She's exquisite. Her eyes haunt me. The feel of her body . . ."

The longer he sat the more his eyes adjusted to the darkness. Rebecca went back into the cabin. He imagined her lovely mouth.

He could look back and be glad Naantam ruined his plans to kill Leander—twice. It could be looked at as failure, but it led him to her—his prize. She would become his family. The bullet aimed many months ago to spook, which burned the horse's hide and nothing more, would be worth it. He could be grateful.

Now and then, he found that horse and ran

his fingers over the smooth scar everyone else attributed to the tumble over the embankment. *I know.*

He always knew. And he would ruin Rebecca and then offer her hearth and home. Leander would help him, for her sake. And he would always have the memory of the moments in the darkness with her for his dreams.

He could still smell her sweet skin on him.

He clenched his wounded fist. He was not a fool. If she saw his hand, she'd know. He'd have to leave her alone for a while. "Is this what it was like for you, Mother? Did you want the money, the city life, and life's finer things—no matter the cost?"

The two men were down in the barn, without Rebecca. He wanted to hear what they were planning, how they were responding. He wanted to find more of their weaknesses. He considered creeping close, but there was enough light now to try and use his mother's old opera glasses. He reached for them.

He patted and felt, and patted and felt.

They weren't there.

If he'd left them behind and someone else found them, Reuben would know whose they were. They must have fallen away when he had her pinned to the forest floor . . .

He must go back and find them. Without getting caught.

• • •

Clark climbed down off his horse and walked him across the yard and left the large animal to drink his fill while he unsaddled him. He listened to the night that still hadn't given way to dawn. Someone was out there. Someone who wanted to hurt Rebecca. He wouldn't relax until he was caught.

He carried the saddle into the barn, stopping in the darkness to listen. A light glowed from inside the pen with the new pigs. Was the man back? Why would he be in here? He marched over to the pen and looked over the wood railing.

"Ahhhhhhhhhhh!" A scream rent the air.

"Rebecca?" She was in there with his pigs.

She flung up, jumped the rail, leaving the lantern behind and was scrambling toward the door.

She staggered and tripped, knocking the feed bucket. It rattled and crashed on the floor beside her.

"Rebecca."

Sobs broke in the night.

Tears. She was crying.

She scrabbled to her feet and was in a full-blown run for the door. He caught her around the waist. She was shaking all over and fought against him, but didn't scream.

"Shh. Shh, I'm not going to hurt you. I'm sorry." He held her firm around her waist—her back pressed into his gut. She slowly quit lunging for the door.

How could he let her go, when he'd caused such pain? She was so terrified. Would she get through this? If he let her go, she would run from him physically. Would she take her heart with her and never trust it to him? He would understand. But he couldn't let her go like that.

He scooped her tininess high on his chest. Her feet couldn't touch the barn floor and her hair tickled his nose. "Shh. It's me. I'm sorry." He pressed his lips against the top of her hair.

Over and over he kissed her head. "I'm sorry." Kiss. "I didn't mean to scare you." Kiss. "Please don't be afraid." Kiss. "Please don't run from me." Kiss. "I won't hurt you." Kiss.

How could he hurt her? *I love you.*

He said he would marry her to Eddie down at the pond that first day, but this was different, this was more. If she ran from him, he would split, deep and long, like the split-rail fence—never to be whole again.

"Please." His words created a warm spot on her head where he spoke. He turned his head and laid his cheek on it and slowly bent to put her feet back on the floor, hoping. He kept his arm about her but loosened the restraint. She stayed encircled for a long second.

The sound of another horse coming into the yard had Clark moving forward, one arm around her, one hand on his Colt. She matched his steps in silence.

"Clark?" Eddie's familiar voice came out of the darkness. "Is that you? I didn't expect anyone to be up yet. Are the pigs farrowing?"

Rebecca's voice still held a quiver of fear if you were listening for it, "Yes. The second one is farrowing now. That's why we are down here."

"They are? We are?" he whispered. Clark watched the shadows as Eddie dismounted and put his horse to trough. Rebecca squeezed his hand and slipped from his hold. The pressure in his chest doubled.

"Thank you," she said.

Pressure released from his chest at her gentle tone. Then empty coldness flooded in the wake of her warm body. He started forward after her and then stopped himself.

"I'll put on an extra-large breakfast in a couple hours. Leander wore himself to a nub yesterday. I'll ring the bell when it's ready." She left both men standing in the barn.

"I'm going to eat and run again. Still more trips. I have a lead on a few more head of cattle. I came back for the wagon and supplies."

Clark said, "I'd offer you a hand, but I'd need to stay close to Rebecca . . . and Leander."

"Rebecca and Leander? That's new. I didn't know you even noticed my uncle with the glow of the halo you put on her blinding your eyes."

"A lot happened when you were away. And I just got back from town myself. Father is hurt." Clark filled Eddie in on everything as simply as he could, protecting Rebecca as best he could. He concluded with "I'll hang here and see if I'm needed."

Eddie, brow furrowed, agreed. "We should see if we can track him when it gets light."

"Good idea." Clark liked having Eddie there to help—too much was at stake.

A little while later, opera glasses found, Joe watched the slim fingers of one of her hands playing with her hair at the nape of her neck. He'd gripped both of her hands in one of his and felt her lithe body squirm.

One of the other men moved and blocked his view of her. "Move. Move! I want to see her." He muttered to himself.

He checked around him for Naantam. He'd almost been caught out earlier by Otis. Good thing he was caring for his jugs like a mother with newborn triplets, or he might have had some explaining to do.

Rebecca lifted the cup to her mouth. He sighed—her lovely mouth. He'd have to think of a way to be close to her. To have her.

He wished he could be the one sitting next to her. He didn't want to stop looking at Rebecca through the opera glasses, but he did want to be closer. He'd have to wait until it was dark to slip up to the window.

Again, more patience. He thumbed over the surface of the hard-boiled egg—his supper—white shells crumbling to the ground beside his boot.

He'd bide his time. Nothing could be done with the two fellows around, but they wouldn't stay for long. He could outwait them. He'd already been patient for years.

He bit into the white orb—the yellow inside coated his lips. A pack of coyotes yipped. He scooped dirt with the toe of his boot to cover the eggshells. Nothing to chance. He'd gotten away with his spying so far—no need to grow careless.

Joe went silent and waited for the next coming of darkness. Yes, the darkness was his closest friend—his sweetest confidant.

CHAPTER TWENTY-FOUR

Rebecca tried to lie on her new bed in the larder and sleep after she went back into the cabin. Sleep wouldn't come.

She opened her mother's diary instead. Tiny script with looping l's and t's crossed the page. The date went back to before Rebecca was born, before the trip around Cape Hope.

All these years she wanted to know. All these years she'd waited for Pa to say—to give her something to hold on to, to cling to.

And now she held it in her hands, knowing it wouldn't give her what she wanted, because it couldn't give her what she already had.

"I'm not trying to take something from you. I'm trying to give something to you." She said the words aloud that came from the quiet place at just the right time, so many times in the past weeks.

She closed the journal. She held it close. Her time to read it would come, but she wouldn't tarnish it with this dark day's memory. Instead she thought about Clark. They way he'd held her and kissed her head.

He was back. How was his father? She hadn't thought to ask.

And the question she didn't want to think came too. Would he stay?

She left her space and began to prepare a breakfast feast. She would feed them all so much it would take an hour to eat. She wanted these men around her table. *My table.*

She ran a hand over the heavy wood surface before she lit the lanterns. She wanted them to make their plans, to dream, and to figure out who jumped her over ham steaks and eggs. Pa slept on.

After a big breakfast, they all, except Leander and Pa, walked the trail back to the spring and collected her crushed basket filled with now-dirty laundry. She led the way and then watched as they scanned the area for boot prints or marks. All they found was a cedar bow branch used as a broom to sweep the marks free.

"He came back and cleared up behind himself?" Rebecca shuddered. She wasn't alone. She wouldn't be alone again. But she crossed her arms over her chest and repressed all the memories.

"Was that smart or stupid? Clearing up behind himself seems less random," Eddie said. He picked up her crumpled bow. "I bet Naantam would make you a new one. He's made me more than one over the years."

Rebecca didn't want to think the attack was more than random. "Would the sheriff want that?"

"I don't know. I could take it to him. Give him

an update. I'm not sure what he could do, that we haven't done. But if I go to him on my way back to town, then he will get the information faster. Maybe there will be a clue in the goings-on in town, maybe we should ask more of the neighbors. I don't know, but maybe the sheriff will have heard something. And if I go, that means you can stay here, Clark."

"That might be all we can do, for now," Clark said.

Eddie walked around in one big looping circle after the other. When he was nearly to Baron's fence, he stopped. "Whoever it was is local enough to know that's a bull pen."

"They live around here?" she asked before she pressed her lips between her teeth, stubborn against panic. *The Lord is my Rock.* He knew she was here. He knew who the evil man was.

"Not necessarily. They would simply have come by in the daylight. Any man worth his weight can tell cows from a bull." Clark stepped closer to her.

Eddie came back through the brush and stood on the path with them. "I should probably go. There're two weaner pigs to grow out up for sale at the same place I'm collecting the cattle. Should I bring those back?"

"Yes," Clark answered fast.

She almost laughed. But nothing felt funny inside.

"I will buy as many pigs as you would allow me on this place. I need to make my mark, as a businessman. Could you check in on Father on your way through too? I just left, but if I can get an update from him, when he is more awake and prepared to answer, that would put my mind more at ease."

"I can do that easy. I'll stop in before I go get the cows. And this farm is not just mine. It's big enough for quite a bit more. Fit as many as you can, for now. My pa let me do the same with his place. It's the only way to get started. I should check the assayer's before I come back, too. If there are any local homesteads available close to us, you should be ready for that."

Rebecca looked at the scuffed dirt trail while the two men talked over the incidentals. There was nothing here, nothing left. Other than the bruise on her back and the tender spot on her forehead, she had nothing to say that the attack really happened. If she could trust the man wouldn't come back, she could walk away and never speak of it again—as silent as Pa's daughter had been trained to be. But would he come back?

They went to do morning chores, milking and counting the piglets in the new litter.

Eddie left for town. Clark stayed close to Rebecca—whether she was at the barn, garden, or cabin. He watched her fuss over Leander and gently talk him into spending the rest of the day in bed. Leander was worn out from all the comings and goings.

Rebecca worked on projects outside, right around the house—like she was guarding Leander. Clark did the same, only protecting her instead of him.

He'd fetched water, stacked enough wood along the smokehouse wall to last the whole of next winter, mixed and added a batch of chinking to the log cabin walls. Later, he joined her when she planted potatoes for Christmas new potatoes—food for the coming winter. Rebecca worked so fast she was a row ahead of him the whole time.

He stayed close when she worked Sheba and Samson, but not close enough to smother. When she finished brushing the drafts down, he put them out to pasture. When he was through, he came back to the yard. Naantam stepped out of the forest and came to him carrying a basket. Clark didn't know if Rebecca saw him. He didn't want her to be frightened. He put his arm around Rebecca's shoulder. "Naantam!"

"Oh. Naantam."

Clark only felt a slight jolt.

"What's that?" She went forward and looked in. "Fish. Thank you."

Naantam made a few gestures with his hand after scanning Clark head-to-toe, including his arm around Rebecca, moving nothing but his piercing eyes. "More." Naantam moved away back toward the trees.

"He caught more than these? We should go fishing sometime. Do you think he'll show us?" It felt good to talk about a future with her—about normal things.

Clark didn't think Rebecca heard his question. She hefted the basket of fish into Clark's arms and trotted after the Indian who was halfway across the field.

The last he heard clearly was Rebecca call Naantam. Clark watched. She looked down and rubbed the toe of her boot in the dirt, wringing her hands. She looked like she was confessing sins. She must be telling him about her broken bow. Naantam gave her some words. She came back with a serene smile and a twinkle in her beautiful brown eyes.

He wished it was him that put the twinkle there.

"He said he'd take us fishing later on. Will you help me fillet and clean these? Naantam is bringing us more soon. Fresh fish for dinner."

How could he say no? He kept the basket and followed her. "These are big. Where will we clean them?"

"Down at the creek. The crawdads love the tailings."

She led the way. Rebecca was all tiny-sweetness in front of him. Her lithe form moved with quiet freedom in her buckskins. He would follow her forever. A root caught his foot and almost sent him sprawling. *Focus. Watch your step.* But his eyes and heart couldn't or wouldn't obey.

Clark tried to make the day as normal as possible. When they finished cleaning the fish, Clark joined Rebecca in the evening chores. They worked together in quiet camaraderie until all the troughs were topped and the grain and hay dispensed.

Darkness was making its shadowy presence known. They leaned against the fence together and watched her milk cows graze.

The birds grew silent, and the frogs sang.

The moment couldn't have been more perfect if he'd planned it. "Sorry about startling you this morning. How are you holding up?" He felt better just asking.

"No need to apologize."

He waited.

"I'm finding my way. I feel like so many things have changed since yesterday."

He waited for what felt like forever but was only a few long seconds. "I hate that you got hurt," he said.

She turned her head so she could see him. She rested her chin on her arms, which were still stretched along the top of the rail. "Bruises heal. It's nice I'm not alone. I know that better now than I did last night."

Clark read all the emotions that blinked through

her large eyes—fear, panic, resignation, and finally resolution.

She went back to watching her cows. "I want it to become an old memory. That's all. Nothing more."

"I'm glad I was here to understand how things were."

Her fidgets and wiggles made him nervous. "I decided something last night."

He moved one step closer to her, still leaning on the rail. Afraid to touch her and break the mood.

Dusk cloaked them.

"I don't have to leave next year. I'm not sure how things will fall out, but I'm staying here with Pa, Leander . . . and you."

"That's good news. *Great news.* I don't have to help with Father's bank. Max has it covered."

"So he's not sick? Sorry, I forgot to ask with everything."

"He hurt his ankle. He can walk, but he needs a cane." Clark inched closer again. This time his elbow was up against hers. He had to clutch the railing to keep from reaching out and holding her in his arms.

She must've sensed it in him. She rushed and repeated her words. "I won't run from what happened. I won't run from the secrets about my real father. I'll stay and learn and grow. I should replant my rose."

In the twilight, he could see the ring of purple bruises that wrapped her wrists. Why hadn't he seen them earlier?

He slipped his hand under hers on the railing and traced the bruises, wishing he could thrash the beast who did this to her. "I'm sorry you had to go through that. I'm grateful you got away."

She looked up at him. He could see the hint of honey-amber in her eyes. She squeezed his hand. He really couldn't leave her. He didn't think he could ever leave her. He didn't *want* to leave her. He leaned down and kissed her temple and slipped his arm around her to hold the base of her neck and kissed her temple a second time—savoring the floral scent of her hair and the warmth of her skin.

She didn't shy off. She rested into him.

Joe punched the tree with his good hand and then jammed said fist into his mouth. *Blast you*. How could she let Clark so close—even after cleaning smelly fish?

Clark wanted his Rebecca as bad as he did . . . only Joe was hampered by a setback. He untied the stocking covering the gouge on the back of his hand and then retied it tighter. It was about as healed as it was an hour ago when he checked. His patience took a hit with the lack of sleep all night. And when he realized Clark was sniffing after Rebecca even harder than before—like a buck in rut—he grew angry. *I need to join them.*

Joe could see how the wind blew.

He promised himself he would keep his bandaged hand in the wide pocket of his denims. They'd probably head back to the cabin for supper once it grew completely dark. She would be afraid of the dark. He sat unseen in utter silence, like a cougar, at his favorite watching tree.

From his vantage, he could see right into the cabin's living space. She would be inside there soon. She always cooked there. His stomach growled. One day soon, she would cook him supper.

He looked around and listened in all directions. Naantam had darn near walked up behind him earlier. If he hadn't been carrying the fish baskets, Joe was sure he would've seen the sign he left. He'd have to pick a new tree soon or the pressed dirt and broken brush would give him away.

He watched the way Rebecca and Clark leaned against the fence rail. If Joe was down there with them, she wouldn't give Clark the time of day. He sneered when Clark said something that made her smile. "You think because you have fresh, city-boy charm, you can dance her off right under my nose." He spat. "She's mine . . . not yours."

"Who's yours?"

Joe whirled and squatted low. His eyes found the person and the escape path at the same time.

Otis looked in the direction Joe was spying on. "You looking at my girl?"

"Otis . . ." *Phew*. His heart banged in his chest. He could handle Otis. But he was slipping. He let Otis get the drop on him. *Not good.* And Otis wasn't even quiet. He was juggling three tankards like newborn triplets.

"Not yer daughter. Keeping an eye on Clark. With Leander down, someone needs to make sure he isn't taking advantage of the situation. Especially now, since they are alone and Eddie went back to town."

Otis came and sat by him, weighed down by his three favorite jugs.

"You make some more?" Joe pointed to them.

"Yup. Still getting used to apples. Sweeter than corn."

"Is it as good as your last batch?" He needed to keep Otis here. If Otis went to the cabin now, he would surely mention who he'd seen. "Your last batch would be hard to beat. It was better than Stewart Besley's, and he's had forty years of practice."

"Besley is as old as dirt, and his drink tastes moldy. Mine sets tongues a-waggin'. Like a try?"

That was the invitation Joe was after. Otis was as proud of his drink as a first grader with a McGuffey Reader. It wouldn't take much to get him to indulge, and a drunk Otis he could work with.

As Otis settled himself and his jugs, he watched Rebecca, Clark still at her heels or nearby. He couldn't do anything about Clark now, but soon there would be a reckoning. He dug his fingers into the bandage on his hand. *Soon.*

Otis set two jugs down and was working on the cork of the third. He tipped the jug and swallowed several loud gulps and gasped, wiped his lips on his crusted sleeve, and belched, leaving enough signs scratched into the dirt to cover any Joe left.

Eventually, he offered a swig to Joe. Joe drank some and gasped. "Good." Smacking his lips, he said, "Boy, that'll grow hair on yer chest. What's that aftertaste?" There was no aftertaste, but if he was going to get Otis to drink enough to be manageable, he had to drink more than normal. The man was always two-thirds pickled as it was.

"Aftertaste?" Otis downed another swallow and smacked his lips. "Nothing but glorious nectar."

Joe pretended to take another sip, "Right after the burn, there's a hint of . . . what is that?"

The ruse had Otis drinking and testing. He sat down and leaned back against the tree and opened his other two jugs, using Joe as a tester.

Joe moved so he could see the cabin and keep the man drinking. It didn't matter if Naantam came upon them now. He would see two men enjoying the fruit of their labors.

Rebecca left the cabin and went to the barn. Clark never left her side. This would work. There was nothing but an innocent story here. He fed Otis's fire. "These aren't the same batch, are they?" He couldn't tell the difference, but Otis took the bait.

"Why you ask that?" Otis scowled at him like Reuben's dog protecting his food dish.

"Nothing really. I can just tell they aren't from the same cooking. This one has a little extra and that one you have, has that aftertaste."

"No aftertaste—" Otis took big swigs of both and the third for good measure.

Joe used his distraction to slip out his opera glasses. The opera glasses he'd gone back for. Such a big mistake—neatly averted. Soon he could see the barn from here, but not Clark and Rebecca. The glasses brought them into sharp focus.

He watched as she removed the old hay from the chickens' nesting boxes. She pulled a strand of her thick brown hair from the corner of her mouth—hair as smooth and brown as a cattail flower.

Corners of her mouth. The mouth he'd tasted.

"An' twist 'em up a tune called Turkey in the Straw. Turkey in the Straw. Turkey in the Straw." Otis bobbed his head up and down.

"Shh. Quit yer singing. If you're caught yowling, Clark will catch wind of us. He won't show his true colors."

"Song got stuck in my head after my last taste. I've never had liquor as good as this since the barn raising at Aunt Sally's place. Met my Ophelia there before we came here. Before she married Albert." He blew out a sad gust. His shoulders, always sloped, dropped farther. "Perttiest lass in the room." He drank again.

Otis offered Joe the jug and then pulled off his coat and unbuttoned his shirt, revealing a sweat-stained nightshirt. Joe swallowed as little drink as possible and made a loud gulp, enough for Otis to hear, even while the man pulled his arms out of his overshirt.

He needed to keep his head clear, but from the look of things, Otis was already half-out of his.

"Want more?"

"Sure. Don't mind if I do. It is good." Otis tossed his shirt aside, accepting his own drink.

Movement by the barn caught Joe's eye. They were coming out. They didn't head into the cabin but leaned against the fence rails overlooking the pasture. He ground his teeth.

He could tell from across the field she was letting her guard down—letting Clark and his baby-blues bamboozle her.

"Is it hot out here to you? I'm sweatin'. Can I have some more?"

Joe turned to shush Otis. Otis was standing with his back to Joe, undoing his belt. What was the crazy drunk doing? It wasn't that warm. Why was he taking off his pants?

He flipped the opera glasses back into place

and turned to the couple, trying to read Rebecca's lips. Lips that should be his and his alone.

Closer to my prize. He wished Leander would come out and call for her, as he did occasionally when he needed her help. He wished that crazy-old-Indian would bring them more fish. *Anything.*

Then they would have something to keep their hands busy . . . their eyes busy. They wouldn't look at each other like lost hound dogs.

He punched the tree trunk next to him, again. This time blood sprang up on his knuckles. "By Jep."

"Whatcha do that for?"

Joe wished Otis to the moon until he remembered he was better cover than ten tree trunks. No one would question him for drinking with him. Joe ignored Otis's question, and his scuffling behind him.

He watched Clark move close enough that his and Rebecca's elbows touched. Joe growled and glared. Clark hadn't touched Rebecca like *he'd* touched her. Joe wouldn't allow him to. He would soil her first and only. He would make her desperate and then save her. He closed his eyes to better picture it. But then he opened his eyes to see what Clark was doing. "Don't you do it."

Even from here, Joe could see Clark watching her lips—lips as full and fresh as wild strawberries. *His* lips—the lips he owned. "Don't you do it. Don't you kiss my Rebecca."

"Kiss? Kiss. Rebecca, did you say?"

Joe growled again. All he needed was for Otis to go out there and spoil everything. *Hey.* All he needed was for Otis to go out there and spoil everything! This wasn't a methodical plan, checked and rechecked, but since he couldn't step forward until he healed, it would work.

"Clark is going to kiss *your daughter* unless you do something. He is taking advantage. You need to protect her. Now! Are you going to sit by and watch that city boy steal her virtue?" Joe gushed all he could think of to motivate Otis's slow, intoxicated mind.

"Nobody's stealing nothin' of mine." Otis clanked the jugs as he picked all three up into his arms. It wasn't until he'd trudged past Joe that he realized Otis had taken off all his outer clothes and was left wearing a stained nightshirt, the short summer kind.

One of the jugs slipped from his grasp and was sliding down his thigh. Otis bent to catch it before it crashed on the ground, but not without flashing Joe the full glory of his pale behind. "That'll stop the kissin' if nothing else will."

Joe used the glasses again to see everything unfold. It had been a long time since he'd grinned so big. The smile hurt his face. His knuckles throbbed. The back of his hand hurt, but he ignored them. He slipped up behind a different tree—a thinner one. He wanted to watch it all happen.

Usually, he wouldn't risk it, but he was sure they would all be entirely preoccupied as soon as Otis reached them. His hand had to heal. He had to get back in there. He needed to be close to her. He needed to smell her sweet scent—to touch her soft skin, to claim her and his future home.

He savored Rebecca's initial squeal of protest when she spied her father. But his satisfaction was short-lived. Some commotion out of his sight, around the front side of the cabin, claimed everyone's attention.

He didn't know what it could be, but he didn't have long to wait. A wagon jangled up and a new man—the spitting image of Clark, only taller—came into view.

The newcomer was more upset than Joe was. He scolded Clark loud enough the whole hillside could hear. Joe leaned into the tree and gloated like a fat cat in a sunny window.

The man ranted, "Are you really planning on taking out a loan for a homestead before your business even has an income? Haven't you learned anything from working under my tutelage at the bank?"

Joe gloated. "You watching, Mother? You proud of your boy? All my schemes. Look at this one unfold. You thought I was out of luck when she marked me, didn't you? Don't count Joe Curl down-and-out until he stops breathin'. Right?" His mutterings were quiet secrets spoken soft enough he could hear every word of Clark's pa's tirade.

The angry man stood in the wagon, yelling, "Are you trying to break your mother's heart, and spoil the Sutherland name, so none of us can hold our heads up in town?" His face was red.

Joe could tell the argument flummoxed Otis when he wobbled and stepped to keep his balance and failed. White skin shown to all.

"Oh, no." Joe shoved his left hand with the scraped knuckles into his mouth to block the sound of his laugh.

Clark said a few things back to his father that Joe couldn't make out. He focused on the conversation and looked through the lenses again. The opera-glass view slid across Rebecca's cheeks, which had gone as white as a chicken egg. Mr. Sutherland's angry shouts rang through the surrounding trees.

Joe took in every word.

The man ranted on, "Eddie gave me half the story of how things were out here. Said you were looking to buy land. Thought I would come and give you my help. Don't want you picking a place too far from town—too far from your mother. I even braced up my sore leg to get here, and told your mother she and your sisters could follow tomorrow, after I'd had a chance to talk with you." He shook his head. "But I can't believe my eyes. I rolled up here in time to catch you kissing her in plain view. How could a Sutherland, my own flesh and blood, treat a lady with such disregard and not make it right? I would never be able to hold my head up in public, let alone run for mayor." He chopped his hand in the air and turned redder still. "You *will* marry her, if I have anything to say about it. Good thing your mother will be here tomorrow, and I heard the parson he'd be making his rounds out this way too. Good thing indeed!"

Did he say "the parson?" Joe cursed full. Things were going so well. Why did this man meddle? Joe was out from behind the tree and halfway across the yard before he remembered to shove his bandaged hand into his pants pocket. He couldn't stay back any longer. Rebecca and his farm were slipping out of his reach. *I must stop this. But what could I say?* What could he do? Nothing except break up this insane little tantrum, but how to do that?

CHAPTER TWENTY-FIVE

"Father, you have it all wrong." Clark felt Rebecca recoil beside him, whether from his father's cruel assessment of her character and his, or her father's indecent show. He gripped Otis around his upper arm to help balance him. Otis's missing clothes made the whole thing seem tawdry and cheap.

Rebecca didn't deserve any of it, especially when she was still reeling from the attack. Clark had to stop this. Even if marrying her was his real desire, this was the wrong way to begin.

Rebecca beat him to it, "Mr. Sutherland, there is no need to react so. Your son has treated me with every propriety."

Otis lurched forward. Clark kept ahold of his arm. *Lord knows we don't need him to bend over and pick up another jug.* Clark scooped one of the three drink containers into his own arms.

"Thank you." Otis coughed and cleared his craggy throat. "Yer as fine a gentleman as can be, Clark. No one should come 'round here yelling loco like that, but don't expect different. When Leander and I met him, he was giving the boat master a chew down for something he didn't know nothin' about. Come on, Rebecca, let's go inside."

"You know me? Leander is still in there? You live with Leander?"

Otis answered, "Yes, and you know me. I'm Otis, you dunder. Quit hollering till you split my head."

Did Father not recognize him? Otis had been around when Leander and he were cronies.

"Father, if you give me half-a-second, I'll explain. You've read the situation wrong. This is Leander's niece, Rebecca, and he's her father, Otis Packwood, from your trip around Cape Hope. Don't you recognize him?"

"Know him or not, I can't have got it all wrong if a man is gadding about in his ill-fitted nightclothes before it's even dark outside."

"Enough!" Clark was done. Father came into the situation, as he did everything in Clark's life, assuming he had a better answer than Clark could come up with—like he was the fount of wisdom and everyone else was his lowly subjects. Every reason Clark had to escape Father's banking business filled his soul in this crowning moment. He was right to leave. He wouldn't back down, and he wouldn't marry Rebecca under Father's terms.

His father stood silent, obviously seething at Clark's rebuke. Why was Father even here—to lead him by a ring in his nose, like Baron the Bull? He even came with an injured foot.

Clark gave Otis a gentle shove toward the

cabin, hoping he would stay on his feet. "Wait for me here. I'll explain, Father. Rebecca needs help with her pa, first."

"Nice to meet you, Mr. Sutherland. I'll go and fix supper for you." She didn't look his father in the face.

That made his gut burn.

Her fingers trembled, yet her words were sweet and meek. Her fear and pale fright broke his heart. He was so mad at Father he wanted to physically fight him.

Father was acting the master—sending them to the gallows. *I won't be pushed around. Not here. Not with her.*

Rebecca aided her pa to the cabin.

Clark watched until they were balancing on the steps.

Rebecca continued to appease his father, talking over her shoulder. "I'm sure you're hungry, Mr. Sutherland, after traveling so fa—" She gasped. "Clark!"

Clark thought Otis must be losing his balance, but he wasn't. She lunged toward *his* father. He whipped around in time to see his pa, eyes white in their sockets, slumping from his stance on the wagon bench and tumbling toward the ground. He lurched to catch him. "Father?" And narrowly kept his head from crashing the rocky-dirt road.

Clark pulled his father's head into his lap and watched his chest for breathing. He was so focused he took a few blinks to register the moccasins next to his thigh where he sat, and the end of a long, black braid.

Naantam crouched beside them. "He chicken of me. I go." Naantam turned and lifted a second basket of spring salmon into Rebecca's arms and then left. As Clark watched him walk away, the Indian puffed his chest at Joe. Where had Joe come from? Both men gave each other a glare from head-to-toe, on their way past each other. And if Naantam's craggy face was any indicator, he found Joe wanting in every way.

Naantam disappeared into the woods, like he always did.

His father stirred in Clark's lap, reviving from his faint. Slowly he climbed to his feet, wincing at the pain in his ankle. He leaned heavily on Clark.

Clark studied the disappearing Indian and then his father. "That's how Leander saved your life, isn't it?" he asked. "You fainted when the natives accosted you and Leander on your Cape Hope crossing. And Leander kept you from getting yourself killed."

"My ankle. Find me a place to sit down." Father grunted but didn't look Clark in the eye or say anything else.

Rebecca stayed back, giving them cautious space.

His father never admitted to weakness. Never

missed a chance to bring correction, if he was right, but he hadn't defended himself.

Clark must be right—Father fainted when he saw Indians.

There was a weakness. Clark had no intention of exploiting it. Nonetheless, it was wonderful to know it was there. They were about to have a talk that would make it very clear just how much of the Sutherland pride Father had taught him.

Clark led his father to the porch and helped him sit on the low step. He left his father dusting his pants and went to Rebecca before she retreated into the cabin.

He leaned close to her ear. "Don't worry about the threat of a wedding. I won't let him push you . . . even if I think the idea is charming. You all right?"

She looked up at him with her liquid brown eyes and nodded. She didn't recoil but leaned a little closer. He closed the space and kissed her temple, then her cheek. "I need to talk to Father."

Otis wobbled on the steps. Leander made it out to the doorstep. "Welcome, Sutherland. We have a lot to catch up on. Why don't you all come to dinner?" he called to them all. "We have plenty. Joe, there's enough time to fetch Reuben, if you like. Fish for everyone."

Rebecca nodded.

Clark didn't expect anything but kindness from Rebecca. He loved that about her. He wished he could say the same about himself, but at the moment, all he wanted to do was punch the smug fox-in-the-henhouse smile off Joe's face.

"Reuben will like that. I'll fetch him. Fresh salmon sounds good."

"We'll make it a celebration of sorts. Mr. Sutherland is well enough to travel here for a visit." She paused and swallowed. "That's an occasion to celebrate." She raised the heavy basket to her hip and followed her pa and Leander into the cabin.

Otis yelled back through the doorway too loud for her standing so close, "And Old Orchard! Shared to you all." Otis moved to raise a jug in cheer.

Rebecca shook her head "No, Pa—I mean yes, Pa. You can share if you'd like. Don't lift your arms. We need to make you a different nightshirt. Let's go inside. You can pour them all a drink."

He wobbled forward. "Use the small glasses. I don't want to share—don't have much left. I should go make more—entertaining guests."

"After supper, you can if you like." She turned back. "Dinner in about an hour? Nice to meet you, Mr. Sutherland. I leave your son to help you settle."

Joe lifted a hand to her, his other stuffed in his pocket. "I'll be back with Reuben." He stared for more time than was comfortable.

She went inside.

When Joe moved off, Father spoke. "I stand by my word. You will marry her, and I won't loan you any money." At least his father had the decency to stage whisper instead of bellowing as earlier.

"You're wrong." He wanted to say that for years. "I will marry her, if she'll have me. And I haven't asked you for money and I never will." He was determined to make that truth. "But I will not be forced to marry her because of your tyrannical fit. If she'll have me—if you haven't scared her off—she will marry me when and where she wants."

"Yes, bu—"

"Stop. You are a businessman, the finest. And you taught me to be the same. You never give loans without all the facts. Why would you let your arrogance lead you into handling this situation with anything less than your usual excellence?"

"Clark." The warning in his father's voice was one he'd heard a thousand times growing up. Usually, he knuckled-under. But this was the last of that. He'd tried nice words. He'd turned the other cheek more times than he could count, and he'd tried removing himself from his father's managing fingers, and was even prepared to support Father when he thought him too ill to run the bank.

Now it was time for brutal honesty and maybe fisticuffs. "Rebecca is special. She deserves better, and I will give it to her. I don't care if Mother comes. I don't care if she figures out a way to drag the parson into accompanying her. There is nothing going on here that I need to repent of. If you had been cordial enough to get to know her before you accused her of impropriety, then you would've seen for yourself that she is as sweet as they come."

"Careful, Clark. I saw her in your arms. And her father—"

"*You* be careful. And I mean that. Yes, her father is a drunk, but despite that, she found her way across the Oregon Trail, to be Leander's arms and legs. We never came out to help him. She's the reason Leander can stay here. This is her home. Leander would shoot you, if he saw how you treated her."

"But—"

"No buts. I will do everything in my power to support Rebecca and all she does for her pa and uncle—marrying her amongst them. Also, the Indian you saw is the reason Leander is alive. Your fear of him is foolish."

Clark's soul felt like it grew two inches speaking up to his father. He loved Father, but he was done bending to his demands. He hadn't just learned to be a pig farmer, he was his own man and there was no going back.

Father's face was still purple-red. "Are you finished?"

"Depends. Are you ready to see reason?" Clark clenched his fists, stood and faced him. Would Father take this too far? Would he make him cross the boundary lines of respect?

Then, like a sunny break in the clouds, his father smiled. He grinned wide and white.

"What?"

"I've been waiting for this moment since I first held you in my arms as a baby."

"What?" Clark shook his head.

His father rubbed his sore ankle. "Five girls and then you. I wanted you to know your limits. I wanted you to be tested and tried. I wanted for you what my own father failed to give me—courage and strength born of experience—not limited by fear at every turn and filled with self-doubt." He looked off in the direction Naantam disappeared.

Before Clark could quite take it all in, Father stood without weight on his bad ankle and hugged him, glad-clapping him on the back. "A man, born and raised amongst women, knows a few things to his advantage—pampered, for sure. But if he has a weak character and is smothered by their love—if he doesn't get his fat in the fire a few times, he may shrink from the moments of conflict that will take his measure as a man. I know."

"Was that what all the hovering and smothering at the bank was about?"

"Yes."

"I wish I'd known. I'd have spoken up sooner. I rather liked banking." Father shook Clark's hand but didn't let it go. "I held my tongue to honor you. I value your respect."

"My respect is freely given. I'm glad to see you aren't a shrinking violet when push comes to shove . . . and not a fainter either." His father's bushy-silver eyebrow arched.

Clark had never known him to mock himself. Was he capitulating on the forced wedding? Clark settled his legs in a wide stance, ready to go to battle with his father for Rebecca's sake a second time, if needed. "We are agreed about the wedding? Mother may come, but the wedding only takes place if I can sweet talk my darling around. No bullying?"

"No bullying. But I hope things work out. When you're settled, I'll only have Gwen left at home. I need you settled so I can rest easy. And it won't matter if I turn old and gray and . . . soft."

"I love her, Father. Hit me like a falling brick the first time I saw her, and she was aiming a gun at my chest." His father's eyebrows arched even higher. "And no. I didn't faint."

Father groaned. "I should have expected that. Fainting—can you believe it? Don't tell your sisters."

Clark saw the twinkle in his father's eye be replaced by uncertainty. That was the last time he would put it there, if he could help it. "They won't hear it from me. Let's get you cleaned up, while I explain to you the *truth* of the situation. We'll share the loft in the barn."

"If I know your mother, she'll bring the parson and as many of your sisters as she can manage. We must think of arrangements."

"And we will. But not before I show you the place, my stock, and we eat a fantastic meal." He paused for emphasis. "Giving you a chance to apologize. Naantam's salmon will taste like manna from Heaven."

Father nodded but didn't say anything. Clark was convinced he would make things right.

"Will he . . . be at the meal?"

"Naantam? No, sir. But he will come around again." Clark offered an arm of strength to his limping father. He had no wish to embarrass him.

They walked toward the barn.

"Did she really point a gun at you, your first day out here?"

Clark grinned. He could think of no better way to spend his time between now and supper than talking about Rebecca. That is, if he was denied being by her side.

CHAPTER TWENTY-SIX

Heat still burned her cheeks at the things Mr. Sutherland accused her of. Rebecca flipped the salmon and tossed the slices of potatoes so they wouldn't scorch. Food was sizzling as she filled a wooden bowl with twice the applesauce they usually ate. As upsetting as it all was—Pa's nightdress and all—she pressed her fingers to the spot Clark had kissed. How many times was she going to touch her cheek?

She placed a loaf of bread in the oven to warm. *A dinner party.* She'd never hosted one before. She'd never been to one before. Unless the company at Mrs. Mabel's or the sewing bee counted. *He kissed me.* When he'd kissed her temple at the fence rail, she knew he was trying to comfort her. Maybe he was simply comforting her now, on the front porch, too.

His father embarrassed them both—not that Pa wasn't embarrassing enough.

She set the bowl of applesauce in the middle of the table and filled Pa a coffee cup, again. He was on his second refill. She was determined to have him sober by supper. Was that even possible?

Maybe Clark didn't know any other way to comfort. Maybe he went around giving comforting kisses to all the gals in Oregon

City. And there she was again, touching her cheek.

She wished she could talk to Cora Mae, Rose, and Heather. She'd write to her friends soon. Being attacked—a kiss—those would be the last things they would expect. It was the last thing *she* expected.

She wished she could leave the men to their meal and close herself into the larder to shore up with her Bible and Mother's journal. She wished she knew what Clark was thinking when he kissed her. How was she supposed to know?

Growing up in the shack with Pa, she went days without talking and no one ever explained anything. If anyone who came to buy or trade with Pa lingered to watch her, she disappeared into the woods until they were gone. She had a handful of books for company, but they didn't talk about this kind of thing.

Clark said he liked the idea of marrying her. Did she like the idea?

She stirred the potatoes again and slid the cooked fish off onto a chipped porcelain platter and loaded the hot skillet with several more pieces—the fish bright pink. "This is the last batch. You can go round-up the others if you are up to it, Pa."

"Leander! Supper's on!" Pa yelled to the back of the cabin.

"I could've done that easily enough."

"Why didn't ya?" He scraped his chair back

and went to the front door, dressed in his second set of clothes. Where was his first?

Rebecca moved to Pa's cot and folded all the blankets tidily and stowed his jugs underneath. They fit perfectly. She hoped he would forget about his offer to share—no need for more chaos.

"Clark! Sutherland! Supper's on! Reuben and Joe are coming up the drive. We won't have to wait to eat. Cold fish ain't no good."

Rebecca went back to the stove to finish her work. She'd made enough fried potatoes to feed the whole wagon train. "Hope they're hungry."

Pa came back from the door and sat in his usual place. "Fellows are always hungry. And if they aren't, they can keep their grubby mitts off this fine meal and leave it for those of us who is." Too bad the coffee didn't sweeten Pa's disposition. Leander came out from his room looking rested and groomed and moved to his chair—a little stiffly. His stays protested when he sat.

"How's the pain?" This was her world. She wanted to be here for him. She touched the place where Clark kissed her.

"No more, no less than usual—albeit an uncomfortable companion. Never a good day, once a draft horse rolls over you. Sure smells good in here. I'm looking forward to chatting with Sutherland."

She talked about the fish that Naantam brought as Clark and Mr. Sutherland made their way in the door, followed directly by Joe and Reuben.

"Curl brothers—Joe and Reuben—have you been introduced properly to Clark's pa?" Leander greeted them all and invited them all to sit.

"I have." Why did Joe sound like meeting Mr. Sutherland was like eating poison? Joe was always hard for her to read.

Rebecca moved the potatoes so they wouldn't stick to the pan.

"We met," Mr. Sutherland added. "How are you holding together, Leander?"

"With stitches and glue, if you must know. Please take a seat."

Pa crinkled his nose before he swallowed another bolt of coffee.

The men filled in the rest of the chairs, minus one saved for her. She'd already left her glass next to Leander's chair. Leander was safe. She could trust him to be the same kind man he was day-in and day-out. He didn't confuse her with courtesy kisses or strange looks.

Clark was charming, but who was to say he wouldn't follow his father back to town after all that was said? If he was going to leave, she didn't want to lower her guard and love him. *Love him? Did she love him?*

She better not. It wasn't safe. She pressed her lips together. She'd spent so much time looking for roots and a place to belong, she never considered love. Was it worth it? Love hurt.

She placed the platter of fish on the corner of the table closest to the stove—right in front of Joe. Joe was on her other side.

She wasn't excited to be stuck next to Joe for the whole of the meal. He had no sense of space. Or maybe it was just that she needed more space than usual, after growing up with her distant pa. Regardless, she needed Joe to scoot over and let her breathe.

She wanted to shove him back, but that would require touching him.

"Did Clark show you around?" Leander asked Sutherland.

"He did. Filled my ear with barn animal updates, repair needs, cross-fencing projects, and expansion plans. And he is far more excited with all that than he gets with a list of numbers before him, I can tell you."

Leander said, "I never thought Clark would come back to the farm after spending those summer weeks with me. I thought he would only remember the poison oak and the hornet's nest and digging post holes. He sure knew how to find trouble."

Clark said, "All good trouble, now."

She caught Clark gazing at her. She touched her cheek again. He noticed, because his smug grin was one notch away from gloating. If he would tell her what the kiss meant, then maybe his smile would be justified.

But as things stood, she sat by Leander. *This is where I belong.* To love and lose would be worse than leaving and starting over. She tried to dampen the hope that kept flaring to life in her chest.

She had to lean slightly away to keep Joe from brushing into her.

"Would you like applesauce?" She held the bowl out to him. His hair was slicked back and wet and he smelled like . . . ?

"Yes, please. Thank you." Joe's black eyes never left her face the whole time he dished.

Hurry up. She leaned away as far as she could.

His stare bold, he filled the second spoonful so full, it slopped over the edge of her plate. He moved his plate to clean the dollop of sauce. When he turned the ladle to manage it, she saw the bandage on the back of his hand. It didn't cover all of the gash.

The gash I made.

And that was the smell—fennel.

Joe was her attacker.

She stood so fast her chair crashed over. "It was you! You attacked me! I did *that* before you got away!" She pointed to his hand.

Joe looked like he would make an excuse. She couldn't bear it if they didn't believe her. Hot tears flowed. "I smelled you! You had fennel on your breath then too!"

Joe reached to grab her. She dodged away—closer to Leander.

He didn't try again. Joe pulled out a revolver and aimed the gun square at Leander. "You can't have her and the farm."

Everyone stood from the table except Leander, who had his hands where Joe could see them.

"Joe?"

"Shut it, Reuben, if you know what's good for ya. You're late to the party, as usual. Mother never wanted you involved in the details—you and your wholesome conscience would've given us away every time." He clicked the hammer back on the gun. "This property is ours. Leander stole it from us."

Rebecca gasped.

"What do you mean?" Reuben asked.

"Not my property?" Leander kept his hands out. "Why would you think I stole it? I gave you first choice all those years ago."

"Did you? Did you give me first choice? More like you swindled me. You pretended to care about a couple of orphan boys. But as soon as you realized this piece of property would be easier to make a living from, you guided us to the other one. If it wasn't for that fool-blame Indian, I'd have had my hands on this place months ago." Joe stepped away from his chair, still holding the gun on Leander. "The rockslide . . . being crushed by the horse . . . sound familiar?"

Leander seemed slow to understand.

Rebecca pointed at Joe. "You did that?"

"I did. And more. The wrecked corn, the pigs in the garden."

"Joe . . . I . . ." Leander was out of words.

"And when you survived, the least you could do is show a little gratitude for those who cared for you throughout your weakest times."

"I remember little from those first weeks. I don't remember you being there at all. I'm sorry. Naantam cared for me. And Reuben cared for me." He shrugged, his hands still out.

Joe stepped closer to Leander. "Come hell or high water, I wouldn't have tended your wounds for anything. I wanted you dead. But brother here, he was your knight in shining armor. And how did you reward him?"

"He let me graze our animals on his land," Reuben said.

"Shut up, Reuben. That's my point. It isn't his land. It's ours. And she isn't his anymore either. She's mine."

Rebecca felt like a spectator. Was this really happening? Her limbs shook. She'd called him out with too many people around and no way out. He had to shoot. Leander would die. Her home would be ripped from her. *Home.*

"And if I can't have her, neither can you." He adjusted his grip on the gun.

At his movements, Rebecca charged his arm at the same time Pa leaped in front of Leander. The gun went off. Pa jerked. "Pa!" she cried.

Reuben and Clark knocked the table over in a clatter, in their attempt to help. It banged at the same time the window crashed and shattered into a hundred tiny pieces as Naantam broke through. He hit the ground in a low crouch and rolled to his feet, making a protective stance between Leander and Joe.

"You dag-blasted Injin!" Joe screamed.

Mr. Sutherland—fainting dead away—slammed to the ground.

"Father?" Clark bent over him.

Joe used the distraction to dart toward the door.

Clark was after him, only a few feet ahead of Reuben.

"Pa?" Rebecca went to him.

"I've got Otis. And Naantam has us both. Go after him. Take the shotgun." Leander clutched Pa to his chest. Rebecca hesitated for only a moment before she grabbed the gun and chased after the men to see what would happen.

She rounded the corner of the porch and saw Clark catch Joe by the smokehouse. They grappled over the gun. Clark flung it wide and punched Joe several blows in the face before Joe fell in the dirt.

Blood spurted out of Joe's nose.

"If you ever come near Rebecca again, I'll have reason to kill you!" Clark shouted

Joe grabbed the meat hook off the smokehouse wall and swung it at Clark's belly.

"Look out!" She screamed and broke into a run to try and help—to get a clear shot.

After taking a few swings, Joe threw the hook at Clark. Clark ducked, narrowly missing getting hit in the face.

She was close enough now. "Stop!"

Both men looked at her and froze.

Before she could get a clear aim, Joe ran across the yard before Clark moved to chase. Joe leaped the split-rail fence in one bound and was looking back over his shoulder as he crossed the pasture. Baron the Bull was already there. He came charging from around the side of the barn.

"Looook outttt!" Running, Rebecca warned.

"Jooooe!" Reuben screamed for his brother and ran lightning fast for a big man.

At the same time Clark and Reuben crossed the fence, the bull hooked Joe with his mighty horns, tossing him in the air like a rag doll and snagged him again before he had time to hit the ground. The bull tossed him a second time. Joe collided with the trunk of an oak tree, sliding down to the base with a limpness that wasn't human.

He lay on the ground with his neck at an unnatural angle. Baron gouged and tore and stomped until Reuben and Clark distracted him with waves of their hands.

When the bull was fatigued enough to be distracted away to his dinner, the two men carried Joe's mangled body out of the pasture and brought him into the cabin and, after putting down a protective sheet, laid him out on Pa's cot where Mr. Sutherland was sitting as he recuperated. Otis was in Leander's bed with his shoulder already bandaged.

Rebecca's trembling turning to quakes, she ran ahead of the men to her pa's side. Would her father make it? She tried to look under his wrappings.

"Leave him be, Rebecca. We got him settled. He passed out from drink, not blood loss." Leander's words made her breath release in a gush.

"Where's Naantam?" she asked.

She looked around and found him with Leander, mixing something in a bowl that smelled of herbs and spices.

A gentle hand slid onto her shoulder. She turned into Clark's arms and buried her face to cry into his shirt, fitting low over his heart. Her attacker was dead. She fought for freedom and caught him, but it was her family that kept her safe.

The soft beat of Clark's heart secured her more than anything else could. He fluttered his fingers through her tangled hair. "It's over. It's all over. He can't hurt you now. Leander said your pa is fine, just winged—he will be fine. He'll heal."

Clark stood with her and held her the whole time Reuben fetched his wagon. He never let go. Not when Naantam and Mr. Sutherland helped put Joe in Reuben's wagon bed. Not when they cleaned up the table and glass, not when they discussed bringing in the sheriff.

He didn't release her until the house was quiet and all was cleaned and settled. "Tomorrow's a new day. There will be much to do. Eddie, Ma, the parson, and whichever sisters braved the trip could roll in. This was a sad end to a sad life—worth no more worry."

Clark lowered his head and kissed her temple and cheek—he lingered on her cheek. "We have things to talk about too. Try to sleep, would you?"

She sniffed and looked up into his crisp-blue eyes. His gaze was serious. She didn't know he could be so serious. How was she to reassure him? What did he need her to say?

What would she want someone to say to her? "This is my home. I'm home." She sobbed and hugged him tight with how true it was. Home wasn't in the past with her mother, or in the quiet Pa protected. Home was in her, when she lived and connected to the people who loved her. Home was love, that's why she felt it with Heather, Rose, and Cora Mae.

Joe can't take that from me. "Sleep might be hard, but I'm not alone. God is my Rock and I know how to take refuge. He has saved me before." Had she done it? Was he reassured?

He squeezed her, and she smiled at him before she turned from him to her larder.

She went in and dropped the lock into place and waited until she heard the cabin door shut behind him and for all to grow quiet. She would survive. She would find her way through. Tomorrow would come.

She touched her cheek. Her thoughts went numb. She dressed for bed and clutched Jules's Bible and her mother's journal to her chest, trying to fall asleep, hoping not to dream, valuing home.

CHAPTER TWENTY-SEVEN

Time ground past, her sleep never deep and true. The sun rose, bringing with it a fresh day, whether Rebecca was ready for it or not. She went through the motions of caring for those around her; feeding everyone, cleaning up, milking, and doing any barn chores that came to mind.

She carried a breakfast tray and Pa's favorite jug into Leander's room and placed them on the small table in the corner. Had Pa not jumped in the way, would Leander be here? Had she not upset the shot, would Pa be here? Too many questions that were too big for her heart to comprehend.

She sighed.

Pa spoke first. "Don't turn all weepy on me, daughter. Things could be worse. Leander told me what Joe did to you. Death was too good for him, if you ask me."

She still wasn't used to it when he burst forth with words. She handed him his jug. He patted her hand. *Home.*

She nodded. No words would come through her clogged throat. She moved the tray onto the bed he shared with Leander. Leander was fully clothed and propped up against the pillows. A pair of reading glasses perched on the end of his nose. "It's good to see you, my dear. Did you find Jules's Bible comforting?"

Home. The word echoed inside her again. It was all around her. She nodded.

"Have you read your mother's journals yet?"

She shook her head.

"I think it's high-time we told her, Otis. She needs to know. Albert can hurt her about as much as Joe can. I'm ready to admit some more selfishness for not explaining things to her when she first came, cause I wanted the help around here, but now it feels wrong and it feels like a waste to leave things the way they are. You agreed?"

Pa said, "Yes. Tell her. She should know. I want to build my shack, by her, over there."

What were they talking about? Afraid of Albert?

Leander cleared his throat and settled a kind gaze on her. "Albert wasn't a good man. I'm sure Ophelia left you a clear picture of how that was for her in her journal. I'll let her words speak for themselves. He owed me a lot of money when he said he was leaving, I demanded he pay up with the deed to his property. At first, I kept the property so Ophelia could have a place to live. There is a small cabin no bigger than the larder on the place, but then when the reports came back that Albert was lost, and Ophelia's Isaac passed . . . Ophelia thought everything that Albert touched was ruined by his greed. She didn't want anything to do with the property, and she didn't want you to be around it. She was so afraid, for so long. Your pa offered to marry her and take her away, which was a kind mercy."

Pa said, "She was happy. She started to smile and laugh again. Then she got sick." Pa said his piece and then lay back and closed his eyes.

"What we are trying to say is, you have land. It's in my name, but it's yours, and it abuts this farm. The pond is shared. You have a place to live that is yours, as long as you want it. I'm sorry I didn't explain that before when I was telling Eddie about coming to the farm. I was thinking that you would live there in my head, but I hadn't said it out loud. I didn't realize bringing Eddie along put you in such a hard place."

"So that was the inheritance in the letter? And not telling about Albert and the property was the secret you both promised Ma not to tell me?"

Both men nodded like guilty schoolboys.

She smiled. "I have land, and pasture for my milk cows?"

"Yes. There's a lean-to sort of outbuilding, no barn, and I'm sure the fences need work. Albert didn't like homesteading, that's why he left. He grew up a rich man's son and didn't understand the work that went into life out here. He was chasing fantasies and was disappointed to the point of becoming mean."

Rebecca soaked up all the stories to sort later.

She knew now that she could ask any question and they would tell her, and she would read Ma's journal without it feeling like she was losing her all over again. She would live here. She had property—land. If she built a big enough house, she could let her sister-friends come live with her or stay with her.

"Thank you for telling me, neighbor." She hugged both men in turn.

Pa grew restless with the raw emotion. He squirmed in the bed and changed the subject. "Leander is making me listen to him read an adventure book. As if yesterday wasn't adventure enough."

"I have a book of sermons that might be uplifting." Leander jostled the bed.

Pa moaned and added, "Watch the arm. Watch the arm. Can't abide sermonizing . . . Nothin' good comes from it 'septin' it puts me to sleep faster than laudanum."

The front door opened and closed. They all expected to see Clark, but Reuben came in puffy faced, with red-rimmed eyes.

They all came to attention.

Leander moved to get up. His stays groaned, and his face pinched.

"No. Don't disturb yourself." Reuben took off his hat and mashed it into a wad. His black hair still looked unwashed. Shifting his weight from foot-to-foot, Reuben looked sheepish. "The thing is, I have a favor to ask, that I have no right to. I spent all night building his pine box. I shouldn't ask . . ." His shoulders bent like a hundred-pound feed sack settled there.

Leander helped him. "I can't answer a question that hasn't been spoken. Last I checked, no was as easy to say as yes."

She didn't know why, but Leander's word stabilized her own thoughts.

Reuben continued to wring his hat.

Leander's gentle tone and practical outlook made it possible to see some sort of normal on the other side of all this. She needed Leander. The oddness of seeing both him and Pa side-by-side in the big log bed gave her a reason to smile.

Pa and her uncle both would give their all to see her safe on life's journey. With them to count on, it would be enough. She wouldn't think about Clark's kisses and his possible conversations until they happened. As Leander said, "No was as easy to say as yes."

After wrestling with the weight of burden for a long minute, Reuben rushed, "Seeing as it was Joe's biggest heart's desire to own this land, I thought it fitting to give to him in death what he couldn't have in life. Can I bury him on your property?"

Joe buried here? Could she handle the constant reminder of that dark night?

After a long moment of pause, Leander looked

at Rebecca before he answered. "I think we can give that to him—on one condition."

"Yes, sir?" His poor hat would never be the same. "What's that, sir?"

"Find a place suitable, but keep in mind our plans for expansion. And you may find a place anywhere exceptin' beside my Jules."

Long eye contact between the two men said all that would have been uncomfortable and awkward out loud. "I'm ready to do it today, sir. Can't abide to have him at the house. Him not being really there."

"Suit yourself."

Rebecca left and brought breakfast to her pa. He tucked into it with his good arm as if it was any other day. As he finished up, he said, "Place in the trees out back he preferred. Outta the way, like. He'll rest there undisturbed." Pa handed his empty plate back to Rebecca and pushed to his feet. "I'll help you find it." He walked outside, presumably to lead Reuben to the right place.

"And when we're done moving Joe to it, I'll help you dig," Clark offered.

"Clark?" She hadn't even heard the door. He would be excited about the land too.

Reuben kept his gaze on the ground. "I don't think we should have a service. God's probably got plenty to say to Joe."

Leander shook his head. "Nonsense, Reuben. The parson should be here soon. He was coming by anyway. He'll know how to handle such a thing." Leander began to eat.

Reuben looked so relieved that Rebecca was mollified. Things would get better—easier. There was a quiet lull where everyone collected their thoughts.

Leander put his meal aside and moved to the trunk and shuffled the things off the top, placing them on different shelves. "While you're busy lifting and carrying, would you mind helping me move Jules's and Ophelia's trunks into Rebecca's room? They are hers. And we'll need to have a pallet made up for me and Otis in the barn, if your ma and sisters are due to drop in on us. It won't do to have ladies bunking in the barn."

Clark agreed.

"I can help you all with that," Reuben offered.

The whole room broke up as each man went his separate way. Leander prepared to have the trunks moved. And Clark left with Reuben.

Rebecca left them to it. She moved to clear a place for the trunks in the larder. When all was settled in the cabin, she walked across the field, looking at the trees that were her future home. At the last minute, instead of walking to her new property, she went to the dig site.

They'd already cracked the earth ankle deep. Beads of sweat pooled on Reuben's forehead.

A respectful silence settled heavily.

Rebecca leaned against the tree and looked

back at the farm. Her home. She could see the dinner table from here and the outline of Jules's dusty cross-stitch on the wall. And if the barn door was open, she could see right into Samson and Sheba's pen.

She stood tall away from the tree. *Wait a minute.* That was the point—wasn't it? He'd watched from here? That's why it was his favorite place. Rebecca bit her lip and held back a shudder.

Mr. Sutherland crossed the pasture with a heavy limp while rolling his sleeves, bringing his own shovel. "My turn, Clark. You're in my way—move," Mr. Sutherland bossed. "And take the pretty miss away from this dismal business, I can tell by the look on her face that she's thinking on rotten things."

"No argument from me." Clark stepped out of the hole.

"She should focus on rainbows and roses, not on a dead man's frozen dreams. Now git—off with you both. And don't let her back into the cabin. She shouldn't spend another minute drudging for us."

"Yes, sir."

"Imp." Before he put the shovel to work, he leaned on it and said, "Miss Rebecca, I owe you a deep apology in several turns. I do, sincerely, beg pardon. And I do, sincerely, ask you to tell me all about the day you met my son and held him at gunpoint." He smiled.

Rebecca smiled back. It was enough.

Clark made a show of coming to her, taking her hand, and tucking it into his arm. He led her away like he was a duke on parade—if dukes carried shovels. She wanted to giggle, but who knew what he would do if she encouraged him.

Peace settled over them both.

Clark said, "I've always loved this place when I was here with Eddie when we were kids. It seems so quiet compared to town, but once you're here for a while the birds and the breeze through the trees make their own kind of noise. I prefer it. I always planned on coming back. I would have sooner, if my sister Gwen hadn't got hurt. She's the one who got me out here. Gave me a kick in the pants."

"I should thank her, then?"

"You might get your chance soon enough. She's probably on her way. I should hope she will make a better first impression than Father." He pulled her closer to his side.

Clark was treasuring her. She soaked it up.

She was at the center of his attention. She swallowed on a gulp. She'd never felt so valued. Not the day Pa told her he loved her, and not the day Leander taught her to shore up.

Clark wanted to be with her. But would he stay? What if he needed to get his own land? "You planned to come back . . . for a visit or to stay?"

"To visit, then. I'd love to stay. I came to help

Eddie with the animals. I didn't know I was going to pig farm until I came. It feels like such a good fit." He looked at her with so much longing, like he wanted to say something more, but couldn't.

She was about to direct his attention to the smokehouse that needed stoking, when he turned his attention first to the front of the cabin.

"I wonder . . . ? Come on." He tugged her beside him—taking advantage by lacing his fingers with her own.

If he left, would she turn hollow inside like her pa did when Ma was gone? Probably. It was a good thing she knew how to shore up.

Lord, help me.

Clark missed her distraction. He was too busy rolling a large, round river rock out from under the foliage of the lupine patch that backed the water pump. "What are you doing?"

"You'll see. Or at least I think you'll see."

He lifted the shovel to point and pressed his foot to its back in the soft earth beneath the rock. "When I was here last, I buried something. I can't remember what all's in it, but I put it here, as a promise to my boy self to come back."

Thunk.

The shovel hit tin. "See. I loved it here. I loved the earth between my fingers and the smell of the barn on a warm spring day—the fact that most every seed you plant grows. I could work for Father at the bank, but this fits me. And now you're here . . ."

Now she was here what? Maybe if he stopped and looked at her, told her plainly what he saw for the future, she could know her mind. She wanted to love like Leander—and her pa. Pa was still broken from losing a love. The pain of it brought him to ruin. Was it worth it?

Clark had a dirt-covered, rusty lunch tin out and opened before she could sort herself. The first thing he pulled out was a perfect coyote skull.

When she wrinkled her nose, he laughed. The sound warmed her like warm cocoa.

"I was a boy—barely thirteen. This was impressive back then. Still neat now, for that matter." A crawdad pincher came next, along with three or four arrowheads. "Found these down by the creek. I was always impressed with how they were made." He handed each one to her, one at a time, after setting the coyote skull on display at the foot of an Oregon grape plant that was blooming with several clusters of yellow blossoms.

"This is the last of it, my favorite treasure." He poured several rocks into the palm of his hand, picking through until he found one.

He held up an orange-ish rock with swirls of clearness through it. "I found it the first day I got here. It captured me enough that I spent the rest of my summer keeping my eyes out for more.

I found these as well, but none as pretty as this first one. And now, all these years later, I found you on the first day I got here, too. As long as I look, I'll never find your equal."

He plucked the arrowheads from her hand. They rattled the tin bottom when he dropped them and the other agates back in. He set the tin down and then held his first-rock-prize out for her to take.

She took his rock and held it in her palm. *How did he know?*

"You can ask Eddie, I loved you at the pond that first day. I didn't know I could. But as soon as I saw you—and your rifle—I knew. I've even wondered if the sense of knowing was from God. He knows I can be thickheaded, at times, but loving you is as easy as breathing, and I want to treasure you for years, like I have all these things."

He closed her fingers over his rock and drew her close. His eyes were filled with so much caring and certainty, she could drown in them. *And he gave me a rock.* His rock—of all things. *Lord, you knew.*

She swallowed back tears and quoted, " 'God is my rock, in whom I take refuge, my shield.' " The scripture Jules underlined in her Bible and the whispered words of comfort came to her again.

I'm not trying to take something from you. I'm trying to give something to you.

Peace filled her. She finished quoting the verse. " 'And my salvation.' "

His lips crushed her whispers as he gently pulled her in and kissed her firm and sound. Every doubt she had shut its mouth on the instant. She would love him. She already loved him.

He squeezed her closer, never breaking the kiss. She could feel the warmth of his body and the race of his heart under her hand.

When he'd kissed her long enough, he asked, "Will you marry me? I don't know how we'll get along, but between the pigs and the milk cows, we'll pull enough together to find some property. But I don't want to wait. Too much can happen, as the last few days proves. I'll stay here with you, as we help run this farm and keep the burden off Leander's back. Will you learn with me, grow with me, take me to yourself and, Lord willing, bear our children?"

She let herself be happy. "Yes, yes, yes, and yes." She let the joy pour through every fiber of her being. She clutched the agate so tight it left a mark on her palm and threw her arms around him and kissed him with all the yes-ness in her.

They were kissing when a lady's voice said, "Looks like we are just in time."

They broke apart. "Mother, you made it." He squeezed Rebecca and kept her tucked to his side. When the wagon stopped, Clark laced his fingers with hers and put her forward to greet his mother.

• • •

The next three days felt like continuous time floating away as fast as the water in a stream. Rebecca found herself standing under the oak trees beside the garden with the parson standing between her and Clark.

The day was perfect.

Beatrice and Gwen fussed with the bustle at the back of the yellow muslin dress with soft flowers covering it. It was Jules's wedding dress, which made the elegant high-ruffle neckline that trailed down to a fitted row of buttons feel almost like the hug Leander gave her when he first saw her in it. He still wept openly at the sight of her. Pa stood silent and sober. He looked uncomfortable.

She surmised that had more to do with the crowd and the string tie cinching his neck than pain in his injured shoulder or the fact she was getting married.

Mr. Sutherland gave his wife a gentle squeeze, which he probably thought was unwitnessed. Rebecca snuggled Jules's Bible close, careful not to rumple the ribbon and roses that Gwen used to decorate the cover. How could Gwen ever know the meaning of the two simple gifts? It made it seem as if Heather, Rose, and Cora Mae were here with her on this special day. She missed them dearly.

Tomorrow, when she woke up for the first time as Mrs. Sutherland, a letter would be her first priority—and what a fat letter it would be. She walked forward to meet Clark.

He kissed her hand. "Here, let me help you hold that since you are a tiny little lady and you need my help and all." His impersonation of their first meeting made her smile.

"Clark, do I need to beat you?" Eddie's warning went unheeded.

Clark drew her closer than was proper. No one objected. Beatrice and Gwen sniffled in their hankies, and Clark's parents held each other.

Clark's voice rang loud in the outdoors and even louder in her heart. "In the name of God, I, Clark, take you, Rebecca, to be my wife, to have and to hold from this day forward, for better . . . for worse . . . for richer, for poorer, in sickness and in health. I will love you and cherish you until death parts us. This is my solemn vow."

She echoed the vows, and the parson declared them husband and wife. Clark kissed her deep and sweet, and the flood of family rooted the promise with a sense of home greater than anything Rebecca ever experienced.

Clark's mother was the first to hug her. "You must come to stay with us in town sometime." When she kissed her cheek, their tears mingled.

"That would be nice."

Clark's father came to stand right behind his wife. "We hate to rush off after such a beautiful moment. We've stayed away from the bank for long enough."

His mother added, "And he needs to get off that foot. The doctor is going to have his hide." The men embraced at the same time Rebecca hugged her mother-in-law again.

Clark smiled at his father. "And your leaving has nothing to do with bunking in the hayloft . . . without Mother?"

His father settled his hand on Clark's shoulder and gave it a squeeze before he moved off. "No one would ever accuse you of being a stupid man, son. Let's go, dear. Say your good-byes, girls. We have a long day of travel ahead. Parson?"

The preacher shook Clark's hand and followed his parents to the wagon.

Eddie gave Clark a bull-like hug. "Keep your eyes on this one, Rebecca. Sleep with one eye opened." She could only laugh at his tease.

"He's got a point." Beatrice came in close and kissed her cheek. Gwen joined her and produced a small, wrapped square from inside her sling. "This is from all of us sisters. You might find it useful."

"*No!* You didn't." Clark eyed Gwen and blocked her from giving the box to Rebecca.

Rebecca laughed.

"Did. It was the only thing that ever worked—even if it took all five of us." Gwen smiled at Beatrice.

"Good thing Rebecca is sweet on me. She'd

never be so cruel—not even on her worst days."

"Give her time." Eddie thumped Clark on the back. "You want me to show her how to wield that weapon?" Eddie moved closer to Gwen and reached for the square gift.

"Don't even," Clark said.

Gwen laughed at Eddie's sally. "Just in case . . ." She handed the gift to Rebecca.

"Thank you . . . I think?" She looked between Clark and Gwen as she opened it, trying to peek and see what it was.

She could see the love Clark had for his sisters in the tiny dimple in his cheek that danced with their teasing.

Could he be more handsome? She opened the box. "Soap?" They all dissolved into laughter around her.

"Yes, soap." Clark feigned indignation. "They ganged up on me, pinned me down, and scrubbed my mouth with that horrid stuff."

Rebecca laughed. She felt so light and free.

"He deserved it," Gwen blurted, her short curls blowing in the breeze.

Eddie moved to her good arm side and offered Gwen his own as they ambled toward the wagon.

"He practically begged us to, with his antics," Beatrice added. "It was our way of taming the shrew."

Gwen called back over her shoulder, "I give you one year."

"One year for her to use the soap on me?" Clark asked.

"One year to make me an aunt," she crooned.

"You're already an aunt," Beatrice added.

"I am. But this spinster needs an excuse to come play out here in the wilds. I can't work in the barn, but I can be a nanny-aunt."

Eddie scowled. "Spinster? Just because you cut your hair short doesn't make you a spinster."

"My hair has slightly less to do with it than this does." She wriggled her crippled arm. Eddie's alarm matched Clark's.

She added, "Stop, you two. Don't cry for me. I'm at peace with my future. I took a heaping spoonful of my own advice before I shoved it at Clark. It's good advice, isn't it, brother? Look what it brought you." Gwen turned around and left before either could respond.

Eddie caught up with her and whispered something that made Gwen laugh. She called back over her shoulder, "You should plan on coming to meet Abigail's newest. She'll want to meet you, Rebecca."

Warmed by Gwen's invitation, Rebecca smiled. "We'll plan on it."

Clark held Rebecca to his side while the others loaded up and moved on down the road. Leander had already escaped to his bed, and Pa wandered off to nurse his shoulder and a jug.

Clark laced his fingers with hers and kissed

the back of her hand as he watched his family's wagon roll out of sight. "Nearly a perfect day."

He traced a heart on the back of her hand with the square of lavender-flecked soap that his sisters gave.

"Nearly? I'm not sure if there will ever be one to top it. I must write to Cora Mae, Heather, and Rose."

"It's only missing one thing."

She could hear the sarcasm in his words. She smiled up at him and let herself be pulled into a hug. "And what could that possibly be?"

He framed her with his strength, and whispered, "They couldn't know I *want* you to use this." He tapped the bar of soap on the back of her hand.

She ignored the twinkle in his eyes and giggled. "You want me to wash your mouth out with soap? Strange . . ."

"That's not quite what I had in mind." He kissed the tip of her nose. "I want you to take me to wherever it is you go when you come back clean and fresh with braided hair running wet down your back—the scent of lavender about you. I want you to take me there . . . with this." He held up the soap.

He wanted to see her spring? She blushed as scarlet as the rose tied to the top of her Bible. He kissed her full and hardy.

When she could catch her breath, she looked at the cabin and the barn, and then before her confidence left, she snatched the soap from his hand and started down the path to her spring, laying her Bible with its rose and ribbons on the bench beside the smokehouse as she passed. The spring would be a great place to tell him they owned the neighboring property.

His heavy steps were so close behind her she giggled again. Scooping the muslin of her dress out of the way, she whisked down the path. It was her time to show she'd learned lessons from Leander and Pa's past—*love as hard as possible every day I have—like they did.*

You never knew what tomorrow would bring.

ACKNOWLEDGMENTS

I went on a birdwatching adventure with my friend Cheri Faulhaber. While we were scanning with our binoculars, a whole flock of diving water birds called Coots flew in and landed together and preceded to float, dive, and forage along the bank of the river. They stayed together. They were stronger and safer together. Some led. Some followed. And some were inseparable from each other. After being entertained by their crazy feet (worth looking up), Cheri and I learned that a flock of birds floating together are called a raft.

So here are my very heartfelt thanks to the Coots that have made up my Raft for the last nine years of this book journey. Yes, nine years.

Angey Lovenburg, Lynn Large, Kathy Bergstorm, Danielle Kendall, Tricia Halverson, Jodi Halverson, my agents Karen Ball and Bob Hostetler with the Steve Laube Agency, my editors Naomi Rawlings, and Julie Swarzburg. My Critique friends Savanna Kaiser, Cynthia Roemer, Tara Johnson, Audra Kearney, Stephannie Hughes, Darlene Panzera, Kate Breslin, Julie Lessman, Camille Eide, Kathleen Denly, Voni Harris. Roseanna and David White, and WhiteFire Publishing for their hard work. My fellow authors . . . all of you, My Country Church family. Oregon Christian Writers Conference and American Christian Fiction Writers Conference.

My parents, my Halverson/Grandle family, my kids and my husband Tim Grandle . . . babe, without you none of this would be possible.

These people have all helped me not be afraid to do the hard thing. They've helped me learn what it is to respect the dream, and they've listened to it Allll for years and patiently floated the river with me.

And my whole journey started with a very special moment at a church women's retreat where I heard the still small voice of the Lord say, "Everybody needs to know what it feels like to finish something." Mother's Day Weekend, 2012.

And to my sweet Jesus, I love you most.

DISCUSSION QUESTIONS

1. If you were forced to find a job to support yourself in the 1840s, what do you think you would be good at? What would you want to be good at?
2. Rebecca is in pursuit of home. Do you think she found it? Or do you think she had it all along and her perspective changed when her circumstances did? Has that ever happened to you?
3. If you lived before modern technology and invention what would you love about it? What would you like least?
4. Have you been or known of someone whose life has been impacted by their parents' secrets?
5. Have you ever had a season of life that was so hard that you had to "shore-up"? If so, what helped you? Have you revisited that help in another season?
6. Did you learn anything from Rebecca and Clark's story? If so, what?
7. Have you felt like you have lived in someone else's shadow, like Clark? Have you felt like your life was unwitnessed or undervalued, like Rebecca? How has that affected you? What have you done to ensure history doesn't repeat?

8. Do you have heart-friends or sisters-of-your-choice? Do you think the Lord put you together? What would you say to someone who was lonely for that kind of friendship?

AUTHOR NOTES

One time, my mom had a gathering at her house that blended our neighbors and the ladies at the church. She baked, had plants and flowers to exchange. People brought other things to share, and she had a coffee table with free books. By accident, she put out one of my collection of Historical Christian Romance books she'd borrowed. I made a mental note of which lady chose that book to take home over cookbooks, self-help, and teaching books.

I knew the lady.

She was in the middle of a really long season of caring for a husband whose body was failing. I went to her a couple months later and asked if she'd had a chance to read the book. She had, and she went on to tell me that it was the best escape from the responsibility, pressure, and general heaviness that was part of her real, everyday life.

That's the kind of book I aim to write.

Don't get me wrong, this lady served her husband well with grace and dignity until the end. But her appreciation for a healthy, "escape" story that left her encouraged made an impact on me that day. Life can be hard. A retreat can be good medicine.

My books tell stories of times past. Many of

you will know the historical facts better than me. I hope you will take any mistakes in stride, when you hear that my heart is to truly write a book that lifts the pressure, allows the reader to catch their breath, and find hope no matter what is on their plate.

Thank you for reading, and thank you for your grace and support.

Center Point Large Print
600 Brooks Road / PO Box 1
Thorndike, ME 04986-0001 USA

(207) 568-3717

US & Canada:
1 800 929-9108
www.centerpointlargeprint.com